T0367625

Starting Over

Starting Over

CLAIRE NADEN

ARCHWAY
PUBLISHING

Archway Publishing books may be ordered through booksellers or by contacting:

Archway Publishing
1663 Liberty Drive
Bloomington, IN 47403
www.archwaypublishing.com
1 (888) 242-5904

ISBN: 978-1-4808-8480-9 (sc)
ISBN: 978-1-4808-8481-6 (e)

Library of Congress Control Number: 2019917843

Print information available on the last page.

Archway Publishing rev. date: 12/06/2019

To David

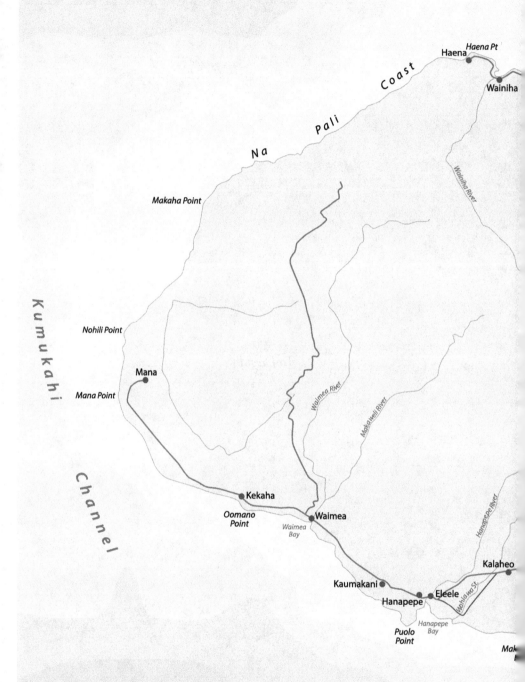

Haena
Haena Pt
Wainiha

Waininha River

N a
P a l i
C o a s t

Makaha Point

K u m u k a h i

Nohili Point

Mana
Mana Point

C h a n n e l

Waimea River
Makaweli River

Hanapepe River

Kekaha
Oomano Point

Waimea
Waimea Bay

Kalaheo

Kaumakani
Eleele
Hanapepe
Kahioula St.

Puolo Point

Hanapepe Bay

Mak

PACIFIC

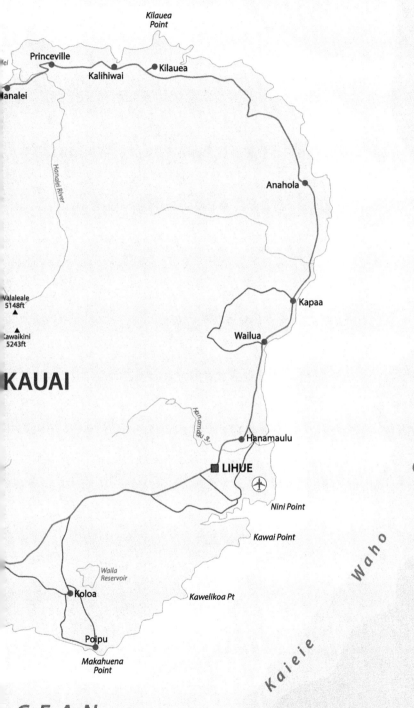

Kilauea
Point

Princeville

Kalihiwai

Kilauea

Hanalei

lei

Hanalei River

Anahola

Waialeale
5148ft
▲

▲
Kawaikini
5243ft

KAUAI

Kapaa

Wailua

Hanamau St.

Hanamaulu

■ LIHUE

Nini Point

Kawai Point

Waila
Reservoir

Koloa

Kawelikoa Pt

Poipu

Makahuena
Point

Channel

Waho

Kaieie

CEAN

CHAPTER ONE

Jack continued to walk our condominium even though he'd been dead for several weeks. My psychologist told me to tell him to go away whenever I had visions of him flitting down the hallway. Easier said than done.

I recalled those days before he passed away. It was all I could do to tolerate the memory of the mental and emotional abuse he'd inflicted on me. To make matters worse, after he passed away, his psychiatrist divulged that my husband had been bipolar. This revelation was intended to make it easier for me to accept and understand his unpredictable outbursts and mood swings but didn't rationalize his foolish mistakes. I realized our marriage was over some time ago what with his lies and deceit; all I'd ever asked of him in the fifteen years of marriage was, to be honest, and loyal. But to lie about a $250,000 income tax debt was something I could not forgive. It nearly cost us our home – our sanctuary.

Jack's death hadn't been unexpected. When I recovered from the shock of his passing and the funeral, I reflected on how we met and what my life would have been if we hadn't gotten together. *Be careful what you wish for* had become my mantra. As a divorced woman, I hoped for a secure, honest man, someone who would love me and share his life with me into our old age. Then I met Jack and got that and a lot more, including heartbreak and despair.

As I tended to my geraniums on my balcony, I recalled coming off a couple of heartbreaking, failed relationships. My first one was a summer romance. He was headed to the Marine Corp, and I was working, fresh out of high school. Sadly, it was short-lived but oh how I fell for him. Trouble was his parents had grandiose plans for him that did not include me. Shortly after that breakup, I married Richard. This union lasted short of twenty years and was fraught with non-communication and indifference, much of it to do with my daughter, Brooke. Then there was Michael, a boyfriend of eight years, who reneged on a promise he made to me even after I had accepted an attractive job offer as a paralegal at a prestigious San Francisco law firm. Promises broken, I felt a stabbing pain across my chest recalling how I felt humiliated and heartbroken when I notified the firm I was withdrawing my acceptance of the job offer. I kept asking him, "Are you sure you want me to make a move, and will you be moving in with me?"

His answer was always the same, "Sure, why wouldn't I?"

Hell hath no fury like a woman scorned. I allowed the anger and disappointment to take over and, impulsively, I called his ex-wife whom he had reconciled with due to pressure from their spoiled and petulant teenage daughter. All he could say was, "Why did you have to do that?"

"Simple, I'm not the only one to suffer and be hurt; you are not coming out of this unscathed." Perhaps, it was to teach him a lesson. Sadly, I still loved him with all my heart.

Hard as I tried, seeking out new friends and meeting single men, I still yearned for Michael until I met Daniel at a singles function. He swept me off my feet in one fell swoop. In retrospect, I realized that meeting him only six weeks from the break with Michael hadn't been a good idea. If only I had kept it as mere friendship. In hindsight, it could very well have been a rebound romance. But there was a strong attraction, and the sexual pull was too great to ignore. I fell hard and totally in love with him. But he also lied. Assuring me that he and his wife were divorced, he left out one tiny detail. They had remarried and were newly separated for the second time. He fell to the pressure exerted by their children, adult men, who could not mind their own business.

A double whammy! Admittedly, I was only going to date for the fun of it and not take anyone at their word. My motto became 'Loves music, loves to dance'. Weaning off men was easier said than done. All the heartbreak from the two breakups had thrown me to seek the services of a psychologist whose words I should have heeded. "Men speak in headlines. Pay attention to what they *don't* say."

Fast forward through the summer and following Labor Day, I decided to place a singles ad in the local paper. It only took a couple of days, and I had a response from a man who owned a condominium. Jack urged me to accept a dinner invitation, and the wooing began in earnest. The following year we were married in a lovely Jewish ceremony, and the fun began. We had one good year, and then his health took a nosedive. Hip replacement surgeries, a liver transplant, and pulmonary problems took him down bit by bit. Not a strong man, he succumbed to his myriad of health problems.

Now, after all the family and friends have gone home following the funeral, all I'm left with are the memories and the nagging question, *Where do I go from here?*

CHAPTER TWO

I sat in my favorite chair on a sunny morning in Pasadena, and thought *nothing is holding me here.* My daughter, Brooke, lives on the east coast and we see each other so seldom due to her demanding career as the editor of a high-fashion magazine. I can move and start a new life without a man. I always have my writing – an ongoing project for me, and if I need to, I can always fall back on my paralegal work. However, while the condominium would be easy enough to sell, where would I go? *Don't make rash decisions but think it through.* Confiding in no one because I didn't want to be influenced, I started out researching where I would like to move to. I always loved the beach and the mountains, but what location would allow me to make a living? But first things first, I must put the condominium up for sale and see how much I can realize from the sale. This location had always been popular with buyers for its proximity to shopping, restaurants, and the California Institute of Technology. The real estate market was brisk even for January.

I pulled out my laptop to search the internet for names of real estate offices, and it occurred to me that I already knew the perfect person to call. I looked through my business card file and found the one for Judy Cole. Dialing her number, I started to have second thoughts. What am I doing trying to sell my only security for retirement? But then, if I don't do this now, I will never have the chance to do it. I will get stuck in this rut.

The number rang, and I asked for Judy.

"Judy Cole, how can I help you?"

"Judy, it's Maggie Langham. Happy New Year! I know it has been a long time since we talked, but I need to ask your professional opinion about selling my condominium."

"Maggie, Happy New Year to you, too, but you aren't serious, are you? At this time, so soon after your husband's passing? Maybe you should give it some thought. Selling your home that you have lived in for so long will be a big adjustment for you."

"I have given it some thought but, to be honest, there is nothing here for me. I need to do something for me. Whether it is wrong or something I will regret, I must give it a shot. I'm not getting any younger, and I feel I need a change. If I stay here, I will only feel smothered."

"Well, if you're sure? When would you like for me to come over and we can start the process?"

"When do you have some time? My calendar is wide open today."

"How about this afternoon at 3:00 p.m.?"

"Sounds good. Remember to ring from the box downstairs, and I'll buzz you in."

"Got it. See you soon."

"Thanks, Judy."

Well, fancy that! I've taken the first step towards starting over. If it is a mistake, then I will be responsible and no one else. I had better get busy and straighten up around here before Judy comes.

A couple of hours later after restoring some order and disposing of some clutter, the phone rang. I quickly ran to answer it.

"Hello. Hi, Judy, let me buzz you in."

There was a knock and I walked to the front door to let Judy in. Still with luscious red hair and a figure to die for.

"Hi, old friend. You look great! How do you do it?"

"As do you, my old chum," Judy said as we embraced.

I invited her in and gave her a tour of the condominium and noticed that in addition to taking copious notes, she had her iPhone out and was taking lots of pictures.

"Would you like a glass of chardonnay or a cup of tea?"

"A glass of wine would be lovely."

"Let's sit at the dining room table so you can spread out your papers. Remember I was in the business once and know the routine."

"I must say, you have done all right for yourself. I don't think it will take too long to sell your lovely condominium. Are you sure you want to do this, and you aren't doing this on a whim?"

"I'm sure, and no it isn't a whim," I replied as I pulled a chilled bottle of chardonnay out of the wine cooler along with two wine glasses, a corkscrew and placed them on the dining room table. "Shall we get started with the paperwork?"

"We can, but I'm curious. Where will you go?"

"I'm not sure. I want to do something out of my comfort zone, even if it means making a big move and starting over. I've always loved the Hawaiian Islands and am thinking about moving there."

"That's a big move. Although I can't blame you, who wouldn't want to live in paradise? But are you sure you haven't made this decision due to post-holiday blues? You know how we always get after the holidays when everything goes back to normal."

"No, I don't think it has anything to do with post-holiday blues. I often think of my career in real estate and miss the people contact."

"You're not thinking of going back into the real estate business?"

"Oh, heavens, no!"

"Glad to hear it. It's a much different business than when you were active."

As I poured our wine, Judy pulled out papers and forms that looked all too familiar to me and asked, "What about Brooke?"

"What about her? We hardly see each other – she's too damn busy with her career! But I must say she's good about calling."

"Maggie, get real. She deserves at least a phone call from you, and

I wouldn't send her one of those 'My Address Has Changed' cards. Take a leap and reach out to her."

"You could be right, and I will give it some thought. Maybe a text?"

"NO, not a text. Make it personal, like a phone call."

"Okay, okay, you have made your point!"

"I apologize if I struck a nerve. But let's get on with this. I've prepared a competitive market analysis of your condo and noted the number of days each one was on the market before it sold."

As I perused the analysis and noted the market time, I realized that if I was going to make this change, I should get ready to do it now. Judy and I discussed the time it would take to sell the condo.

"I've decided to go for it and want you to get it on the market."

"Okay, but first things first. I need you to do some things for me. We will need to stage it."

"Stage it? That's a new term for me."

"Let me explain. It's essentially stripping all the clutter and presenting your property to a potential buyer in such a way that they can envision themselves living here without all your accouterments."

After we had finished completing the plethora of paperwork necessary for listing a property in the state of California, Judy packed up her things and made to leave.

"What do you think about a bed and breakfast property? It would provide you income, and you would have people around you."

"I've thought about that, but would there be available properties in the islands, and could I afford any of them?"

"A friend of mine is a realtor in Hawaii. His name is Dean Kalima. Shall I have him get in touch with you?"

"Sure, why not. I have to start somewhere."

CHAPTER THREE

I woke the next morning earlier than usual and looked at the clock on my night table. It read 8:00 a.m. I threw back the covers of my spacious king-size bed and noticed that the day had dawned bright and clear. I looked out my bedroom window and recalled the previous day and my conversation with Judy. Maybe I'm being too hasty, and I should sit on this for a while? No, I don't want to do that. I've made up my mind, and I'm ready to take this leap. As I was preparing my morning coffee, the phone rang, and I thought this couldn't be the realtor for it's too early in Hawaii at 5:00 a.m.

"Hello?"

"Good morning, Ms. Langham, this is Dean Kalima in Kauai. Our mutual friend, Judy Cole, gave me your name and number and told me you want to make a move to our island."

Not only is he a fast worker, but his voice is very reminiscent of someone I used to know in Kauai.

"Yes, that's correct. To be honest with you, I am surprised you called so early. Well, perhaps early for you?"

"No, not at all. I'm an early riser and have already been for my morning swim. May we discuss when you might be arriving on our beautiful island?"

"That depends on a few things. I need to get my condo prepared for showing but in the meantime, will check the airlines for travel arrangements and, of course, lodgings. So, if everything goes as I hope, I plan to fly out within the next two weeks, by the 15th of the month."

"Sounds like a plan. In the meantime, I can arrange to show you some of the listings when you get here. Do you have a place to stay?"

"I do. The Island Garden Inn is quite lovely and centrally located."

"That it is," Dean replied.

"Once I've booked my travel, I'll let you know. Perhaps you can provide me with contact information?"

"Sure, let me email it to you," he said, and I proceeded to give him my email address.

"Before we hang up, maybe you can tell me how large a bed and breakfast you are interested in?"

"That is going to depend on the price and, of course, the net on my condominium when it's sold. However, I do have funds that I could use to get the transaction started."

"Sounds good. Until I hear from you, I'll email you pictures of properties that are available."

"Thank you for calling, Dean. I'll be in touch soon."

"You're welcome. Mahalo."

After I had hung up the phone, I walked into my office and pulled out a legal pad and began to make a list of things I needed to do ASAP. Sitting at my desk, I looked out my window and smiled to myself. I've made the right decision, and I'm excited. Suddenly the phone rang. I recognized the number for Judy Cole and answered it.

"Good morning! Your man in Kauai is a real go-getter. He called this morning just after I got up and is gung-ho to get started on my quest for a bed and breakfast."

"He's been known to be an aggressive salesperson, so be prepared. I don't doubt that he will work his tail off to make this deal. Listen, the reason I called is to offer my services. If you need help with downsizing and staging, please don't hesitate to call on me. I'll be happy to help. I know you want to make that trip to Kauai soon. For lodging, I suggest the Island Garden Inn."

"Yes, soon like yesterday. Today, I will spend time making additional travel arrangements. We think alike. I've already made a reservation at the Island Garden Inn. Can you make it over tomorrow?"

"I'll check my calendar and let you know."

"Thanks, Judy."

"Oh, Maggie! Please don't forget to call Brooke. Bye for now, my friend."

Ignoring her comment, I turned to my computer and started to search the internet for airfare. Knowing where I would stay was one less thing to worry about. Planning for this all-important trip took most of the morning. I settled on taking a one-way direct flight on American Airlines that would depart at 9:45 a.m. two weeks from today. I booked it straight away.

CHAPTER FOUR

The next seven days were a flurry of exhausting work, but I was eager to get it all done and be on my way. I included a phone call to my daughter, Brooke. Needing to allow for the three-hour time difference, I awoke early the next morning at 4 and dialed up her number on my cell. It rang and rang, and just as I was about to hang up, I heard "Hello?"

"Hello, Brooke. It's Mom. How are you?"

"I'm good. Just stepped out of the shower. Happy I caught the phone. It must be very early in Cali."

"Yes, it is, but not too early to call my daughter. I wanted to catch you before you head to your office. I know how busy your day is."

"Never too busy to talk to my mom, but I'm wondering, what's going on with you?"

"I've made a life-changing decision. I'm selling the condo and moving to Kauai."

"Okay. But why Kauai and what in the world will you do there?"

"You know how I have always loved Kauai, and I will continue my writing."

"Is that it? Can't believe you don't have anything else cookin'. It wouldn't be like you to head off like this without some idea of what you will do."

I took a deep breath and forged on, expecting a rash of negativity from my daughter. "I'm going to buy a bed and breakfast and become the innkeeper." There was a long silence, and finally, I said, "No comment?"

"I'm speechless. Don't you think you're biting off more than you should, especially at your age?"

"What do you mean *your age*? Brooke, I will not let age deter me from doing what I want to do. If I don't do this now, then when? Should I sit in this condo with all the bad memories and drift away into nothingness without anything to excite and challenge me? I think not. I will not live my life for you, or what you want me to do or not do! Enough said. I'll give you my address once I'm settled."

"Okay, sounds like you are bound and determined to take this giant leap."

"Yes, I am, but also excited – please don't take that away from me with your negativity. I will look to a visit from you once I'm settled in."

"I will do that, Mom. Bye for now."

"Goodbye, Brooke."

After I hung up, I was relieved that I had taken that big step to call her, but not so pleased that I'd allowed her to break my spirit. *I hate it when people can only point out the negatives and not the positives. Why can't she be happy for me? She should be for, after all; she will have a place to stay in Kauai.* As I sat thinking about our conversation, I heard a knock on the door. Getting up to answer, I recalled Judy had said she was coming over to help me with the laborious task of down-sizing and sorting through my possessions.

I answered the door to find Judy standing there with her arms full of packing boxes. "Good morning, my friend. You're certainly early. What is that I smell?"

"Good morning, Maggie. I plan to get an early start today, and that smell happens to be from Einstein's bagels with, of course, cream cheese. Figured you could use some sustenance."

"Yes, I could, and especially after my talk with Brooke."

"Really? How did that go?"

"About as well as I expected. She isn't thrilled with me moving to Kauai and couldn't muster up a compliment, which isn't surprising to me considering our history."

"Did you ever tell her about her real father?"

"Only that he had disappeared from my life, and I wouldn't give her up for anything. I have delighted in having a daughter, but it hasn't always been easy."

"Kids never are, or at least seldom."

"Enough about Brooke, let's sit and have those bagels. I have coffee ready."

Judy sat nibbling on her everything bagel and drinking her coffee, which she always claimed was like sludge. "Maggie, are you still using that strong brew? Have you ever thought of switching to a more mellow coffee?"

"Yes, and no. I happen to like my 'sludge' as you call it. Just add some hot water or more Coffee-mate."

"I already did that, and it's still too strong for my taste, but I will struggle through it."

I smiled and finished up my cinnamon and raisin bagel and indulged in a second cup of coffee.

"How about we get started with packing?" I suggested, "And then I'll treat you to dinner, if you're available?"

"How about a rain check? I have a – what you might call a date."

"Good for you. Anyone, I know?"

"No, someone I met while showing houses."

"Have a good time but be careful, especially on your first date."

"Oh, I will, but you shouldn't project your fears onto me. I haven't had some of your experiences."

"Be glad you haven't," I said with the utmost sincerity.

We made short order of a lot of my belongings: those that were treasured, those that didn't hold any particular significance to me, and others that were just ho-hum – "I think I can live without that."

In the afternoon while we were making order in my office, Judy asked: "What are you going to do with all these books?"

"I'm going to pack them and take them with me. Many of them are research for my writing, and others are books that are part of my collection. No way am I getting rid of them."

"Why would you start writing at this time of your life?"

"What is that supposed to mean? Besides, I have been writing. Are you saying I'm too old?"

"Well, don't people usually start at a younger age?"

"Not always. You see, when Jack got sick and later when I saw our marriage dissolving, writing became a form of therapy for me. It gave me a path in which to set aside what was happening with our marriage and his health and allowed me to do something for me. I lived in his shadow for so long that I felt like I was suffocating. He was a difficult and overbearing person to live with. Writing became my refuge."

"You are an amazing woman, and I'm proud of you for being able to move on. You could have very easily had a breakdown, or worse, been driven to drinking or using drugs! I know your marriage was not a bed of roses, and you'd been unhappy for a long time."

"That's true, but I was all he had. He lost his business, and then he became ill. I promised him that I would take care of him and provide him with medical care. But I was determined he wasn't going to take everything out of me. I've always been strong, and this was a time in which I had to show what I was made of. Of course, it helps that I'm financially independent having the proceeds from his life insurance policies and my profit sharing from the law firm. So, I should be fairly comfortable."

"But back to being realistic, do you realize what it is going to cost you to ship those books?"

"I know it'll be expensive, but they are a part of who I am, so I'll grin and bear it – the cost I mean. Now let's get busy with packing them. I will also be packing a few things to take with me in case I don't find a place right away, and writing will fill my time."

I could see Judy grimace at the thought of shipping books, but I couldn't care less. I'm going to be selfish and have what I want.

"Besides, books don't talk back," I replied with a wide grin on my face.

I struggled at times with the decision-making process and would stop what I was doing with my mind wandering off in another direction. My home holds so many memories – some good and some not so good, and there are ones I would like to erase from my mind. Will I regret making this big move and all that it entails or live happily ever after? Well, I certainly won't know until I try it.

CHAPTER FIVE

I woke to the sounds of the smooth jazz radio station I had come to love and admittedly would miss when I moved. I'd need to convert myself into listening to Hawaiian music! I looked at the clock and groaned; 4:00 a.m.! I should be ecstatic that my big day had arrived so why am I groaning when this is the start of my brand-new life? I turned off the alarm, threw back the covers and, with a smile on my face, walked into the bathroom to get ready for my shuttle to the airport that was due to arrive in exactly one hour. I was pleased that I had laid out my clothes the night before – white sneakers, white slacks, a red t-shirt and, just in case of rain, a navy-blue windbreaker.

Fortunately, I had done most of my packing yesterday after fits and starts about what I should take and what I would need to wear on the island. I reconciled with myself that if necessary, I would resort to buying some clothes upon arrival because most of what I had in the closet was not appropriate for Kauai. When I become the innkeeper of a bed and breakfast my wardrobe would change altogether. I finished putting the last of what I had set aside to pack, hoping it would all fit, and I wouldn't be charged for extra weight. Shoes were no problem as I'm a sandal gal, and I threw in a pair of sneakers and flats.

I placed my laptop in my carry on and packed all my toiletries in a waterproof pouch. Double-checking to make sure I had everything

I could need, the phone rang. Knowing it had to be the shuttle driver, I answered, and this strange voice said, "Hi, I'm Bernie, your shuttle driver. I'll wait for you to come down."

"That's fine; I'll be down in a few minutes."

I quickly closed my luggage and carry on, double checked the sliding door and turned off lights. Fortunately, Judy had said she would come over to check on the place while I was gone, and I needn't worry about anything. I worked my way down the hallway to the elevator. *This is the last time I'll be in this building.* Certain memories came flashing back, but I quickly pushed them aside. After sorting through everything, I had made a detailed inventory of the things I wanted to be shipped to Kauai. Judy had a copy of the list along with instructions. What a lifesaver she was in addition to assisting me with downsizing and staging the condominium. Once downstairs in the lobby, a man with a crazy beanie hat came charging up the steps to the front door to assist me.

"Ms. Langham. I'm your driver, Bernie."

"I'm pleased to meet you and thank you for being prompt. Let's get going."

"Okay, but first we need to stop for coffee to go at Starbucks. I saw one nearby on the corner."

"Really? Well, if you're going to get one, I'll take one as well. A medium latte with two equals would be great! Let me give you some money, Bernie."

"No need. It's on me."

"Thanks."

"What airline are you flying on today?" Bernie asked.

"American Airlines," I responded.

"Headed to Hawaii?"

"Yes, how did you know?"

"A lot of my early morning passengers fly to Hawaii, so it was just a good guess. When will you be coming back? I will be happy to make you a reservation."

"Thank you, Bernie, but that won't be necessary."

I specifically ordered an executive car so that I could enjoy a quiet, conversation-less ride to the airport without a coffee stop or idle chit-chat on the way to the airport! I hadn't expected my driver would be so talkative.

"Mind me being nosy, but I'm going to ask it anyway. Are you going to be living there?"

"Yes. I'm moving – starting over, you could say."

"Wow! You are brave to be making such a move at your age."

Not knowing how to respond, I ignored Bernie's comment.

"Sorry if I misspoke."

"I'm sure others will wonder the same thing. It's never too late to start over."

"Guess not," he replied. "I admire your courage."

"Thank you."

Bernie drove the rest of the way without engaging me in conversation, which was a relief, for I still had things to sort through my mind.

CHAPTER SIX

Bernie stopped at the terminal for my departure and assisted me with my bags. I tipped him generously and said, "Thank you for getting me here on time and safely. It was nice talking to you." I checked my bags with the skycap and walked into the terminal to check the departures and arrivals board. I noticed that my plane was on time and proceeded to my designated gate to depart LAX.

Loving to people-watch I sat gazing at the army of passengers from different walks of life scurrying around in search of their flights. I listened for the announcement that my plane was boarding and stepped into the line awaiting my turn.

Once ensconced in my window seat, I settled in for the five-and-one-half hour flight to Lihue. I pulled out a novel I had been reading and my journal to review my notes for features I would be looking for in a bed and breakfast. I dozed off and felt the hand of a flight attendant gently shake my shoulder, "Ms., we are starting our descent into Lihue."

"Thank you," I mumbled in the middle of a yawn. *My goodness, how could I have slept the entire way? Guess I'm more tired than I thought I was. It will be good to get settled and hopefully into a routine.*

Stepping off the plane, I was immediately struck by the warm tropical breeze and the overall feeling of tranquility. *Oh, how I have missed the islands.* The immediate sense put me at ease, and I breathed in the scent of the tropics.

Upon arriving at the Lihue airport, I was greeted with a fragrant plumeria lei and made my way to baggage claim and retrieved my checked bags. I dragged them over to the Hertz shuttle bus that would take me to the car rental area. I had previously reserved a cute red Volvo convertible and took care of all the necessary paperwork; I began the short drive to The Island Garden Inn where I'd requested a first-floor room with access to the pool and a view of the ocean. With some assistance to my room, I was happy to see that I was afforded my request. I quickly unpacked, stretched out on the king-size bed, and reflected on my quick decision-making prowess. I dropped off to sleep and woke to realize that it was almost 5:00 p.m. – happy hour. I freshened up and decided to get into the spirit of the islands and picked out a long shocking-pink dress with a short cardi to match; slipped my feet into my white sandals and headed to the restaurant area for a bit of libation.

Not wanting to sit at the bar, I found a table and sat waiting for a server to take my order. Suddenly a handsome man with electric blue eyes approached my table, "Have you been helped?" he asked with a recognizable Scottish brogue.

"I was waiting to order a glass of white wine, but so far, no one has come over."

"My apologies, miss. Let me introduce myself. Paul Sinclair, I'm the innkeeper and at your service. I'll get you that glass of wine."

I watched him walk over to the bar area and pour a glass of white wine. Mr. Sinclair appeared to be in his early fifties and was well built – he obviously works out. Dark brown hair, blue eyes, and a killer smile. But what am I thinking – I'm not looking for a man! I'm here to start over sans men. Still, he's easy on the eye.

"Here you go."

"Thank you, Mr. Sinclair. Do I detect a bit of an accent?"

"Yes, you do. I was born in Scotland and came to the United States when I was a teenager. Please call me Paul. May I sit?"

"Sure. My name is Maggie Langham, and I arrived this afternoon from Los Angeles."

"Are you here on business or for pleasure?"

"A little of both. I'm here to meet with a realtor and hopefully purchase a property. I plan to move to Kauai as soon as my condominium in Pasadena sells."

"Really? I can tell you from my experience that I came here to escape the hustle and bustle of the city and wanted a better quality of life. Now I'm happy to say that I have it and I enjoy living here."

"Well, my situation is a bit different," I said as my cell phone rang. Paul got up and excused himself.

"Hello."

"Aloha. Maggie, this is Dean Kalima. I hope you are getting settled in at the hotel and finding everything to your liking."

"Yes, so far."

"How about if I meet you for breakfast in the morning and we can start your search for a bed and breakfast?"

Frankly, the word 'search' caught me off guard. I had hoped he would have properties lined up to show me.

"Yes, Dean that would be fine."

"9:00 a.m.?"

"See you then, and thank you for calling."

"Na'u Ka Hau'oli."

I sat feeling the excitement build. My new venture was becoming a reality. As I was looking around to order another glass of wine, Paul reappeared, this time with two glasses of chardonnay. Sitting down, he said, "I left because I didn't want you to think that I was eavesdropping on your conversation."

"Oh no. Not at all. It was about setting a time to look at some properties."

"When your phone rang, we were discussing our situations, and you were about to tell me all about yours."

"Yes. Mine. Well frankly, I lost my husband six months ago after a not so pleasant marriage. I don't want to bore you with all the details for they are difficult for me to talk about and you probably wouldn't be interested anyway."

"Why don't you try me? I make an excellent listener and have a good shoulder if you need one to cry on."

"My crying days are over. I don't mean to sound so cavalier, but my husband put me through the wringer. I'm fortunate to have survived the financial debacle and the mental abuse. Maybe some other time. I don't want to spoil the high I'm on right now. I'm excited to be moving forward even though I know I will be up to my ears in work."

"What kind of work may I ask?"

"Afraid you were going to ask that. I'm looking to purchase a bed and breakfast that will give me some income."

"Why would you say that? I don't feel like we will be competitors. We'll be working with different markets. So, does your plan include staying on Kauai?"

"Yes, it does, but only if I can find the right property."

"I have every confidence you'll be successful."

"You hardly know me. Why do you say that?"

I can read people well, and you seem like a very determined woman and independent, which will see you far. Listen, I'm finished for the day. How about some dinner? Not here, of course. Give me some time to show you a bit of the island? Unless you're too tired from traveling."

"No, that would be great. I'm wound up and excited to be here. I should probably change?"

"No, you look fine. Let me get my briefcase, and we can head out."

Paul was gone only for a couple of minutes which gave me time to look around and get familiar with the lobby and the small sundries area which offered every conceivable item a guest would want; even healthy snacks and sparkling bottled water.

"Ready?"

"Sure," I replied as he took my arm, leading me out to the parking lot.

We walked out to his car, a white BMW convertible. He assisted me as I got into the passenger side.

Driving out to Kuhio Highway, he turned right and after a short drive pulled into a parking area. The sign read 'Parking for Bull Shed customers only'. *Hmm. Bull Shed in Kauai. This is going to be interesting.*

Paul helped me out of the car, and we walked into the restaurant. I was pleasantly surprised that it didn't have any atmosphere reflective of the name. A hostess seated us on the oceanfront patio with an exquisite view of the Pacific, waves crashing onto the beach.

"Paul, this is a stunning view."

"I thought you might like it. It's a local establishment that has been serving some of Kauai's best steak and seafood for the past forty years."

"You have selected the perfect restaurant for my first night in Kauai."

"I was hoping you would like it."

We looked over the menu, and Paul asked, "Wine?"

"Yes, that would be lovely. I'll leave it up to you to make a selection."

Our server appeared, and Paul ordered a bottle of chardonnay and said, "Give us a few minutes to take our order."

"No problem," he said and went off to get our wine.

"What are you hungry for?" he asked.

"Considering it's my first night I'm going to splurge and have the lobster."

"Great choice," he replied.

Our server, whose name tag read *Kimo*, appeared with our wine and Paul deftly placed our dinner order after giving his approval for the wine.

He is smooth. Wonder if he greets all of his guests in this manner?

"Paul, you have certainly made my first day memorable. The wine is delicious, and I'm looking forward to the lobster."

"Just so you know, I don't treat all my guests this way."

"I was wondering about that. I'm not concerned at all, just enjoying sitting out here and soaking up the atmosphere."

"Good," he said, smiling.

We ate our dinners, and upon finishing, Kimo appeared and asked, "Dessert?"

"Lappert's Kauai Pie," Paul responded.

"I don't think I can eat a whole slice. How about if we share?"

"Fine. Kimo, bring two forks if you would."

Kimo returned and along with our dessert, placed the check on the table and said, "No rush. Take your time."

I smiled and reached for the check, and Paul quickly grabbed it from me.

"Paul, please. Let me get this."

"No, my treat, I insist."

I couldn't argue with him as I was starting to feel tired from my day of traveling and then this scrumptious dinner. We finished our dessert and left the restaurant. Walking to the car, I felt completely at ease and anxious to tackle my task of finding the property for my bed and breakfast. On the way back to the hotel, Paul asked, "You look deep in thought. A penny for them?"

"A penny wouldn't cut it. Thinking about my property, I want to purchase, but I need to be patient and wait and see what comes."

"Good thinking."

As I said that, we pulled into the inn's parking lot and Paul came around to help me out of the car.

"May I walk you to your room?"

"You may."

"I don't like to presume anything," he said, placing his hand on the small of my back as we walked towards my room.

"Here it is," I whispered not wanting to make noise, disturbing the other guests.

"Maggie, no need to whisper," he said with a broad grin. "We have outdone ourselves soundproofing rooms, so guests are not disturbed."

"Oh," is all I could think of to say.

He took my room key and opened my door and I stepped into my room.

"Paul, it has been a lovely evening. Thank you. I'm sure I will see you tomorrow?"

"Definitely. Breakfast in the dining room," he said, turning to leave and handing me my key.

I reached out and grabbed his arm, saying, "I so enjoyed dinner. I sense you went out of your way to entertain me, and I appreciate it. Been a long time since a man made me feel special."

"So I have been told," he replied.

"Wait a minute. What do you mean exactly?"

"Let's just say that someone gave me a heads-up," and with that, he turned and strode off down the hall. "One other thing don't forget to secure the door with the additional locks," he said over his shoulder.

"Oh, I won't. Thank you, Paul."

And then he was gone. I closed the door and complied with his instructions. *He is such a gentleman. But obviously, it was a setup. The only one who could have tipped him off was my good friend, Judy. I will certainly have to speak to her about that. I am not a charity case by any stretch of the imagination. But it was a lovely evening!*

I was grateful that I had already unpacked and walked into the bathroom to prepare for bed. As I finished brushing my teeth, the room phone rang. I quickly went to answer it.

"Hello?"

"All tucked in?"

"No, not quite but just about."

"Door double locked?"

"Yes, sir, just as you instructed."

"Good. Then I will say goodnight and sleep well."

"Thank you and goodnight to you as well. Until tomorrow."

I heard a click and hung up the phone.

I pulled back the bedcovers and slipped in between the soft sheets, luxuriating in the feeling. I left the sliding door open and listened to the waves splashing onto the beach and felt the tropical trade wind breeze float into my room. As I drifted off, I felt contented that I had made the right decision and was starting my life over. Sometime during the night, I woke to hear rain lightly falling outside my window, soothing me back to sleep.

CHAPTER SEVEN

The next morning a rooster awakened me at the ungodly hour of 5:00 a.m. *This bed feels so good* – I turned over and decided a little more sleep wouldn't hurt. Suddenly, I awoke, glanced at the clock, 8:00 a.m.! Bright sun blasted my window! I threw back the covers: *I have one hour to get ready and eat some breakfast.* I dressed quickly but took care, selecting a navy-blue cotton skirt and a white t-shirt with flats to wear for my appointment with Dean Kalima. Makeup and hair all done – I looked in the mirror and said, "I'm ready to get on with the day."

I took the elevator down to the lobby area and walked with a spring in my step past the front desk to the restaurant area. Paul was there, which surprised me, and he had coffee waiting for me.

"Good morning, Mr. Sinclair," I said as I sat down opposite him. "This is a surprise. How did you know I was up and moving?"

"I asked my front desk person to call me when he saw you. I was up early and decided to come in and see you off with your realtor. Since you are alone, I want to make sure you aren't going off with some questionable stranger. You know, we Scots are quite protective of those we're close to."

I smiled and started drinking my coffee.

"How did you do this?"

"What do you mean?"

"My coffee is fixed just the way I like it."

"Lucky guess is all. May I get you something to eat?"

"I'll look at the buffet and see what it offers. If you will excuse me, I'll be right back."

I got up and approached the buffet. I chose several slices of the orange papaya, chunks of honeydew melon and a handful of grapes. Deciding against waiting for the waffle maker to free up, I ambled over to the table loaded with all types of pastries and bread, selecting an English muffin to complement my fruit.

Once my muffin was toasted, I grabbed some butter and strawberry jam and walked back to the table where Paul was patiently waiting for me.

I sat down and quickly consumed fruit and muffin.

"Maggie, excuse me. I have a call to take."

Just as well for now. I enjoyed talking with him but as hungry as I was, I needed to finish my breakfast. As I was looking to refill my cup, Paul appeared with a fresh cup of coffee for me.

"Thank you. Amazing how insightful you are."

"You forget, service is my area of expertise."

"Do you treat all your hotel guests this way?"

"Not all, just the attractive single ones."

I smiled and glanced at my watch. It was five after nine and Paul, not missing a beat, said, "Don't worry. Hawaiians have their own clock."

As he said that a very handsome thirty-something Hawaiian dressed in a blue floral aloha shirt walked in. I could only assume it was Dean Kalima and he carried a beautiful lei of pink and yellow plumeria blossoms. As he approached my table, I could sense a change in Paul's demeanor, which was a bit off-putting to me.

"You must be Ms. Langham. Aloha, I'm Dean Kalima," he said as he placed the lei around my neck and kissed me on each cheek.

I looked up at the most handsome man I had ever seen. Thirty-something, nearly black hair and deep-set slanted dark brown eyes that could be considered bedroom eyes. I could hardly find my voice. Finally, I spoke, "Thank you for the beautiful lei, and you needn't worry, you are right on time."

"I try to be. It wouldn't be professional if I were late," he said, smiling broadly and displaying a perfect set of white teeth.

"Please sit down. Would you care to join me for breakfast or perhaps coffee?"

"Coffee would be fine."

As if on cue, the server approached with the coffee carafe and cup and saucer in hand. Placing them on the table, Dean commented that it was his first visit to the Island Garden Inn.

"It's lovely. Light and airy, allowing for the guests to appreciate our trade winds."

"Yes, I agree. I love sitting here. It's so relaxing and peaceful."

"That's what Hawaii is all about," he replied.

"I'm very excited to learn about the properties you have lined up for me to see. When will it be possible to preview them?"

"The one I think you'll be the most taken with we will see today. It's located near Hanalei. Are you familiar with that area?"

"Yes, but only to the extent that I've stopped there for a meal and to shop."

"Okay, so you are aware that it is a bit of a drive from here. I think you will appreciate the property. The owners of the bed and breakfast, for personal reasons, find that they must return to the mainland. This property just came on the market within the last week. There has been some activity, but so far nothing of any substance; no offers. But I'm confident it won't last long. When the 'right' buyer comes along, it will be snapped up very quickly."

"Can you tell me about it, as I know it is a bit of a drive out to Hanalei."

"Sure."

Reading from his book, Dean went on, "The bed and breakfast consists of the big house, which is quite spacious. It features five bedrooms and 6-1/2 baths. There is a fully equipped gourmet kitchen and pantry, available for guests to use, as is the gas BBQ, washer/dryer, and refrigerator with ice maker/water. A TV/VCR/DVD are available in the great room. For beachgoers, boogie boards and snorkel equipment, beach chairs, towels, and coolers are provided. It has a spa and a full bath in the hot tub area that is recommended before guests enter the spa. A computer notebook and printer are available for guests to use. It's a smoke-free establishment, but a guest may smoke outside the building. Social drinking is acceptable."

"It sounds fabulous, but I'm sure so is the price."

"Well, I'm sure you're aware that the price is negotiable."

"What are they asking?"

"A million two."

"With some maneuvering, I can come close to that."

"I have it on good authority, that because of their situation, they will entertain any offer; they're most anxious to relocate to the mainland."

"I guess there's no harm in looking at the property. It will at least give me something to go by."

"Yes, that's true. Shall we go?"

"Yes, but first I need to go to my room for my bag."

"Go ahead, and I'll be waiting for you right here."

I'm sure you will be. If you can wrap up this sale, it would be a nice hefty commission for you.

Back in my room, I pulled together what I thought I would need when my cell phone rang. "Aloha."

"Wow! You're getting adjusted to living in Hawaii."

"Hi, Judy. What's up?"

"What's up is that I showed the condo to a couple in their late sixties yesterday afternoon. They're both retired professors and doing research at the Huntington Library. They loved your condo, and I have an offer to present to you. When would be a good time?"

"I would say now except that I'm on my way out to look at a bed and breakfast. Maybe it would be a good idea if you could fax or email it to me, so I can read it along with a breakdown of my costs and what I will possibly net while we talk."

"Okay, let me send an email. I think that would be more appropriate and safe. When you've had a chance to look over the offer, call me so that we can discuss it. Please keep in mind that people do get impatient; if they're considering other properties, and you take too long to respond to their offer, you may lose them."

"You forget, I was in real estate once, and I know all about fickle buyers. By the way, on another topic: did you set me up with Paul Sinclair? He was very attentive last night, and he took me to dinner, which was lovely. I must say, I've not been wined and dined like that in years. It seemed he had been given some inside information, and while I enjoyed dinner, it seemed like a setup. Judy, you should know better. I'm not ready for another relationship or romp in the hay, even a one-night stand. Besides, I was tired after traveling and didn't feel like being romanced. Makes me wonder if you know Paul?"

"Oh, all right, I did go overboard, and yes, I know Paul but don't want to go into any details. I apologize but honestly thought you could use the special attention from a handsome, sexy man."

"I'm not a charity case, but you can be sure I appreciated all the attention. But it was too soon. And then again, I wouldn't want to spoil anything for the future. I don't want to belabor this, and Dean is waiting for me. I'll talk to you later and good luck with selling my condominium. Ciao," and with that, I hung up.

As I left my room to meet up with Dean, I felt elated but told myself not to get too excited. I had no idea what the offer could be, but otherwise, Judy did sound upbeat about it.

From the elevator, I walked towards the restaurant but noticed that Dean was standing near the front desk, talking quietly with Paul.

"Hi, hope I'm not disturbing your conversation? You both look so serious."

"No, not really," replied Dean. "Paul was just warning me to take care of you."

"Paul, that's very kind of you, but…"

"Don't say it. I take care of my friends. Look, I need to get to work. Good luck with the property. I'll see you later?"

"Sure. I'll let you know when I get back."

Dean and I walked out to the parking lot, but I turned around to catch a glimpse of Paul standing in the same spot staring at us. I waved and walked on to where Dean's white Land Rover was parked.

"I guess real estate here on Kauai must be quite profitable?"

"Because I often show remote property, it's best to have this type of vehicle. Don't want to get stuck."

He opened the passenger door and helped me in. Despite what he said about visiting remote properties, I couldn't help but think Dean's business must be doing quite well for him to be driving this vehicle. Unless he comes from a family with 'money'.

CHAPTER EIGHT

As we drove out on Kuhio Highway towards Hanalei, we passed what was left of the Coco Palms Resort which was ravaged by Hurricane Iniki that devastated the island in 1992.

"Maggie, you seem a million miles away."

"No. I remember how the Coco Palms looked way back in the '80s."

"Was that the last time you were here?"

"Oh, no, I've been here on a couple of occasions since then, and every time I drive by, I wonder why something hasn't been done. Such a shame to let this property deteriorate. The palms are still standing proudly despite the havoc from Iniki, but I can see how devastating the storm was to the entire resort."

"Yes, it is a shame, but I have it on good authority there are plans to redo the entire property. As always, things get mired in bureaucratic red tape."

"So true."

I knew there were questions I should be asking but decided to wait until after I viewed the property. As we drove the winding road up to Hanalei, I was taken by the lush green tropical foliage and the clean, fresh air that follows the rain. I was beginning to think we would never get to the bed and breakfast for we kept driving and driving, passing through Princeville and traversing over a double metal bridge before making a turn on Alamihi Road.

"Dean, how far is this property? We seem to have been driving a good while."

"It's a bit out of the way from Lihue and a few miles from Hanalei, but worth the drive once you see it," he answered.

We drove a short distance and approached a property that appeared to be on stilts.

Dean said, "Don't look so taken aback. I know you think this must be out of your price range."

"Yes, that's exactly what I was thinking."

We got out of the car and were met by an older couple, tanned and smiling as they walked towards us.

"Hi, I'm Mac, and this is my wife, Sara. You must be Dean Kalima, the realtor." He nodded in my direction, "And you are his client."

Dean responded quickly and said, "Yes, this is Maggie Langham, who has moved from the mainland."

"How do you do."

I smiled and said, "So nice to meet you both, and I want to thank you for allowing us to come and preview the property at such short notice."

"No, problem," said Mac as he reached out to shake my hand, and his wife stepped forward and said, "Aloha."

"Aloha to you both."

Mac said, "If you don't mind, let me lead the way, and I can tell you all about the property, of which we are extremely proud."

As the elevator took us to the upstairs area, Mac described all the amenities of the property. He talked about the importance of being close to the beach – only 110 steps!

"Mac, that's amazing. I'm sure your guests find that very convenient."

"Yes, ma'am, they do."

Mac pointed out all the amenities of the property and mentioned

that Ona assists them with preparing breakfast and other kitchen duties. "After all, breakfast is the most important meal of the day, and
we want our guests to be well nourished when they set out for their
day's activities."

Sara took over the conversation and said, "I enjoy lei making, reading, cooking, and gardening. I stay very busy, but most of all, Mac and
I take pleasure in our guests sharing our Hawaiian hospitality, island
history, and legends."

"Sounds lovely," I said as they proudly showed us the Plumeria,
Hibiscus, Anthurium, and Pikake suites each with private baths and
decorated in a unique color.

"Mac, these guest suites are lovely, but no one is here. Is that
unusual?"

"Ms. Langham, we had the rooms occupied for two weeks, and
all the folks left about the same time. Rest assured, we have reservations booked well in advance, and it's not often that all four suites are
unoccupied at one time."

Nodding, I said, "Okay. Where do you get your guests from? Is
there a service or an agency?"

"Ms. Langham, that's a good question. Initially, we hooked up
with a national travel agency, but then, after a while, we had a lot of
repeat customers and then referrals from them. It rather snowballed.
We were lucky that way," replied Mac.

As we continued, I observed the dining room, gourmet kitchen,
great room, TV and reading room, and outside the lanai and picnic
area adjacent to the hot tub.

"Your property is lovely. Well cared for and maintained but it
seems as if it would be a tremendous amount of work for one person.
Is there help available to assist with cooking, cleaning, yard work, and
the like?" I inquired.

"Ms. Langham, thank you for asking that question which is an
essential one. We do have Ona and her husband, Keoki, who live
here on the property in a small cottage to assist us with those things.

Otherwise, we couldn't handle everything and be gracious hosts at the same time."

"Thank you for providing that information. It's a relief to know that," I said.

As we finished our tour, I asked: "Where do you two live?"

Mac spoke up and said, "Sorry. I wasn't sure if you plan on residing here or having managers and living elsewhere."

"I plan to live on the property. I guess I could always take one of the suites, but that would take away from potential income."

"No need to be concerned about that, Ms. Langham."

"Please call me Maggie."

"Okay, Maggie. Follow me, and I'll show you our living quarters."

We followed Mac and Sara to the front door and down the steps. He led us through an area of lush green foliage and bamboo trees.

"Here it is," he said proudly.

Dean and I looked with our mouths open. From the outside, the cottage looked brand new, and I was taken aback, wondering how much more this would add to the price.

"Let's go inside."

We walked up a few steps, and Mac opened the door for us, which led into the pristine kitchen which had been freshly painted a porcelain white and updated with ocean blue Caesar stone countertops. The cabinets were a bright, clean white. I looked around and noticed the appliances looked new.

"Come on this way, folks," Mac led us into the dining area which had a large bay window overlooking the beach. We walked on into the living room and found another large window alongside the front door that led out to a wraparound porch.

"May I go out?"

"Certainly."

I walked out and was overwhelmed by the view. The ocean and sparkling white sand were so inviting, and I wanted to take a swim.

"Mac, if I could, I would move in today! This property is incredible."

"Let us show you the rest of the inside."

We walked back in through the living room into a hallway that led to the master bedroom. I noticed a sitting room adjacent to the bedroom that would make an excellent area for my writing. A large window provided a stunning view of the surrounding landscape. I could picture myself sitting at my desk, looking out onto the lush grounds.

"This room would make a perfect office where I can do my writing and be inspired by the beautiful view," I said with a broad smile.

"What do you write, Maggie?" asked Mac.

"I'm currently working on a historical novel about a Hawaiian woman who made her mark in history."

"Sounds interesting. This would certainly be a quiet retreat for you to pursue that," he commented.

"Maggie, this is the master bath," Sara said, taking my arm and leading me through another doorway that featured a large old-fashioned bathtub looking out onto a vast expanse of beach.

I noticed the enclosed stall shower, double sinks, and a private closet with the commode.

I stood, too amazed to speak.

"I don't know what to say. This is all so beautiful."

We started walking back out through the hallway to the kitchen, and I marveled at how beautifully maintained the entire cottage was, much like the inside of the main building.

Mac spoke about the utilities on the property that included a satellite dish with internet access. "Back about 100 yards is the cottage where Keoki, our handyman, and Ona, our maid and cook, reside," offered Mac as we found ourselves back out by the cars.

Dean, extending his hand to both Mac and Sara, said, "Thank you for your time and hospitality."

"I appreciate you taking the time to show us your lovely property; you have been most gracious," I said, stepping forward to hug Mac and Sara.

As we walked to Dean's Land Rover, Sara was anxiously following us and asked, "When do you think you'll make a decision?"

"I'm not sure. Some things will affect which way I'll go, but I will let you know as quickly as I can. It seems you are most anxious to return to the mainland?"

Sara clutched Mac's arm and said, "Yes, we are. Family requires us to be close. If we could, we would stay, but we're needed back on the mainland."

"Thank you again for your time."

We drove off with Sara and Mac watching us until we had turned onto Alamihi Road, when I said to Dean, "Didn't you think they were a bit anxious? Maybe they'll be flexible on their price?"

"Could be. However, I wouldn't count on it. I believe you're the first potential buyer to see the property, so naturally, they're encouraged. I must admit this is an in-house listing, so I have the first crack at it. But that doesn't mean you can drag your feet thinking about it."

"Dean, bottom line. What is the property listed for?"

"$1.2 million."

"About what I expected, but since this is a business, I presume that once we present them with an offer, they'll allow me to look at their books? I certainly would need to know what their profit and loss look like. Although I must say from the appearance of everything, they must do well. Otherwise, the property couldn't look like it does. Let's face it. The Inn on Alamihi Road is an extraordinary property and not what I expected. To be quite honest, I thought it would have a lot of deferred maintenance and such, but it looks well maintained and cared for. The only drawback is that it is so far away from Lihue."

"True, but remember you are very close to Princeville and Hanalei. Yes, you will have access to their books."

CHAPTER NINE

Dean and I didn't engage in much conversation as he drove us back to the hotel. I kept thinking about the property and how perfect it was. I couldn't find any fault with it and was imagining living there when he interrupted my train of thought.

"I have another property to show you, which is in Poipu Beach and much closer to where you indicated you would like to be. If you're not too tired, would you like to see it today?"

"Sure, why not? I'm not tired at all. In fact, I'm encouraged and upbeat about my prospects. Besides, it's early enough in the day. Let's do it."

"Great. First, may I suggest I take you to lunch, and I can set up the viewing while we are eating?"

"Perfect."

Dean drove on the Kuhio Highway towards Poipu as I texted Judy and let her know what was happening. As I finished texting, we pulled into the parking lot of Kalapaki Joe's, a restaurant Dean claimed to be the westernmost sports bar in the U.S.

"We're here," announced Dean as he got out of the Land Rover and walked around to my side of the car to help me out. We headed into the restaurant and were shown to a lovely table in a quiet corner, which was saying a lot. *The noise level was several decibels from where I felt comfortable, but this was Dean's choice and who was I to complain?*

The Hawaiian hostess was very attentive, greeting Dean by name. She mentioned the specials of the day as she handed us menus. It didn't take long for me to decide on the Fresh Fish Island Sandwich with iced tea. Dean ordered the Pulled Pork Stack and iced tea as well. He excused himself to call the owners of the bed and breakfast that we were to preview. I sat looking through my email messages and noticed that Judy had asked me to call ASAP.

Dialing her number, I grew anxious, but she answered on the second ring.

"Hi, Judy, it's me from the beautiful garden island of Kauai."

"Hi, Maggie. You obviously got my email."

"Yes, I did. It sounded urgent. I hope this isn't bad news?"

"No, it isn't, and in fact, you are going to be ecstatic! I now have in my hands three offers, all of which you will be happy with. I can tell you that one of them puts the pinch on you because they want possession very soon and, as an incentive, they have come in way over the listed price."

"Really? Like how soon?"

"Two weeks. But before I get ahead of myself, we need to set a time for me to present these offers."

Dean appeared from having made his phone call and indicated with a thumbs-up we were good to go to preview the next property.

"Judy, we're having lunch and are headed to preview another B & B. Can it wait until I get back to the hotel?"

"Sure. In the meantime, I'm going to try and figure out how to use this Skype thing."

"Okay. Sounds good to me. Talk to you later."

"That was Judy, and she has two more offers to present to me. I'm beginning to wonder if this is all a dream."

"No, Maggie, I would say that when things are meant to be, they happen very quickly."

As we ate our lunch, Dean described the Poipu Bed and Breakfast.

"According to the listing, all of their suites are decorated in vintage Hawaiian decor. Guests are provided with a luxurious king-size bed with a private bath. Quality linens, plush pillows, and natural bath products that are handmade on Kauai. A light, nutritious breakfast is served daily on the outside lanai area where guests may socialize. Guests will experience all the amenities they would expect from a luxurious hotel, but with personal service. The vintage Hawaiian decor is simple and stylish. The artwork is provided by local artists and are available for purchase."

As I munched on my Fish Island Sandwich, I contemplated what Dean had just recited.

"Well, what do you think?"

"What I think is, that since we came all the way to Poipu Beach and made the appointment with the owners, we should show them the courtesy of previewing the property."

"You don't sound too enthused."

"Not sure what I feel about this property, but it deserves a look. If I don't, I may regret it later."

"Good. I'm glad you think so."

Dean summoned the server over to our table and asked for the check. He pulled out a credit card and without glancing at the check gave it back to the server to ring up.

Soon we were on our way amidst the big fluffy white clouds that had turned to a grayish black color, indicating rain.

"I hope we make it before the rain starts." No sooner had I said that and raindrops began to appear on the windshield.

"Don't worry; I grew up here and driving in our rain – even torrential downpours is a common occurrence."

"That's comforting," I said, looking out the window as the rain began pelting the Land Rover.

"It isn't much further," said Dean sensing my unease.

We continued with the rain pouring down when he said, "We're right here," turning onto Hoonani Road.

Dean introduced me to the owners of the inn, Tony and Anani, who were not as charming and gracious as the couple I had met earlier in Hanalei. Reluctantly, they escorted us around the property, and Tony explained that their Hoonani Road Bed & Breakfast Inn, is located near the famous Koloa Landing Diving & Swimming location on Kauai's sunny south shore. The entire house was decorated with tropical furnishings, fine art and woodwork. I sensed the warm, aloha feeling they offered with every amenity a guest could need.

"Maggie, our inn is the perfect location for guests to enjoy their time on Kauai, close to Kukui'ula Shopping Center and a short walk to snorkeling with Hawaiian monk seals and turtles. We serve a delicious island continental breakfast every morning," Tony said enthusiastically.

Walking around the property, I saw a large mango tree, sunrise papayas and apple bananas that complemented the lush gardens. I had to admit that there were many lovely features to the property, and the proximity to the beach was key. After a short tour, Dean and I thanked our hosts and walked out to the Land Rover to make the drive back to the island. He had given me a lot to ponder, but I questioned his judgment, even showing me the property after sensing the wife's less than enthusiastic reaction to our visit.

"Dean, by the way, you didn't tell me why this young couple want to sell their bed and breakfast. From all appearances, they don't seem like they're eager to rush off anywhere and, in fact, I noticed they were a bit reticent about showing us around and giving me any information I would need to make my decision. I also noticed that none of the rooms were occupied, which made me wonder if something was going on, and we were intruding."

"To be honest, Anani doesn't want to sell. She has lived here all her life, and it is home to her. But Tony is from San Diego and misses all the creature comforts of life on the mainland."

"Well, truthfully, is the property available or not and if it is what are they asking?"

"They would like to have $1.5 million."

"However, I didn't find the rooms that appealing, and it didn't have the charm that the other one did. But back to the question: is it or is it not for sale?"

"For the right price but Anani is going to need some convincing."

"To be honest with you, I'm not sure I want to get involved in this situation. It seems there are problems. I have had my share of challenges and would prefer not to get involved."

We drove back to the Island Garden Inn, and I told Dean I would be in touch very soon. What I didn't say was I would call him after I conferred with Judy. But as I walked into the hotel, I glanced around and, not seeing Paul, walked to my room. I had hoped that I could get his spin on the property I saw and get his opinion.

CHAPTER TEN

Once in my room, I muddled over the events of the day, and after taking a short nap, I called Judy, and she told me that Dean had called, concerned that he 'blew it' with me.

"Maggie, Dean knew that the second property would be a stretch, he didn't realize that you would see through his feeble attempt and he admits he hadn't given you the credit you deserve for being so astute. Give him another chance to make up for this snafu and let him show you what he can do for you. There is much more to him than meets the eye, and I think you will be pleasantly surprised and pleased."

"Maybe you're right, and I'm not giving him credit. Frankly, I feel worn out, and my brain feels frazzled. I'll give him another chance, but he better not blow it."

Judy presented the offers to me, and while they were all close to the asking price, the one I was the most inclined to accept was all cash and a very fast escrow, however, I had concerns.

"Why are they so anxious for a fast escrow? Have you checked these people out?"

"They're clients of one of my colleagues, and I feel confident they are reliable. Don't worry about the packing and shipping what you need for Kauai. I'll make sure only the things we discussed will get shipped, so you don't have to worry about sorting through things you won't want or need. But you have to promise me a week in one of your suites once the deal is done."

"No problem with that. But in the meantime, I'll sleep on it and call you in the morning. One other thing. Please fax me the documents."

Interrupting me, Judy chimed in, "If you check the hotel's fax machine you will find what you need. Don't worry; I marked the fax CONFIDENTIAL."

"You are covering all the bases. As soon as we hang up, I'll go to the front desk and ask about the fax."

"Until tomorrow then. Try and get a good night's sleep."

"I will, and I'll send you some pictures of the bed and breakfast."

"That will be great."

"Goodnight now."

"Talk to you tomorrow."

We hung up, and I looked at the clock and saw that it was still early, and I was getting a little hungry. But first things first. Must check for the faxes.

I decided to freshen up and picked out a long blue-print dress, which would be comfortable but still attractive. I slipped on my sandals and headed down to the front desk.

"Excuse me. Do you have a fax for Maggie Langham?"

"Let me check."

I stood tapping my fingers nervously on the counter, and I felt the presence of someone behind me and a voice said: "May I help you, miss?"

I turned to see Paul. We were practically nose to nose.

Pleasantly surprised and smiling, I said, "Oh! Hi! Yes, maybe you can help the desk person look for my fax?"

"My pleasure," he responded just as Akela appeared with the fax of numerous documents, a larger stack than I'd anticipated, which she handed to me.

"Here you go. Sorry, it took me a while to locate these."

"No problem. Mahalo, Akela."

"May I buy you a glass of wine?"

I looked at Paul and felt bad that I had practically ignored him but smiled and said, "That would be lovely."

We walked over to a table out of the way of the other diners and sat. A server approached, and Paul ordered for us.

"What do you have there?"

"Gee, I must apologize if I'm rude, but I'm very preoccupied. This fax contains several offers on my property in Pasadena. To compound my confusion, I have to sort out what Dean showed me today and figure out which way I'm going to go."

"Well, I hope you decide to stay here. Do you want to talk it out?"

The server arrived with our drinks, and I was surprised that instead of a glass of wine, there was a glass with a dark liquid.

"Paul, did you order us Scotch?"

Smiling devilishly, he replied, "Yes, I thought you could use it, and you need to broaden your horizons."

"You know, I used to drink Scotch back in the day."

Lifting his glass, he said, "All the best to you in what you decide."

We clinked glasses. "Cheers! Would you mind if I pick your brain?"

"No, not at all," he replied.

I proceeded to tell him about the properties I'd seen and my frustration with Dean over showing one to me that wasn't even available. "More troubling was that the couple who own the property are in the middle of a dispute. The wife doesn't want to sell but stay here on the island. The husband, who is from the mainland, wants to return to be closer to his family."

"Dean certainly didn't use good judgment."

"I think he's close friends with the husband and trying to help him out, but I don't want to get caught in the middle and be the villain."

"I understand your concerns. What are you planning to do?"

"I like the B & B in Hanalei but need another opinion. I should take another look at it. Would you mind going with me?"

"I'm honored that you asked my opinion. When would you like to schedule it?"

"As soon as possible. Would tomorrow morning work for you?"

"Sounds good. I'll let Dean know to meet us out there. I really can't in good conscience go behind his back. I know from being a real estate agent that it isn't a professional way to conduct business."

"You're more scrupulous than I am. Considering what he pulled, I would be apt just to give it a go alone."

"I thought of that too, but seriously, I know I'd be very offended if my client went behind my back. Besides, he is entitled to a commission. What time tomorrow?"

"I'll check with Dean and let you know."

We finished our drinks and Paul excused himself to see to some business.

I sat thinking of the events of the day, as Dean walked up to where I was sitting.

"Maggie, I have behaved less than professionally and wanted to apologize for today. I know after speaking with Judy, you're very offended. What can I do to make it up to you?"

"Dean, at this point, I would like for you to arrange another showing of the property in Hanalei for tomorrow morning. I have asked Paul for his advice, and he is going to drive out there with me."

I could tell from the expression on his face, he wasn't thrilled with the idea of Paul getting involved, but he agreed to set it up.

"Maggie, I would prefer to go with you, but understand your position."

"Tell them that something unexpected came up and you couldn't make it? Besides, I think they like me well enough to make this exception."

"I suppose I can. You are making this very difficult for me, but I suppose I can trust you."

"Yes, Dean, you can trust me. I will not go around you and circumvent your relationship with the sellers."

"Very well. I'll call them and tell them to expect you at say 11:30?"

Paul approached and asked, "What are you two kids plotting?"

"I have asked Dean to schedule a visit to the bread and breakfast for tomorrow morning at 11:30. I hope that's convenient for you. I know you have responsibilities here at the hotel, so if you can't make it, I'll understand."

"I'll make it work," replied Paul.

"Great. I'll call Mac and Sara and ask them if it's convenient for you to come by and I'll let you know. Goodnight, Maggie," Dean said brusquely like a petulant child who isn't allowed to eat with the grownups. He abruptly turned and walked out of the restaurant.

"Well, it looks like he's none too happy about us going out to see the property without him," commented Paul.

"Only to the extent, that I have asked you to come along but, in all fairness, if he wants to be there then so be it," I replied.

"Strange. Why would he be so disgruntled?"

"Good question. I think it's a good idea to see the property without him and make sure that everything he has told me is accurate and not exaggerated. It isn't like you're another realtor about to scoop up his client."

"True. Maggie, how about some dinner?"

"Sounds good."

Paul excused himself to get us menus and a server to take our order.

Approaching the table, he sat in the chair closest to me, and I could pick up the fragrance of his cologne; a combination of citrus and a subtle spice. *He smells great!*

The server, Pua, approached, and asked if we would like something to drink. "What are you in the mood for?" asked Paul.

"I would like a white wine. I certainly don't need anything stronger tonight after that Scotch. Want to make sure I'm super sharp tomorrow morning."

Pua returned with a bottle of chardonnay and glasses. I continued to look over the menu.

"What looks good tonight?" Paul asked as he did the honors of opening the wine, pouring it with a flourish.

"I think the sea bass would be perfect. Not too heavy. I want to make sure I can sleep tonight, so I'm well rested for our trip up to Hanalei tomorrow."

"Good point."

He turned to Akela and ordered the sea bass for me and the prime rib for himself.

"How about we share a Caesar salad?"

"That's perfect."

Akela finished taking our order and walked off as I said to Paul, "I hope I'm not taking you away from your work."

"Don't worry about me. The hotel and I will be fine."

Akela appeared with a cart laden with all the ingredients for a Caesar salad, and I exclaimed "When did this start? I didn't know you had this nice feature of preparing a Caesar salad, tableside."

"Well, it's something new, and I thought it would be good to try out tonight," he said winking at me.

We ate our salad as if we hadn't eaten in days. Our entrees arrived just as we were finishing and we both ate happily.

The conversation was kept to a minimum, as all I really wanted to do was eat and go to bed. I was hoping that tomorrow would go well.

"Maggie, you're so quiet," Paul remarked.

"I didn't realize how hungry I was until the food was set in front of me. It tasted delicious. I think I'm finally getting around to relaxing. I didn't think that this move was going to be so stressful. I don't want to appear impulsive, but at my age, I can't afford to take my time and dilly dally about making decisions. I know now that it's getting closer to reality. I want this very badly."

Paul reached across, took my hand, and I noticed how soft his was. Not expecting his gesture, I looked up into his sexy bedroom eyes and felt my cheeks beginning to flush. Not knowing what else to do, I sat and smiled like a silly schoolgirl.

Pua reappeared and asked "Would you like anything else?"

Paul looked at me, and I answered, "I think I'm fine."

"No coffee or after dinner drink?"

"Maybe a glass of Amaretto?"

"Make that two," he directed Pua.

"Maggie, I don't want to pressure you."

"Before you go any further, Paul, I want you to know that I find you very attractive and I'm most comfortable with you. But after what I have been through, maybe what I need right now is a good friend."

"I understand completely. Please don't worry. I will give you as much time as you want. We need to get you settled here on the garden island first."

Smiling, I said happily, "I'm relieved, but want you to know that when I feel the time is right, I'll let you know."

Pua appeared with our glasses of Amaretto.

As we sipped, Paul commented, "You know that Amaretto has been associated with romance."

"Yes, I know," I responded, smiling, looking into the depths of his eyes. This could go further tonight, but it would be a mistake. But I was oh so tempted!

Pua brought the check and asked if I enjoyed my meal, and I answered: "Yes, mahalo."

Paul signed the check, and we stood up. Starting to walk towards my room, he grasped my elbow, and the nearness of him was almost too much to handle. With the trade winds blowing in the restaurant through dinner and then the Amaretto, I was feeling like I could be easily persuaded into asking him to spend the night.

Suddenly, we were at my door, and I reached into my pocket for my room key, and Paul took it and inserted it into the lock as I stood there wondering... what if?

"A penny for your thoughts?"

"A penny wouldn't cut it. Not tonight. Thank you for dinner and your company."

"Anytime," he said, leaning in to brush my cheek with his lips.

I wanted to become friends before lovers, if that was what was to come.

"See you in the morning," I said, smiling as I entered my room. Closing the door, I could hear him reminding me to double lock it.

Not wanting to be taken in by the romantic atmosphere, I struggled to keep my distance from Paul, but happenstance seemed to put us in the same place at the same time more often than not, and now I was relying on his opinion about the property I may be purchasing.

I got ready for bed, performing my usual nighttime routine, feeling wistful that I would have liked for him to stay the night but knowing deep in my heart, it was too soon.

I pulled the covers back and slipped in between the sheets. Smiling with thoughts of Paul, I drifted off.

CHAPTER ELEVEN

The next morning, I woke to bright sunshine streaming in through the window. A rooster crowed reminding me it was time to get up when suddenly my cell rang. Glancing at my phone, I saw it was Dean.

"Good morning, Dean."

"Good morning to you too. You are all set to go out and look at the bed and breakfast again. Just be careful not to get into a discussion about any potential offer."

"You forget, I was once in the business and know how it works. Besides, if this goes through, you will have a nice fat check at the end."

"Have a good day and give me a call later."

"Will do," I said.

I got out of bed and walked over to the window and looked out to a beautiful morning with clear skies and a brilliant blue ocean pounding the sand.

Quickly, I got dressed, picking out a pair of white slacks, a navy-blue polo shirt, and white sneakers. Finishing my makeup, the phone rang, and I ran to answer it.

"Good morning, Maggie. Did I wake you?"

"No, not at all. I'm almost ready."

"Great. Meet me in the restaurant, say five minutes?"

"Got it."

I grabbed my bag, phone, and I was out the door, running to the lobby.

I saw Paul sitting at a table and walked over to him and greeted him with "Good morning, again."

He got up and, helping me with my chair, I noticed coffee had already been prepared just the way I liked it and said: "Thank you for the coffee."

"I thought you might need it this morning," he said.

"Every morning, but especially today. I'm excited to show you the property."

"Do you want any breakfast?"

"Maybe just a couple of eggs and toast."

"Okay, you got it," he said, getting up.

"No wait, I can get it."

"You just stay there and relax. Next time you can serve me," he said.

Within a couple of minutes, he was back with my papaya, eggs, and toast.

"Paul, I'm amazed you remembered I like papaya for breakfast and the eggs are perfect, just the way I like them."

He smiled and sat down. Looking at me, he said, "Certain things I record to memory."

I ate like I hadn't eaten anything last night, and as I finished, I said: "I'm ready if you are."

"Have everything you need," asked Paul?

"I'm all set. Let's go."

We walked out to the parking lot to Paul's car, and he had the top down.

"I must say you are prepared for our drive to Hanalei."

"Hope you don't mind that the top is down?"

"No. Not at all. It will feel good to have the warm sun and fresh air blowing in my face."

He opened the passenger door and helped me in, and as he walked around to the driver's side, I thought, if only I was ready, he could be the one I would spend the rest of my life with, married or not, and we haven't even had sex yet.

Pulling out of the parking lot onto Kuhio Highway, I tried not to look at Paul's face. He had his own handsomeness in an appealing way.

Driving north to Hanalei, we barely spoke until I said, "Up ahead you want to turn right onto Alamihi Road."

"No problem. I mapped it out last night," replied Paul glancing at me with a smile on his face.

"Well! Think you're smart, eh? Trying to keep ahead of me?"

"Not really. Just like to be prepared."

Driving up to the Inn on Alamihi Road, I felt excited to think this could one day be my property, and I would be an innkeeper!

Paul stopped the car, got out, and came around to help me out.

I saw Mac and Sara walking from the garage area, waving and shouting, "Hello!"

As they approached, I said to Paul, "These are our hosts. Mac and Sara, I would like to introduce a friend of mine, Paul Sinclair."

Exchanging aloha greetings with warm handshakes, I said, "I appreciate you taking the time to show the property again. I hope we're not disturbing you."

"No, not at all," smiled Mac.

Sara extended her hand and placed it on my arm, easing me to walk with her. Paul and Mac followed, and I could hear them chatting.

We took the elevator up to the main area, and Mac said to me, "Why don't you show Paul around?"

"You mean, you don't want to go with us?"

"No, I feel comfortable with you. Feel free to show him the cottage as well."

"Thank you, Mac," I said as I grasped Paul's arm. "Let me give you the tour."

I started by showing Paul the central area of the house and giving him the tour of the suites before we headed out to the cottage.

"There are so many pluses to this property, but the one that sticks out is that the beach is a mere 110 steps from here and it's the best snorkel beach on the island. And, for those guests so inclined, there are two world-class golf courses within a ten-minute drive, and according to Dean, there's an abundance of shops, restaurants, supermarkets and two riding stables. A little bit of everything one could want for a quiet vacation spot. The Inn on Alamihi Road is a house of rest, and I can see that it truly is just that," I said as we approached the cottage.

"This too?"

"Yes, that's what they said."

"You've got to be kidding. What's the catch?"

"There isn't one, at least as far as I know. They're just very anxious to return to the mainland. But before we go any further, let me show you the inside of where I will live."

Giving him the grand tour of the cottage, Paul was virtually speechless until we walked into the master bedroom and, seeing the bathroom area, "This is a fantastic property, and I like the double shower, perfect for a couple," he said, winking.

"It certainly surpasses anything that I'd hoped for. It's like a dream, and if it is, please don't wake me."

Paul placed his hands on my shoulders as we looked out over the lush landscape and said: "I live not too far from here."

"You do?"

"Yes, I do, so if you needed me for anything, I would be close by."

I smiled and said, "I may take you up on that. I think we should catch up with Mac and Sara."

"Good idea," Paul said.

We walked back to the main entrance, and I called out, "I think we're going to head back."

Mac and Sara approached, smiling, and said, "Hope you saw everything you needed to."

"I think we are good. Thank you for letting us impose on you."

Mac piped up, "If coming out here today, helps you make your decision, then it wasn't an imposition. I have a good feeling about you, Maggie."

"Why thank you, Mac. You have been most gracious."

They walked us out to the car, and as we drove off, I turned to see them watching, arms around each other, waving.

On the way back to the hotel, Paul seemed focused on his driving as I had thoughts racing through my mind: all the what ifs.

Pulling into the parking lot, Paul brought the car to a stop, turned to face me and said: "You're sure you want to make this leap?"

"I have given this a lot of thought, and I know this is what I want, although I guess between guests, the inn might become a bit lonely. I plan to keep Ona and Keoki on to help out."

"Good decision. But don't forget you will have me around, too."

I smiled and said, "I hoped you would say that."

Suddenly, one of the hotel employees came bounding out to the car and said to Paul, "We have a problem."

He got out of the car and came around to help me out and took my arm, leading us back to the hotel.

Turning to me, he said, "Would you excuse me?"

"Sure, go ahead and take care of business."

"Thanks, Maggie."

I watched as he took off in a run with the employee towards the rear of the restaurant. I thought to myself *hope nothing serious happened while we were gone.*

CHAPTER TWELVE

I walked back to my room thinking that when I got settled in, I would phone Dean and then Judy. As I unlocked the door to my room, I noticed a strong floral smell. I turned on the light and, placed on the desk was a massive arrangement of tropical flowers, including my favorite plumeria blossoms in pink and white. The card read 'Best wishes for every success, Dean.'

I wouldn't have expected this. Maybe a ploy on his behalf to make sure I continued working with him and seal the deal? I suspected that he felt threatened with the more sophisticated, debonair Paul by my side. I set the card back amongst the flowers and stood staring out the window at the blue Pacific, waves churning and rolling onto the beach.

I picked up my cell and double-checked the time. It was still reasonable to call Judy, considering the time difference.

"Hello."

"Hi, Judy. Hope I'm not calling too late, but I wanted to tell you that I've decided to go ahead with the Hanalei property – provided my escrow is going okay?"

"Good to hear from you – and you sound so upbeat. Better than you have in a while. No problems with the escrow, and it should close the day after tomorrow."

"Do you know what my net will be?"

"In round figures, $700,000."

"I can make that work. I wanted to make sure before I have Dean submit an offer. Are you still planning a trip to see me?"

"Well, of course. I plan on making sure all of your possessions reach you in good shape."

"That would be great, and by then perhaps the escrow will be completed at this end and you'll be my first guest."

"Guess I get to call you Ms. Innkeeper?"

"I do like the sound of that."

"Maggie, let me call you tomorrow after I've checked with our escrow officer. In the meantime, I hope you can get a good night's sleep."

"I think so. It's early here so I'll wander down to the restaurant and see what I can find to eat."

"Talk to you soon," Judy said as she hung up.

I sat on the bed in a daze feeling exuberant but nervous at the same time. So much to think about and learn about the bed and breakfast business. I wondered if Mac and Sara would take the time to show me the ropes. First things first. Must call Dean.

I dialed Dean's number, and it went directly to voicemail. I left a message for him to call me as soon as possible.

I freshened up my makeup and changed into a long lime green dress that would be a welcome change from my white pants and a polo shirt.

Before heading out, I grabbed my tote bag that held my notebook so that I could make some preliminary notes.

Walking towards the lobby, my thoughts turned to Paul and what he was doing. But I had enough to keep my mind occupied with the purchase of the bed and breakfast. Maybe just as well we don't get involved, although each time we're together, I feel a strong pull.

I sat at a table away from the throng of hotel guests and pulled out my notebook. I took out a pen and started making a list of things I needed to check into and questions for Mac and Sara.

"Boy, aren't you the efficient one?"

I looked up, and Paul was standing over me with two glasses of what looked like Scotch.

"I'm trying to get organized for the deal of the century. So much I have to think about including hiring a handyman and maid." Suddenly, I saw a message on my cell phone,

Maggie, I got ticketed for Kauai. I'm arriving tomorrow evening 6:00 p.m. Hawaiian Airlines. No need to pick me up. I plan on getting a rental car.

I looked up at Paul and said, "My realtor is flying into Lihue tomorrow. Big surprise. Didn't think it would be so soon."

"Well, maybe that's a good thing. Tidying things up for you," he said, sitting down and handing me a glass of Scotch, "Cheers."

"Cheers to you too," I replied.

Sipping the pungent, aromatic liquid, I looked at Paul over the rim of my glass, and he was staring right into my eyes. I gulped and started to choke.

"Whoa, don't expire on me," he exclaimed.

"Oh, I won't. Just didn't expect the strength of this Scotch. Mind telling me what I'm drinking?"

"It's from my private collection, one of the leftovers from my days as a Scotch sommelier. Someday, I'll let you in on my secret."

"Well, if you're going to be that way, you know turnabout is fair play?"

Paul placed his hand over mine and smiled "How about some dinner. Don't think you had lunch?"

"No, come to think of it, I didn't. I am getting hungry."

"Give me a minute, and I'll be right back."

"I'll be here."

Judy making this fast trip to Kauai had me wondering what she was up to. She could always have wired my funds. Maybe she wants to give me her excellent professional advice?

I continued making a to-do list when I felt two strong hands grip my shoulders. I looked up into Paul's sexy blue eyes.

Smiling, Paul said, "All ready. Got us in."

"Oh, that was fast. Where are we dining?"

"It's a surprise. I think you'll like it."

I gathered up my things and joined Paul, walking out to his car. As we pulled out of the parking lot onto Kuhio Highway, I noticed we were heading in the opposite direction from the hotel. I felt Paul's hand grasping mine as we drove. He had put the top up in case it might start raining, and I sat relaxing, enjoying the fresh trade winds blowing in through the windows.

I sensed we were headed in the direction of Poipu. It hadn't gotten dark yet, so the setting sun provided a beautiful orange and pink sunset for us to admire as we drove on. Before I knew it, Paul had parked the car at the Plantation Gardens Restaurant and Bar. I was taken by the lovely gardens.

"Did I doze off?"

"For a few minutes, but not to worry. It's a good sign that you feel comfortable with me."

"I so agree with you. It's the first time in years I've fallen asleep in a car. I was in a horrible traffic accident with my deceased husband, and it still haunts me to this day, but for some reason, I feel at ease with you."

Smiling, Paul said, "That's good."

"And you?"

"Let's get dinner," was his response.

He got out of the car and came around to assist me, and we walked hand in hand into the restaurant.

"Good evening, Mr. Sinclair. Right this way."

As we walked through the restaurant to our table, it felt like I'd been taken away to an idyllic getaway with the outdoor lanai seating and views of lush gardens.

We were led to a table overlooking a garden, with the fragrant plumeria blossoms wafting amidst glowing tiki torches. Seated, we began to look over the menu as the server asked if we would like something from the bar. Paul ordered a bottle of their Rombauer chardonnay. I realized how hungry I was. "I'm going to give you the honor of ordering for us. I trust you, implicitly."

"If you're sure. It would be my pleasure. They serve authentic Hawaiian cuisine, and the vegetables are grown organically and sourced from local farmers. All the food is cooked on traditional Kiawe – a mesquite wood which adds flavor to the food."

Taken by the ambiance, I said, "Very impressive."

When the server approached the table, Paul ordered Seafood Lau Lau that came with fresh fish, large shrimp, jumbo scallops, julienne vegetables wrapped in a ti leaf, steamed brown rice with furikake, and wasabi aioli. Sounded delicious. But he wasn't finished for he then ordered the crusted local fish with a smoked quinoa crust, creamed quinoa, asparagus, and tomato chili oil. Our food arrived in good time, and I marveled at the presentation.

"Paul, you've outdone yourself this time. If the food tastes as good as it looks, I won't be able to eat for a week."

He smiled and said, "As long as you're satisfied, I'll be happy."

We started to eat, and neither of us had much to say. It had been a busy day, and I was admittedly tired and anxious to retire to my bed.

"What about some dessert?" Paul asked.

"Not sure where I would put it and frankly, I would prefer we call it an early night. I'm bushed," I replied.

"Okay. I'll get the check."

Once the check was taken care of, Paul assisted me with my chair and took my hand as we strolled out to the parking area to retrieve his car. On the way back to the hotel I chatted on about my plans for the bed and breakfast although prefacing it with "I know all of what I want to do can't be done that quickly, but I am anxious to get moving on this new chapter of my life. I feel excited, and yet I'm a bit nervous."

Paul asked, "You haven't spoken about your writing. What is it you write?"

"Right now, I'm in the midst of writing historical fiction and will be researching Hawaiians who made their mark in history. Perhaps as a start, I will use Bernice Pauahi Bishop, one of Hawaii's most important philanthropists. As an *ali´i*, the last descendant of the Kamehameha line – she held the largest private land ownership in the Islands. At least I think I will start with her. Who knows, maybe once I'm settled, I'll have another inspiration although I have one idea on the back burner that takes place during World War II."

We arrived back at the hotel and Paul walked me to my room.

I opened my door and was about to say goodnight when Paul stepped forward and planted a tender kiss on my cheek.

"I'll see you in the morning," he said smiling and turned to walk back towards the lobby.

I was a bit surprised because I half expected him to want to come in. Just as well he didn't. I secured my door and got ready for bed. As I drifted off to sleep, I thought back through the day and admitted I was happy that Paul had become a friend and I could depend on him. Who knows where this would lead, but for right now, I was contented to keep him as a friend and confidante.

CHAPTER THIRTEEN

The next morning, I noticed that Paul had already slipped out of bed, and I could hear him in the shower. I got out of bed, pulled on my robe and walked over to the sliding door and looked out to see what kind of day we were going to have. I heard my cell phone ringing and turned over to pick it off the night table and realized I had been dreaming. No Paul in the shower! Wow!

"Hello. Good morning, sleepy head."

"Good morning, Paul."

"Are you ready to meet with Dean Kalima?"

"You mean he's there in the lobby?"

"He and I are enjoying a cup of Kona coffee and will wait for you to join us for breakfast."

"Sounds good; I'll be down in fifteen minutes, give or take a few."

"Take your time. We'll wait."

I jumped out of bed and dashed into the bathroom and into the shower. I finished with my usual routine and pulled my hair back into a ponytail. No sense in worrying about hair today. Too much to do. I grabbed a white skirt and red t-shirt out of the closet and hastily threw on my clothes, slipping my feet into a pair of sandals. I picked up my tote bag, and off I went to join Paul and Dean.

I walked into the lobby area and saw both men sitting at a table off to the side where one could have a quiet conversation.

"Good morning, gentlemen."

"Good morning," they chimed.

I sat down and asked, "Mind if I join you? It looked like you were deep into a serious conversation. No smiles this morning?"

"No worries, Maggie. We were just discussing your purchase of the bed and breakfast," said Paul.

"Oh, you were, were you. Isn't that my business?" I responded sarcastically.

"Now, don't get defensive," replied Paul.

"I promise I won't, but why not discuss this in my presence?"

"We were just speaking man to man," said Dean.

"I think I get it. But before I get into a deep dive with you, I need some food," and with that, I stood up and strode over to the buffet. I picked out a plateful of papaya and melon, overlooking the watermelon due to my allergy, and hurried back to the table. The server approached, asking if we wanted to order from the kitchen. I piped up with "Yes, I would. Two poached eggs and toast plus cottage cheese. I think I'll need my protein today."

"Maile, I'll have the same," added Paul.

Dean got up and walked over to the buffet; I wasn't sure if he wanted to give Paul and me a few minutes alone to talk, or if he was really hungry.

"Paul, I'm concerned that you're trying to interfere with my plans."

"Maggie, no, I wasn't, but I did have questions."

"Like what?"

"Well, for one thing, you need to look at their books and check out the inn's profit and loss numbers. I want to suggest that you write the offer contingent on approving the books."

"I would agree with that," said a familiar voice, and I turned to see Judy standing behind me.

I got up and gave her a big hug, "Aloha, my friend. What are you doing here so early? I thought you were coming in this afternoon. I don't even have a lei for you."

"Maggie don't be concerned about that. I caught the red eye out of LAX, so I didn't waste any time. You know me, the early bird gets the worm."

"I'm so surprised you're here, but how did you get here from Lihue?"

"I got a rental car, so I can have some freedom for roaming, if I want."

"Okay, can't blame you for wanting that. I suppose you want to see the property I'm going to bid on?"

"Yes, most definitely, but let's take care of one thing at a time. By the way, if you check your account, you will see the funds were wired from the escrow."

"Why do I get the distinct impression that you two are hovering over me like two mother hens? Don't you think I can make a rational business decision? You know this isn't like I'm purchasing a home for myself. It's a business, a home for me comes along with it."

"Honey, consider us your advisers and maybe partners if you need us," quipped Judy.

"What does that mean?"

Before anyone could answer, our food arrived, and Dean returned from the buffet, his hands full with plates overflowing with food.

Dean gave Judy aloha kisses on both cheeks and asked "Hungry?"

"Yes, I am," replied Judy.

"Here, we can share," said Dean.

"Let me at least start my food before I lose my appetite," I said.

"Now, why would you do that?" asked Judy.

"Let's not discuss the property until we finish and then we can get out pencil and paper and do the usual Benjamin Franklin approach, you know, positives and negatives."

"Maybe that won't be necessary," added Paul.

"What does that mean?" I asked.

"I think we all can concur that you've made up your mind that you want the bed and breakfast. Now it's a matter of looking at the numbers, meaning profit and loss versus your investment and if your income can support it."

"Paul, you've hit the nail on the head," said Judy.

Dean piped up and looked at Paul and said, "You should be in real estate. You have a good business head."

"That's because I have owned and still do own my business. It's in my blood, and the nature of the species is ingrained in my brain."

I continued eating my way through my breakfast, enjoying every bite. Maile came around with the coffee carafe. "Thank you, Maile."

Our server started clearing our plates when Dean spoke up, "I have some bad news for you."

"Now what?"

"It was brought to my attention this morning that another offer may be coming in."

"Oh, great! Just what I need – competition before I even start up as a new innkeeper."

"You will recall I warned you about this," Dean said, pulling out paperwork from his briefcase: "Let's get this offer on paper."

Paul stood up and looked at me and said: "Excuse me while I check with my crew and make sure I'm not needed."

I smiled and said, "No problem with that. I understand."

While he did that, I checked on my phone for my bank balance and saw that the money from the closed escrow had indeed been wired into my account.

"Now that I have the preliminary information, let's talk dollars," said Dean.

"I intend to offer the full price, and it will be all cash."

Judy looked at me and said, "Are you crazy?"

"No, but if it's mine, free and clear, then I won't have to worry about making mortgage payments or whatever they are called for a business of this type. My dear Judy, rest assured I know what I'm doing, and I have funds you haven't been privy to that will be my safety net."

Dean continued writing, and Judy sat shaking her head.

"Judy, what's wrong with you? I thought you were on my side?"

"Well, I am, but I worry about you making rash decisions, you know, after all the stress you have been under."

"What stress? I've been here in paradise, and my stress is below sea level."

Dean handed me the offer to review and added that he had included the provision that a property inspection by a licensed general contractor be done within two days."

"Thanks for including that, Dean. As to a deposit, what's customary here in the islands?"

"At least ten percent of the price."

"Okay. What about liquidated damages?"

"They are included on page three if you read ahead."

"Judy and Dean, I think you two should take a walk or something so that I can focus on the offer."

They chimed in and agreed.

Maile came over and refilled my coffee cup and asked if I needed anything else.

"No, I'm good for now. Thank you."

"You're welcome."

I sat mulling over the paperwork while sipping on my Kona coffee.

The trade winds picked up, and I felt a chill sitting in the path of the wind. I saw dark storm clouds starting to gather overhead and almost simultaneously, rain began to fall. I got up quickly, gathered my things, and moved to a table on the other side of the restaurant. By now, most of the diners had finished and gone on to their day's activities, so I virtually had the place to myself. Quiet. It was lovely to sit and ponder what I was about to do. Am I making the right decision? Before I could even answer my question, my head and heart agreed it was the right thing to do. I signed the documents and motioned for the server to come over.

"Maile, may I have a glass of champagne, please?"

"Certainly, Ms. Langham."

My champagne arrived in a lovely fluted glass, and I said to myself, congratulations – well done.

"What have we here? Are you imbibing in the morning? What's the occasion?" asked Paul.

"My decision-making process has concluded, and I feel ecstatic that I could make this decision on my own and start over. It feels so good. Would you like to join me? I would rather not drink alone and better to celebrate with another."

"Love to."

I motioned for Maile to come over and asked, "Please bring Mr. Sinclair a glass of champagne as well."

As we sat sipping our champagne, Dean and Judy sauntered over to the table and pulled over a couple of chairs and sat down.

"Would you like a glass of champagne?"

Judy piped up, "If I did, I would probably pass out. I never sleep well on planes, and last night was no exception."

"Dean, what about you?"

"No thanks, I want to pay attention to what you have going on here." "I've completed the paperwork. What type of earnest money deposit do you need, a personal check, or would a cashier's check be better?"

"In your case, I would say a personal check would be just fine. I don't think that Mac or Sara will take exception to it."

I reached into my bag, pulled out my checkbook, and wrote Dean a handsome, earnest money deposit, and handed it to him. "Will that be sufficient? I want them to be assured I'm serious, especially if they have other offers. I can sweeten the pot if need be."

Dean studied the check and said, "I don't think that will be necessary. I called them while Judy and I were away and told them to sit tight for an offer was coming in from you. I'll give them a call and tell them I'm on the way to present your offer to them."

"Perfect. Let me know as soon as you can if they accept it. Oh, one other thing, I know we included it in the offer, but if you can remind them to share names with me of those that have reservations?"

"I plan to."

In the meantime, "Judy, do you want to check in and get settled?"

"I think that would be an excellent idea and maybe include a nap as well."

"You go on and do what you need to do."

I looked at Paul, and he took my hand and said: "Let's go for a walk."

"Sounds good," I said, standing up, and we walked towards the rear of the restaurant and took the walkway toward the pool that was deserted. "Look at that. As quickly as the rain came in, it went out. Now it's clear and sunny, which I take as a good omen."

He grabbed a couple of beach towels, and we walked carefully down a rickety flight of stairs and Paul, ever mindful, kept an eye that I didn't stumble considering my bit of champagne. We walked on towards Lydgate Park, adjacent to the hotel. We had the beach all to ourselves, which was surprisingly deserted for the hour. The rain had moved on, leaving the sky a brilliant blue, cloudless except for a few stray white fluffy cumulus ones.

I said, "Mind if we sit? I think the champagne has gotten to me. One thing you probably don't know is that it doesn't take much for me to feel the effects of alcohol. I guess you could say I'm a lightweight when it comes to drinking."

Paul turned to me and, looking into my eyes, his hand touched my chin, and our lips found each other. He gave me a tender and slow kiss full on. Thinking to myself, he can kiss, and he has the softest lips, I came up for air and smiling said, "Where did that come from?"

"Right where this one is coming from," as our lips locked, and he pushed me gently onto the sand where he had positioned the beach towels. I could feel his heart beating against my breast, and I could feel my pulse race as he kissed me long and hard. I pulled him closer with my arms tightly around his back, I could feel his breath against my face as he pulled back and he whispered, "Are you sure?"

"Yes, I'm sure," and again we embraced for a long, slow kiss.

We pulled apart, and I asked him, "Do you want to come to my room?" as his cell phone rang.

He pulled it out of his pocket, stood up, and said, "I have to get this."

I could only hear his muffled comments as I focused on the ocean waves lapping on the shore. I looked up at the blue Hawaiian sky when Paul interrupted my thoughts by saying, "I have to get back to work. There's a problem I need to attend to. May I have a rain check on that offer?"

"You sure can. I think I'll wander back up to the hotel with you and wait for Dean's call."

"Let me know what he says, just text me," he said, giving me his hand to help me up.

He grabbed the two towels, shaking the sand from them, "This isn't exactly what I had in mind. Thought that everything was working fine, but apparently, there's an emergency."

"You have responsibilities, and it is in the middle of the business day. So, I will just figure out how to keep myself occupied while I wait to hear from Dean."

We walked hand in hand back to the hotel with Paul dropping the towels in the bin at the pool. He lightly brushed my cheeks with his lips as we parted, he going towards the hotel kitchen and me walking back towards the lobby area where I decided to sit on one of their plush ocean blue sofas. I put my feet up and kept an eye on my cell phone. I must have dozed off as the ringing of my cell awakened me. I answered, and Dean said, "Congratulations! You are now the owner of a bed and breakfast. They accepted everything – not one counteroffer except they want a very short escrow."

"I have no problem with that. But what do you mean by 'a very short escrow'? Oh, and what about the future guests?"

"I'm bringing their list with me, so you can become familiar with their process for handling reservations."

"That sounds great, Dean. Are you headed back?"

"Just getting on the road now. See you soon."

After hanging up, I sat there transfixed, realizing that I had my offer accepted and had my work cut out for me. Smiling, I got up and sauntered over to one of the tables in the restaurant and sat down. Wonder where Paul and Judy are? I would love to celebrate. I got up and walked over to the front desk and asked for Judy's room.

"Just a moment. If you would like to step over to the house phone, I will ring her room."

I picked up the phone and could hear voices in Judy's room as she said, "Hello."

"Hi, Judy. I hope I didn't wake you."

"No, not at all. Paul and I were just talking."

"Paul is there?"

"Yes, he's been here about thirty minutes. Do you want to speak to him?"

"No, not necessary," I said and hung up.

"Those two dirty rats! How could they? Well, so Judy was Paul's emergency!"

I decided I would wait in the lobby until Dean got back.

CHAPTER FOURTEEN

Paul and Dean, trying to be peacemakers, made arrangements at a restaurant to celebrate my accomplishment, and Dean's as well. With Dean taking so much credit, I felt slighted. Without me, there would be no reason for him to celebrate. I decided not to be so sensitive and put on a good front until the sting of this had cooled off. I wanted to sit back and make plans for taking over the bed and breakfast, but all in good time. Regardless of my disappointment in Paul, I was thrilled!

"Maggie, Maggie, earth to Maggie," said Dean.

"What?" I snapped back.

"We're making dinner plans, and you are somewhere else."

"Sorry, I was just starting to make mental lists of what I need to do to make this transition as seamless as possible. Whatever you guys decide to do is fine with me. Have you decided on a time?"

"7:00," piped up Paul.

"Perfect. In the meantime, I think I'll retreat to my room to gather my thoughts. Could someone give me a ring when you're ready to leave, and I'll join you in the lobby," I said, standing up and gathering my things.

"Sure," replied Dean.

"See you later," I said.

No sooner had I set my things down in my room, there was a knock on the door.

"Who's there?"

"It's Paul. May I come in?"

I walked to the door, looked through the peephole, and saw that it was Paul. I opened the door to let him in.

"Maggie, what's wrong? You should be ecstatic."

Closing the door, I said, "I am, Paul. But earlier when it was obvious you were in Judy's room; I felt a sense of betrayal. However, I shouldn't have since neither of us has committed to the other one. I must apologize for putting so much stock into what I thought we had going."

"Time out," Paul said, placing his hands on my shoulders and drawing me close as he kissed me. I realized I was kissing him back with all the fervor I could. We pulled apart, mere inches and he whispered "Now you tell me. Am I into Judy?"

I looked into his sexy blue eyes that spoke volumes of his interest in me. How could I have been so silly as to think he and Judy had something going?

"Maybe this is too soon. I still don't have a lot to put into trusting someone after what I've been through."

"Perhaps we should talk about that," he said with his lilting Scottish brogue.

I took his hand and led him over to the sofa and sat down, taking a deep breath to dive into all the mess of my history with men.

"Are you sure you want to hear this? Do you have time?"

"Yes. As far as the hotel is concerned, I'm off and out for the rest of the day."

"Okay. After hearing what I have to say, you may not want to have anything to do with me, thinking I'm one messed up cookie."

"I doubt that," he said kissing me lightly on my lips.

I began with explaining about my first husband, and then husband number two, following with the trials and tribulations of my past dating life. I could tell Paul was absorbing every word.

"That's enough for now," I said calmly.

"You mean, there's more?"

"No, not really, but I thought I should tell you how all of this has caused me to be wary about getting involved."

"We can take it as slow as you want," he said with a soft smile.

"Let me make myself clear. You're still a virile man. I can tell you have a lot of passion, and I don't want to frustrate and discourage you, nor do I want you to feel rejected."

"You won't. Because you see, I have my own demons, and I know you wouldn't want anything to do with me if I told you half of my history."

"Maybe, not today but someday when I get to know you better," I said, leaning in to kiss him tenderly.

"That right there tells me a lot."

"What do you mean?" I asked sheepishly.

"You are a very passionate woman, and I feel a strong connection with you. We just have to take it as it comes."

"I appreciate that, but for now, I can only take on so much at a time, and my purchase of the bed and breakfast and getting settled in has to be my first priority."

"I understand. No pressure from me. Just so you know I'm here for you," Paul responded.

"Paul, it's getting closer to our dinner with Judy and Dean. I need to get ready. Would you mind?"

"Oh, no. Not at all," he replied, brushing my cheek with his lips.

"I'll see you in a while in the lobby." I smiled. "I am looking forward to it and moving on to my next chapter."

He gave me one last kiss and then he left. I glanced at my watch, saw that I didn't have much time. I quickly pulled out a long black dress with a splash of Hawaiian flowers cascading down the front.

Freshening up my makeup and hair, I dressed quickly and grabbed my clutch and headed out the door.

When I arrived in the lobby, Judy, Dean, and Paul were waiting for me.

"Ready?"

"Sure," I replied as Paul took my arm, leading me out to the parking lot with Judy and Dean following. We approached Paul's car and, helping me into the passenger side, I sensed a familiarity was surfacing. *Well, I may have to push back on that.* We pulled out of the parking lot and turned onto Kuhio Highway. As we headed west to Lihue, I was in awe of the gorgeous sunset.

"Hope you like Italian food," said Paul.

"Love it. It sounds like you have a place in mind?"

"I do," and as he said that he pulled into a parking lot next to the Marriott Hotel. "Now, you have me curious. The sign says Duke's. Doesn't sound very Italian to me."

"Oh, that. Next door to Duke's on the upper level is Café Portofino. I'm friends with the owner, Giovanni Moretti, an excellent chef. He has wanted me to come and try his food. Thought tonight would be a good night since I won't have to dine alone, and this is a celebration of sorts."

The valet approached the car and opened my door.

I stepped out, and Paul was immediately at my side taking my arm as we headed to the restaurant with Dean and Judy following. The night air was intoxicating with the fragrant plumeria blossoms.

We walked up the stairs into Café Portofino and were approached by an attractive hostess of Hawaiian descent. The striking brunette smiled at Paul and asked if we had a reservation.

"No, but I believe that Giovanni is expecting us."

"You must be Mr. Sinclair. Please come this way, we have a lovely table for your group overlooking Kalapaki Bay."

"Thank you."

We followed the hostess, and she hadn't misspoken as the table was overlooking a white sandy beach with waves gently lapping on the shore.

As we sat, she handed us menus, and suddenly the most gorgeous man said, "Paul, I am so happy to see you. This must be Maggie and the friends you spoke about."

"Yes, Giovanni. This is Maggie Langham who will soon be a resident of Kauai."

Giovanni extended his hand and, taking mine lightly, brushed his lips on the top of my hand, "Congratulations. The pleasure is all mine."

Taken off guard, I managed to mutter, "So happy to meet you. Paul has told me great things about your culinary expertise and this beautiful restaurant."

Paul interrupted our exchange and said, "Giovanni, this is Maggie's friend from the mainland, Judy Cole, and Dean Kalima, a realtor handling an acquisition for Maggie.

"Folks, this is Giovanni Morretti. He and I have worked together before in the food and beverage business."

"How do you do. Paul has been telling us about your restaurant," I said.

"I hope he has been telling you good things."

"Of course, my friend, never doubt that," Paul said with a wink from his cerulean blue eyes.

I was beginning to think they were more than just friends and had a tight bromance going on.

Giovanni said, "Let me give you a few minutes to look over the menu, or would you like for me to use my judgment and have my recommendations brought out to you?"

"What do you think? Shall we trust Giovanni?"

"Sure, why not. I'm an adventurous eater," I replied.

"In the meantime, Giovanni, how about bringing out a bottle of an excellent Italian red. I will trust your judgment."

Giovanni responded with, "Only the best for you, and I'll also have an appetizer brought out as well."

"Wonderful," Paul said as he smiled at his old friend.

We sat and looked out over the bay, sipping our glasses of Setti Ponti 'Saia' Nero D'Avola, a lovely red wine which the menu described as 'Deep violet in color with aromas of dark and bitter red cherry, spearmint, spice, and oak nuances'.

"Giovanni certainly didn't scrimp on the wine selection, and I must say it's every bit as delicious as the menu claims it to be," I said looking at Paul over my wine glass.

"He knows I wanted an exceptional wine for tonight."

Appearing at the right time to break the mood was the server with a plate of the most delectable escargot and bresaola carpaccio. Then our gracious host appeared with a basket of warm bread and butter.

"Paul, I hope that everything is to your satisfaction?"

"Yes, Giovanni. But then I wouldn't expect anything less."

Bowing slightly, he turned and walked away.

"So far, he has gone above and beyond what I would have expected."

Once we'd finished off the appetizers and had consumed another glass of the wine, a server brought out our main courses: scampi, filet of Dover, penne salsiccia and linguine alla puttanesca.

"The food is incredible. I would not have expected such outstanding Italian food in Hawaii."

The server presented a medley of desserts that included profiteroles, panna cota, and chocolate mousse. Almost instantly, cappuccinos were placed in front of us.

"I'm not sure I can eat anything more, but I must at least taste these fabulous desserts."

Finishing up our cappuccinos, Giovanni stopped by our table and asked: "I hope you enjoyed your meal?"

Paul said, "My friend, you have outdone yourself. We will return."

"Giovanni, the entire meal was beyond my expectations for Italian food on Kauai. Thank you."

Dean added, "I will be sure to recommend your fine restaurant to others."

"That is all I wanted to hear and I'm happy you have enjoyed your evening. Until next time, ciao."

"I think it's time we got you back to the hotel," Paul said, "You have a big day ahead of you tomorrow."

"Yes, I do, and thank you for an enjoyable evening."

Walking to retrieve the car, he tenderly grasped my hand, "It's so dark out here, I don't want you to chance tripping and falling."

The valet brought the car around, and Paul assisted me into the car, as Judy and Dean climbed into the back seat.

We were all chatting about the delicious meal while I was semi-lost in thought about my new venture.

I heard Judy say, "Earth to Maggie."

"Sorry," I replied. "A bit distracted about tomorrow and the bed and breakfast."

"As you should be," commented Dean. "It isn't every day that you take on such a life-changing endeavor."

Paul pulled into the hotel's parking lot, and he came around to help me out of the car.

"Goodnight," I said.

"Goodnight, Maggie," chimed in Judy.

"I'll walk you to your room," Paul said, taking my hand. We continued to my room, leaving Dean and Judy to fend for themselves.

"Tomorrow is your big day! Best you get your rest. Make sure you double lock your door."

"I certainly will and thank you for the lovely evening."

"The pleasure was all mine," he said, brushing his lips against mine, he walked back towards the lobby.

I entered my room and felt that something was missing. I guessed I was just excited about my new business and maybe, thought Paul would have been insistent about coming in.

I walked into the bathroom to prepare for bed. As I finished brushing my teeth, the hotel phone rang. I quickly went to answer it.

"Hello?"

"All tucked in?"

"No, not quite but just about."

"Door double locked?"

"Yes, sir."

"Good. Then I will say goodnight and sleep well."

"Thank you and goodnight to you as well. Until tomorrow."

I heard a click and hung up the phone.

CHAPTER FIFTEEN

The rooster's first crow at 5:00 a.m. gave me my wake-up call. No need to set the alarm. Having left the sliding door open and the drapes pulled back I could see the sun just rising and the first light of a new day was inspiring to me and gave me the feeling of getting on with my life. I happily got out of bed as I had a lot to accomplish. I had a whole list of tasks. First thing was to check with the bank and transfer my accounts. Then a trip to the post office to make sure I could get my mail forwarded. Somewhere there had to be a shop where I could order business cards.

I walked into the bathroom to take care of my morning toilette, including a nice but brief shower. I took care to apply my makeup. Besides, now that I was to be in business, I must take care to look my very best whenever out in public, for I would be representing my new enterprise. I dressed quickly, selecting a navy-blue crinkle fabric maxi dress that would serve well my plans for the day. I grabbed the matching jacket, my tote bag, and phone as I headed out the door.

As I walked into the restaurant area, I noticed Paul sitting at a table drinking a cup of coffee and staring out towards the lush, green garden.

Walking over to him, I noticed he was deep in thought, and as I approached his table, he must have sensed me for he turned, smiled, and said, "Good morning. Aren't you up awfully early?"

"Good morning, Paul. I could say the same for you. Don't you usually come in a bit later?"

"Normally, I do, but I had trouble sleeping and thought it best if I came in early. Wanted to make sure I caught you before you set out for Hanalei."

"Is something wrong?"

"Why don't you sit down so we can talk. How about some coffee?"

"Sure, I could use a cup," I said as he got up and went over to the buffet area.

I felt a twinge of anxiety, wondering what he was so anxious to talk about as he returned with my coffee.

"First, I'm happy that you got the bed and breakfast but wonder if you aren't biting off more than you can chew?"

"You think I have great ambitions but not prepared for what this venture entails?"

"More or less."

"I see. Don't you have any confidence in me? I have been in business before and am very confident I will be able to manage the bed and breakfast. It would help that instead of proclaiming your lack of faith in me, you keep those feelings to yourself or change your attitude and give me all the support you can."

"I must apologize," Paul said, looking downcast. "I didn't mean to come off so negative. I must also confess something else. Judy and I have known each other prior to this trip."

"Oh? Are you saying you were lovers?"

"Yes and no. Not in the long-term sense of the word. We had a very hasty and short-lived affair when I was living in Michigan and running the bar. She came in one night with a group of friends, and I don't want to go into details, but things developed I wasn't prepared for."

"Are you saying she initiated the meetup?"

"I was tentative with her, and she had had too much to drink, and one thing led to another as they say."

"No need to go any further. I think I get the picture. Now, this is all coming together. Why she was so anxious to make the trip here, which really wasn't necessary considering that everything was being handled electronically. So yesterday when you were in her room, was that your idea or hers?"

"Hers. Judy begged me to come to her room. She said she'd been thinking about me and wanted us to hook up, but she wasn't sure where we stood with each other. She did make it abundantly clear that she didn't want to hurt you or interfere."

"Interfere? She has a way of putting things that allows her to remain the innocent one and not guilty of anything. How does she think I would feel? I thought she and Dean were hooked up. Or am I wrong about that, too?"

"Not entirely. She and Dean are very close and had gotten together the last time she was here on the island. He told me he was quite taken with her and had hoped when she returned someday, they could resume where they left off. However, he didn't know that Judy and I knew each other until she arrived here, and he could sense something was going on."

"I must admit that I wasn't prepared for this and now must get on with what I had planned for today. I guess it's best to see how this all shakes out. I have a lot on my mind and frankly, as much as I was hoping we had made a connection, now I'm not so sure. Maybe best to just put it on the back burner? I don't know what else to say."

"Maggie, I don't want to hurt you. I do have feelings for you. Ever since you arrived, I felt we had hit it off. Now, with Judy here...?"

"So, who is it to be? Who's the lucky girl to get you as the prize?"

"I wouldn't put it that way."

"How else should I put it? It's clear to me you and Judy still have the, shall I say 'hots' for each other, and I'm just second choice. So, without prolonging the inevitable, do what you want to do and with whomever. I have more important things to focus on and cannot afford this distraction. My business comes first, and I must focus on that. Thank you for the coffee. If you will excuse me, I must get on with my day. I have lots to accomplish. Goodbye, Paul."

"Wait, you make it sound so final."

"It's all up to you and your red-headed friend. You call the shots."

As I got up, Judy approached and I hesitated, not wanting to have a confrontation but also wanting to put her in her place. I walked up to her and said, "Thanks for being my friend and handling the sale of my condo. You went above and beyond. But now that I know you had an ulterior motive; I see why you came to Kauai. I think our relationship has changed. Unless there is some other business we need to take care of, I would rather not see you for the rest of your stay here. I do need to have details of when to expect the arrival of my possessions. Other than that, I think we're done." I felt a lump rise in my throat. I wanted to get on with my business and didn't want her or Paul to see how hurt I was.

"Maggie, wait," Judy said, pleading with me to stay and talk. "We need to resolve whatever it is that's bothering you."

"Paul can fill you in." I saw Paul get up and start walking towards us.

"Goodbye, Judy."

I walked quickly out of the hotel and rushed to my car.

CHAPTER SIXTEEN

I pulled out of the parking lot, gravel flying, and turned onto Kuhio Highway and drove over the bridge at the base of the Wailua River. I decided that since I would be living at the north end near Princeville, it would make sense to get acquainted with the services there. Not at all intimidated with driving in that direction, I felt good about myself. Starting over had been a great idea. Here I was, truly on my own and feeling safe and resourceful. Once on my way, I felt myself relax and pushed Paul and Judy to the back of my mind. I put the top down and savored the warm tropical wind blowing through my hair, and I felt a sense of self that I thought I had lost. Feeling contented, it wasn't long before I reached Princeville and located the Bank of Hawaii, which was situated within the Princeville Shopping Center along with the post office.

Fortunately, the bank wasn't too busy, and I was able to find a customer service person to assist me. I was in and out within thirty minutes. I continued to the post office and my cell phone rang.

"Hello."

"Maggie, it's Dean. I understand you had a problem this morning with Paul and Judy."

"Yes, you could say that. Although I'm not thinking about that now. I'm taking care of business."

"Is there anything I can assist you with?"

"Dean, I appreciate the offer, but I'm up in Princeville at a bank, and my next stop is the post office."

"I'm on my way. I have some papers from Mac and Sara. How about if we meet someplace for lunch?"

"Sure, but may I ask what kind of papers?"

"They wanted you to be aware of a few things as you take over the bed and breakfast. One thing is the list of reservations they have with arrival dates. You will need that information."

"Sounds good. Where do you suggest we meet for lunch?"

"Do you think you can find Tiki Iniki? It's next door to the Ace Hardware Store in the Princeville Shopping Center. It has good food, and you can meet the owner. You'll want to start making some contacts. I'll get there as quickly as I can."

"See you when you get here."

Guess that takes care of lunch and getting some more information I will need for taking over the bed and breakfast. Dean has undoubtedly stepped up to the plate, anticipating what I will need to get started in my new business venture. Since it will be a while until he gets here, I'll take care of my business at the post office. It didn't take me long to locate it as it was very close to the bank. The postmaster was extremely helpful and indicated I needed to contact the post office at home to have my mail forwarded. Once finished there, I decided to take a stroll around the shopping center while I waited for Dean. I stumbled across the Tiki Iniki and walked up the ramp to the hostess station, where I requested a table for two in a quiet area since the bar was in full swing and noisy. I was seated, ordered ice water, and waited for Dean to arrive.

Sitting in the restaurant, I was in a position to get a good view of the shopping center and noticed several shops that looked interesting. I took out my notebook and was making some notes of things to ask Dean when I heard a familiar voice.

"Hi, Maggie."

"Hi, Dean. You must have driven fast to get up here in record time."

"No, not really. Traffic cooperated with me. I see you got a good table away from the noise. The bar is trendy."

Dean sat down across from me, and immediately, the server was upon us asking what we wanted to order. Not wanting to be rude, we told her to give us a few minutes. She did and was back quickly.

"I'll have the fish and chips with iced tea."

"I would like the pulled pork sandwich with a Coke," said Dean.

"Now that's settled. What do you have for me?"

"First, you need to be aware that shortly after you take possession of The Inn on Alamihi Road, you will have your first guest. He's a divorced, middle-aged man newly retired out of the Marine Corps and needs a quiet place to rest. Mac and Sara told me that he's suffering from posttraumatic stress disorder after having served his final tour in Afghanistan. They were notified of his arrival this morning and wanted you to be prepared."

"Sounds like this first guest will either make or break me. Are you sure he's for real or a test?"

"No test. He's for real and already paid up for his two-week stay."

"If he is the real deal maybe I should do some research on PTSD. Wouldn't hurt to have some background info. I suffered from it, but not from having served in the war, and that would make a big difference, at least I think so."

Our lunch arrived, and I realized that I was hungry. We settled back and enjoyed our food, which was delicious. An attractive brunette middle-aged woman dressed in a colorful Hawaiian print dress approached our table.

"How is everything? Dean, I see you've brought us a new visitor."

"Maggie, this is Jennifer Rogers, the proprietor of this establishment. Jennifer, Maggie has just relocated here from the mainland and has purchased a bed and breakfast. I'm sure you will be seeing a lot of her."

"Hi, Maggie."

"Hi, Jennifer, it's nice to meet you. I'm enjoying my lunch. It's delicious. Fun place you have here. Lots of atmosphere."

"Thank you. Hopefully, the next time you visit us, I will have more time to chat. This is a busy time of day. Office paperwork and deliveries plus keeping an eye on my customers require my attention."

"I can imagine, and yes, I will certainly be back."

Jennifer walked away, and I turned back to Dean and said, "Nice lady. A little distracted but understandable considering this is a busy time of day."

"She's a good person to have on your team."

"I'll remember that."

We quietly finished lunch as Dean went over a few details and showed me a notebook filled with pages of what looked to be copious notes from Mac and Sara.

"Maggie, Mac and Sara really like you and are happy you have put in the offer for their bed and breakfast. They wanted to make the transition as smooth as possible and prepared this notebook for you. I have never seen this reaction before upon handling a sale of property. You must have impressed them."

"I hope I don't disappoint them."

"Why would you?"

"I feel isolated and don't want to get discouraged or too lonely."

"Paul won't let that happen."

"Why do you say that?"

"I know him, and he's confided in me that he likes you a lot. Don't pay attention to the Judy thing. Whatever they had didn't last. Paul was looking for a long-term relationship with someone he is comfortable with. He has told me he feels that way about you."

"I'm not sure what to say."

"Nothing at this point. Let Judy return to the mainland and then it will be just you and Paul here, and me, of course, overseeing things."

I laughed at Dean's comment. "Oh, you think we need overseeing?"

"Only to the extent that you two are so much alike that I can see where there might be conflict. But nothing for you to worry about."

"I will take heart with what you have said."

The server approached with the check, and Dean looked at the check and said, "Good to go. Jennifer picked up our lunch."

"That was nice of her."

We stood up, ready to walk out when Paul appeared.

"Hi, Maggie."

"Hi, Paul. What are you doing here?"

"I figured you came out here to take care of some things and, to be honest, Dean said he was meeting you out here for lunch."

I looked at Dean and gave him a look that said, 'What are you up to now?'

"Well, you two, I better get back to Lihue. I have work to do on this escrow and want to make sure it closes on time. Maggie, I'll have documents for you to sign. Can we meet up later today?"

"Sure. I'll give you a ring when I get back to the hotel."

"See you later."

"Bye, Dean."

"Maggie, can we sit for a moment and talk?"

"Do you mind if we take a walk and find a place that is a bit more private and quieter?"

"No, not at all," Paul responded, taking my arm as we walked out of the Tiki Iniki.

We exchanged pleasantries as we walked and came upon a bench situated under a big banyan tree.

"This looks good to me, shall we?"

"Sure," I said, sitting down.

Paul looked directly at me and said, "I would like to clear up what you think has been going on between Judy and me. As I said, we knew each other previously for a short time, but as it stands now, we're merely friends. Nothing between us, except you."

"What does that mean?"

"You're your worst enemy. You must stop creating obstacles and let things take their natural progression. Quit imagining scenarios or, to be blunt, quit making more out of a situation than there is. I'm not sleeping with Judy and don't intend to. But I would like to sleep with you."

Leaning towards me, Paul kissed me ardently and with as much passion as he could considering we were in public. We drew apart within an inch of each other, and I whispered, "I think you have successfully made your point. I'll do my best to try and correct my ways, but sometime I will have to tell you more about my past and why I am the way I am. It isn't that I want to be this way, but my experiences have affected my perceptions whether I like it or not. I think that I'm not entitled to be happy with a man and trust that he is honest and truthful with me. But as I said, that's my problem."

"I can understand that. Having been married a couple of times, I haven't been eager to jump into another serious relationship until you came along."

I glanced at my watch and realized it was time to drive back to the hotel.

"Do you need to go back to the hotel?" Paul asked.

"Yes, I think I better. I have some calls I need to make in private."

"May I walk you to your car?"

"You may," I said, smiling.

Paul took my hand, and we walked to where I had parked.

I pulled the keys from my bag, and he took them and unlocked the doors for me to get in.

Once I was in the car, I put the top down, and Paul leaned in to kiss me and said, "Drive safely. I will try to stay behind you."

CHAPTER SEVENTEEN

During the drive back to the hotel, my thoughts kept flitting between my conversation with Paul and my to-do list. Top of the list was to review and try to acquaint myself with my first guest from Mac's notes. He would be a good test case to see if I could handle being the proprietor of a bed and breakfast. I glanced in the rearview mirror and saw Paul following me just as he said he would. Judging from his comments, I really wanted to believe him and trust what he said that there was nothing going on between him and Judy. Only time would tell.

Big dark clouds were forming the closer I drove to the hotel, and I anticipated they were going to drop some rain. Hopefully, I would get back in time to put the top back up on the car. Once in my room, I would give Sara and Mac a call just to check in with them and maybe set up a time to go out and have them give me a detailed tour of the behind the scenes operation of the inn.

Approaching the hotel, I felt droplets of water falling on my head. I turned onto the property and parked as close to the main entrance as possible before quickly putting the top back up. *I need to turn this car in and see about leasing or buying one since I would be staying here on the island.* Suddenly, the door opened, and Paul extended his hand to help me out.

"Thank you for keeping an eye on me as I drove back, but we better make a dash for inside before we get drenched," I said as the rain picked up.

Paul grabbed my hand, and we hurriedly walked into the hotel.

I turned, still holding his hand, and said, "I'm going to my room to try and make some sense out of the notes from Mac."

"Will I see you for dinner?"

"If you would like. But will it be just the two of us?"

"Depends on what you want to do."

"Let me think about it?"

"Okay, that's fair," Paul replied, leaning in to kiss me on the cheek. "Give me a call?"

"Sure. Oh, one other thing. I'm going to need a new car soon. Is that something you could help me with?"

"I would be happy to help you with that. I'll make a few calls, and maybe later at dinner; you can tell me what you want."

"That sounds like a plan," I said as Paul walked off.

"See you later," I said, turning to walk towards my room when I practically walked into Judy.

"Well, hello there. See you made it back."

"Yes, it was a productive trip to Princeville, and I was able to get some clarification on an issue," I said.

"Oh, really?"

"Yes, but it's something personal that I would prefer not to discuss. I must get to my room. I have some work to do."

"We do need to sit down and wrap up the details of your move here."

"Why don't we take care of our unfinished business now?"

"Excellent," Judy replied.

"Let's sit here," I said, pointing to a table off to the side out of hearing distance from the other guests.

Awkward moments followed before I spoke up, "Judy, do you have the shipping information?"

"Yes, I do," she replied, pulling out a file folder from her tote bag.

"Maggie, before we start on this, I want to apologize for giving you the wrong impression about my relationship with Paul. It has been over for some time, and I intend to keep it that way, although I wouldn't mind a little romp, in all fairness to you, I will stay away. I treasure our friendship and don't want to hurt you or spoil our relationship. I will be returning to the mainland in a couple of days," she said as her eyes welled up with tears.

"Judy, I don't hold grudges, but sometimes I'm not sure about you. I thought we were friends? Do you want a relationship with Paul or with me? It would seem that you would have clued me in on how involved you were with him."

"I told you, Paul and I are history. Besides, I have my eye on that handsome Dean. He has made certain overtures to me."

"Okay, that's enough. I don't need the details."

"Fine then. Let's get on with this. Maybe in time, you'll be able to trust what I say as the truth."

"I'll give it some thought once I get settled here."

Judy provided me with detailed information about the date my personal belongings would be arriving, and I took notes, not wanting to forget anything. After an hour or so, I asked her, "So, how many pieces of furniture might I expect?"

She pulled out a notebook and handed it to me.

"Oh, this looks good. Maybe I'll be able to use some of this in my cottage at the bed and breakfast."

"The arrival date is close to the date the escrow closes. I will have to make sure everything coincides."

"Maybe I should stay on until then?" Judy asked.

"Hmm. Not sure about that. Don't want you sitting around here when you could be back home working on some real estate deals."

"Don't worry about me. I have that figured out."

I looked at Judy with a skeptical eye and said, "We'll work it out one way or the other. I hate to impose on you any further, but I need to be rid of my car."

"No problem. I think I have someone who would be interested. How much do you want for it?"

"The Kelley Blue Book price would be good."

"Consider it done," she said.

"I guess that does it? Do you mind? I really need to get to my room. I have some work to do. I'll see you later," I said as I stood up and walked briskly to my room without waiting for an answer.

As I unlocked the door to my room, I was eager to get to work. I sat down at the same table where I could feel the cool trade winds blowing in through the sliding door. I pulled out the notebook Dean had given me and started reading Mac's notes. I had expected copious notes about my first guest, but what I saw was sketchy at best. Mark Elliott, hmm. It couldn't be the same one I knew years ago, or could it? I realized that I hadn't even inquired about where Sara and Mac got their guests from. Better see if I can take a drive out there to chat with them. Suddenly my cell phone rang.

"Hello."

"Hello. Maggie, it's Mac."

"Hi, Mac. I was getting ready to call you."

"Maggie, Sara and I would like for you to come to dinner. Can you make it tonight? I know it's short notice."

Considering I had just returned from Princeville, I wasn't thrilled with having to drive back out there, but obviously something was on their mind.

"Maggie?"

"Sorry, Mac. Yes, I would love to come out to dinner."

"Great. See you in an hour or so?"

"Sure."

I disconnected the call and went into the bathroom to refresh my makeup before heading to the closet where I picked out a navy blue sleeveless linen dress. I changed quickly, grabbed my bag with all my notes, including Mac's and walked quickly towards the lobby, hoping I wouldn't run into Paul. I wasn't in the mood to explain to him where I was going. But a nagging thought persisted that maybe I should tell someone where I was going in case something happened. Holding me from doing that was I didn't want company on this trip. Just the three of us would do nicely. Off I went in search of my car. Fortunately, the rain had moved on, leaving a lingering freshness to the air.

CHAPTER EIGHTEEN

I backed my car out, looking in the rearview mirror in case someone spotted me. Crazy, but I had this nagging thought that between Paul, Dean, and Judy, they didn't think I could handle driving out to The Inn on Alamihi Road. My stubborn, independent nature took over, and there was no time like the present to give this a try. I'll be having to do this in the future although maybe not all the way into Kapa'a. Fortunately, it wasn't dark, so I had plenty of light for the drive and surprisingly, before I knew it, I had reached Princeville. Wow, twice in one day!

I continued driving toward Hanalei and turned onto Alamihi Road and worked my way towards the inn. I parked, and Mac was awaiting my arrival. I got out of the car and said, "Aloha, Mac."

"Aloha, Maggie. Welcome back."

"Thank you. Where's Sara?"

"She's upstairs cooking dinner with Ona."

"I hope she hasn't gone to too much trouble."

"Now, don't forget, we're in the hospitality business and are used to cooking for people. She does dinner, and I'm your breakfast man. Shall we?" he said offering me his arm.

"Yes, and I have brought my appetite with me."

"Great. I think you will enjoy what Ona has prepared."

Upstairs, I was greeted warmly by Sara.

"We are so pleased you could make it out for dinner, Maggie."

"Your invitation came at the right time."

"Shall we go into the great room for a cocktail?"

"That would be lovely."

We walked into the great room and sat on the plush white sofa as Mac walked over to the bar and started to prepare cocktails.

A Hawaiian woman in her mid-fifties dressed in a beautiful red and white floral hibiscus mumu with magnificent black hair, practically down to her waist, appeared and set down a tray of appetizers.

"Maggie, I would like to introduce Ona, my right hand. She does a lot around here, and you will find her to be invaluable."

"Hello, Ona."

"Hello, Ms. Langham."

Ona smiled and turned to walk back into the kitchen.

Mac brought us our cocktails which he said was his version of a Prince Kuhio, a blend of pineapple juice and rum.

We sat sipping our lush, tropical drinks when Mac said: "Maggie, I bet you're wondering who your first guest will be?"

"Yes. Dean gave me your notes which you so graciously provided, but it doesn't give me much information about Mark Elliott."

"Mark is one of the reasons we had you come to dinner. We wanted to tell you in person what you should be prepared for."

"Really? I can't begin to imagine."

"He's a retired colonel out of the Marines but actually, medically discharged. He was serving in Afghanistan when his battalion of Marines encountered a suicide bomber. Needless to say, the results were catastrophic; not to him physically but mentally. You see, he has post-traumatic stress disorder. The soldiers he lost had been under his command, and he was close to each of them. He took the loss personally, as if he could have done anything differently."

I didn't know what to say in response.

Mac went on, "We're telling you this because we want to be up-front with you. Mark will be staying here for an indefinite time."

Dean gave me the wrong information. I don't understand how he could have done that. "Don't worry about his expenses as he has them covered up front."

"Mac, he sounds like maybe he should be in a veteran's facility. How can I care for him? I'm aware there's a veteran's medical facility here on Kauai."

"There will be no care as such, but to provide an inviting, relaxing atmosphere for him to recuperate. No pressure. He is to be left alone unless he wants to interact with you. He communicates well. You should be forewarned, however, that he also suffers from a sleep disorder, so his sleeping patterns are off, and he may be up during the night."

"Okay. I'll let you know if I have any questions. But I'm curious. How do you know so much about him?"

"He's my nephew," replied Sara.

"Oh," was all I could say. Feeling speechless, which was unusual for me, I felt my cheeks flush.

Suddenly, Mac spoke up.

"Maggie, if this is going to be too much for you please tell us."

"Oh, no, not at all." I couldn't tell them about all I went through with my late husband and that I was fully aware of what it takes to be around someone who is going through a tough time.

"Mac, whatever you can share with me, trust I will keep it confidential. I won't even tell Colonel Elliott what you have told me. All of this will be kept between the three of us and within these walls. Trust me. Would you have a picture of him for me?"

"We do," replied Sara taking Mac's hand and holding it. "Excuse me a minute, and I will get you that picture."

"Before I forget to mention it, my personal belongings, furniture, books, etc., are being shipped over from the mainland and I expect them to be here any day. Is there a storage facility nearby?"

"We have a large storage shed where your things will be perfectly safe and secure," replied Mac.

"That's good to know as I'm not sure what I will keep or discard.

My realtor on the mainland took care of having everything shipped over."

"Also, we have pretty much packed up our things. They will be ready to be picked up for shipping out as soon as our escrow closes."

"I'm happy to hear that. The hotel where I'm staying is very nice, and I'm comfortable, but I'm looking forward to moving out of there and into my own place. I'm not good with staying in hotels for the long-term. So, I'll be anxious to get the escrow closed as well."

Sara appeared and handed me a picture of Colonel Elliott, and I was struck by more than his blond good looks. I was at a loss for words – I knew this man. The question was, do I say anything to Sara or let it go?

"Maggie, is something wrong?"

On the spot, I decided to let it go. "No, Sara, not at all. He is quite handsome and looks like someone I knew many years ago."

"Really? That picture was taken a few years ago, so I don't know how much his experiences of late have affected his appearance, but he will still resemble himself, I'm sure."

"I trust he will," I said, looking at the picture and the deep blue eyes that resembled pools of crashing waves on the shore.

Ona appeared and announced that dinner was ready.

Mac and Sara led to me the lanai where Ona had set up the table for dinner and was in the process of bringing food out from the kitchen.

"We are having Hawaiian shrimp curry with rice," said Sara.

I saw the small bowls of condiments: grated coconut, chopped macadamia nuts, grated hard-boiled eggs, chutney, banana chips, chopped green apples, and chopped green onion.

"Oh, Sara, it smells divine, and I'm hungry."

"Oh, I'm so pleased. I took a chance that you would like this dish. For dessert, we have a surprise which I think you will enjoy."

"Well, let's sit down and eat," said Mac, "I'm starving."

We sat down, and Ona came out with a steaming bowl of white

rice and a lovely green salad. She filled our water glasses and asked if I would like anything else to drink.

"Thank you, Ona, but this will do nicely."

I felt so distracted by the picture of Mark; certainly, Sara and Mac must have noticed that something was on my mind.

"Maggie, would you like wine with dinner? We have a nice bottle of chardonnay chilled," asked Mac.

"No, thank you. Since I'm driving, I'd better not and with the dark road going back to the hotel… Well, I think you know what I mean."

We finished dinner and Sara went into the kitchen. She brought out dessert, and I couldn't help but comment, "This looks intriguing."

"It's called mango floating islands."

Coffee was served, and I glanced at my watch and saw it was later than I thought.

"This has been lovely, but I had better head back to the hotel before Paul sends out a search party for me."

We got up from the table, and I placed the picture of Mark in my bag. I started towards the elevator when Sara said, "Maggie, Mac will walk you down to your car. If there's anything at all you think of, please give us a call or come on out. We are always here – well at least one of us is."

"Sara, I will certainly take you up on that," I said as I leaned in to hug her.

"Goodnight, Maggie and drive safe."

"I will."

As Mac and I went down in the elevator, we exchanged idle chit chat and, walking me to my car, he said "We are so pleased that you bought our place and know you will maintain it as we would. God bless you, Maggie."

I was a bit taken aback by his last comment but rather than ask about it, said

"Goodnight, Mac. Thank you for your hospitality."

CHAPTER NINETEEN

I drove out to Kuhio Highway and took a left to start my drive back to the hotel. It was as I expected; dark and very few streetlights except in Hanalei and Princeville. Fortunately, I didn't feel sleepy but exhilarated! Hopefully, my next trip on this road would be to finalize the sale and do a walkthrough, unless they don't do them in Hawaii? But I couldn't understand why they wouldn't. I turned on a local radio station and heard a report that heavy rain would be coming in, and I felt relieved that I was already on my way back to the hotel. Distracted by all that I'd learned from Mac and Sara about my first guest, I almost missed the turn into the hotel parking lot. I kept thinking about the picture of Mark. Could I be mistaken? Maybe he just resembles the person I knew so many years ago. I parked, sat a moment to come to my senses and the reality of what I had discovered before I got out of the car. I noticed raindrops on the windshield. "Better get inside before I get soaked." Suddenly, the rain was coming down in sheets. I ran towards the entrance and heard a voice.

"Maggie, where have you been? I've been worried about you."

I looked up and saw Paul standing at the front desk with a look on his face that resembled a thunder cloud.

"Is anything wrong?" he asked.

"Of course there's something wrong – I'm soaked!"

"You should have told someone you were driving out and where you were going."

"I don't believe you are responsible for me?" *I should probably apologize for being so abrupt, but this gets tiresome. He really has no right.*

"No, but I do care about your safety and welfare."

"It's been a while since I had someone so concerned about me."

"Remember, you are new to this island even though you have visited before. It can be pitch black out there and hard to drive in the best of conditions. Were you aware the weather report was for heavy rain tonight?"

"Yes, I was. I turned on the radio as soon as I got in the car to drive back and heard about the rain." I could see Paul's patience was wearing thin. *It's as if he owns me, which he doesn't.*

"How about if I buy YOU a drink for a change? I think you could use one."

He smiled at that. "All right. I am off duty, so no problem there."

"Good," I said, linking my arm in his as the front desk clerk handed me a towel to wipe off some of the rain. I steered us towards a quiet table and started to wipe off the excess moisture.

"Now, tell me where you went."

"Well, considering that I am a soon to be new resident I don't have many places to go, but since you insist, I will tell you that Mac and Sara invited me out to The Inn for dinner."

"Couldn't they have had you meet them at a restaurant in Princeville or Hanalei? Why would they have you drive out there on that dark and desolate road?"

"They wanted me to meet one of their employees and give me some insight into my first guest. In hindsight, I can understand why. I believe one of their intentions was to have me experience the inn as I will be living there. They wanted to put me in their place. I hope you can understand that."

Paul looked into my eyes and said, "You may have a point. I will try and understand the situation."

"I would appreciate that."

The server approached, and I said to her, "Please bring Mr. Sinclair a Scotch, two fingers neat, and I will have a glass of Amaretto."

She walked away with a smile on her face.

"Paul, I was okay. No need to worry, but I promise if it makes you feel better, I will tell you the next time I head out to see Mac and Sara. Besides, it is a good idea for someone to know where I'm going."

"Maggie, you need to realize this is a different environment for you."

"I understand that more and more every day. But I'd like to talk about something else, like what am I going to do about getting a car?"

"I called King Auto, who I have dealt with before, and they have a Jeep Cherokee on the lot, I think would fit your needs."

"Okay. Sounds good. When can I look at it?"

"How about tomorrow?"

"Perfect. I need to turn in my rental car, so maybe we can do that too?"

"Sure. I'll have time in the morning."

I heard a female voice from behind me ask, "What are you two so deep in conversation about?"

"Well, wouldn't you like to know," I said sarcastically and then realized how snarky I sounded. "Sorry, Judy, I didn't mean to be snippy, but after all, I'm an adult and don't need everyone treating me like I'm a two-year-old. I've just been through this with Paul."

"I deserve it," Judy answered. "I wanted to let you know that I'm heading back to the mainland as soon as the ship arrives with your personal belongings."

"When do you think that will be?"

"Maybe tomorrow. I need to call the shipping line to confirm their arrival time."

Our drinks arrived, and Judy asked Kale for a dry Martini.

Sitting down, she turned to me and said, "Where were you tonight?"

"I was having dinner with Mac and Sara, and we were discussing business."

"I hope you weren't getting involved in the deal."

"Of course not. No, not at all. We're all satisfied with the terms and, we had other things to discuss, including where to store my stuff when it arrives. Fortunately, they have room and will be happy to help me out when everything arrives."

"Cheers," remarked Paul as Judy's Martini was set on the table in front of her. "To Maggie and her successful venture."

"Thanks, Paul. I think everything will work out nicely," I said sipping my Amaretto. I noticed Judy winking at Paul. "Okay! What does the wink mean, Judy?"

"Just an inside joke. Well, maybe not a joke. We're pleased you're making this transition. You have surprised me!"

"Really! Why are you surprised?"

"Considering all you have been through; I wasn't sure if this was the right thing for you to do."

"Well, guess what? It is, and I'm thrilled that it's working out."

We sat quietly without speaking when Dean appeared.

"Hi, folks. What's up?"

I said to Dean, "Maybe you can tell me. When does the escrow close?"

"It's set to close the day after tomorrow. We need to set a time to do the walkthrough with Mac and Sara. How about tomorrow afternoon after lunch?"

"Oh, Dean, that's fine! It sounds like tomorrow will be a busy day! Things are starting to fall into place. I think it's time for me to turn in. I'm beyond tired but relaxed. It was a good evening."

I got up, and Paul stood, "Maggie, let me walk you to your room."

Extending my hand, Paul grasped it, and I said "Goodnight you two. See you tomorrow."

"Goodnight to you too. Have a good night."

I replied, "I intend to. You as well."

Once at my room, I took my key out, which Paul promptly took from my hand and opened my door. Standing in the doorway, he asked if he could come in.

"Paul, I don't think it's wise, at least for tonight. I would like to get a good night's sleep."

"Maggie, I don't understand you. You come on to me in subtle ways, but when I want to spend alone time with you, you pull back feigning that you're tired and need sleep. If you aren't interested in me, then say so, and I will move on, if not, then I need to know what you want from me."

"Paul, let's not talk about this out here in the hallway. Please come in so we can discuss this." We walked into my room with Paul closing the door, and I motioned for him to sit on one of the orchid chairs next to the sliding door.

"Paul, I am very attracted to you but need some time to figure out where we go from here."

"Are we back to that? I thought I had you convinced that there is nothing going on with Judy. I want you."

"I know what you said, but I'm still hesitant. I don't know that much about you and –" not letting me finish, he pulled me into an embrace and kissed me hard. I kissed him back fervently and pressed my body against his in an attempt to convince him of my desire to be with him.

The kiss was heartfelt and tender, and as I pulled away, I whispered: "Do you want to stay the night?"

"Are you sure?"

"Yes. I am."

He pulled me up and led me to the bed, and as he leaned me back, I collapsed with Paul on top of me, kissing me long and hard.

CHAPTER TWENTY

I opened my eyes the next morning to my favorite rooster's crowing. I was still fully dressed from yesterday – and alone. I sat up and tried to think back to last night and remembered Paul and me in a deep kiss on my bed and nothing else after that. Now I wake up, and he's not here. What happened? Where did he go? Well, if he couldn't at least say goodbye when he left then so be it. I got up and wandered into the bathroom, turned on the shower and took off my clothes from yesterday and the words from an old South Pacific song rang into my head 'Gotta Wash that Man Right Outa My Hair'... but did I really mean that? I finished and, stepping out of the shower, grabbed the terry cloth robe hanging on the back of the bathroom door and wrapped myself in it. I walked out to the sliding door and looked out at the blue Pacific. Smiling, I couldn't believe my good fortune. Moving here was a dream come true, and whatever happens with Paul happens. My phone rang, and I went to answer it.

"Hello."

"Good morning, sleepyhead. I thought we had a date to take care of your car business?"

"Oh, good morning to you too. You're so right. I need to finish dressing, and I'll meet you in the restaurant in fifteen."

"See you then," he responded.

At least he was still speaking to me, so I guess last night didn't end as disastrously as I thought. I applied my makeup with care, hoping it would get me through the day. I pulled from the closet a pair of white pants, a red polo shirt, and white flats. I needed to be comfortable today as it looked like there would be a lot to take care of. First things first. The car.

I walked into the restaurant and saw Paul sitting at our usual table, set off to the side, and semi-private. As I approached, I noted he had already seen to getting my breakfast of papaya, two poached eggs, and whole wheat toast. "You really have my number, Mr. Sinclair."

Paul stood up and said, "Your eating is not complicated and simply consistent, which shows me you are a sensible woman."

"I'm not sure I like the sound of that. It hints of something you're not too keen on."

"To start with, I'm not accustomed to having women fall asleep on me. You passed out. Not sure if you were simply tired or had too much to drink."

"Paul, I'm sorry about that. It won't happen again. I hope you give me another opportunity."

He replied, "I plan to" as Judy and Dean popped up as if out of nowhere.

"Please sit."

"Dean, what time is our walkthrough scheduled for?"

"1:00 p.m. this afternoon, provided you're available."

"Considering it's barely 9:30 in the morning, that shouldn't be a problem."

Judy and Dean got up to hit the buffet, and I devoured my breakfast so Paul and I could take care of my car situation. I finished as they came back to our table.

"Don't like running off on you two, but I must get on with what I need to accomplish today."

"Besides the walkthrough, what could you possibly have to do?" Judy sniped.

"Paul and I are taking care of my car situation, as if it's any business of yours."

"Now, ladies," Paul interjected. "Maggie, let's get out of here."

"Sorry for my curtness, Judy. See you two later."

Paul and I walked out to the parking lot, and he said: "I'll follow you to the car rental place at the airport to return your car."

"Sounds good," I said, stepping forward to plant a kiss on his cheek, brushing against his chest.

"Let's do this."

Driving to Lihue Airport to return the rental car, my thoughts kept going back to last night, and I wondered why I had passed out. If I didn't know better, I would think someone had slipped something in my drink. Enough of that, I told myself. Best keep my mind on track. I looked in the rearview mirror and saw Paul keeping pace with me. I pulled into the Hertz rental lot and took care of returning the car and settling what I owed them. I walked out to Paul, waiting patiently in his car.

"I appreciate you going to all this trouble for me."

"It's no trouble at all. I'll be happy to get you all settled so you can slow down and enjoy life a bit."

As I got into his car, I said, "I would like that. Say, I started thinking, it's not like me to pass out like I did last night. It was as if someone slipped something in my drink. What do you think?"

"Almost anything is possible. Let's focus on getting you your car. We can talk more about that later."

"Okay. Sounds like a plan."

As we headed over to the car dealership, I had the nagging thought that someone had slipped something in my drink. Creepy feeling to think that someone would do that, but who? Maybe I was just being paranoid?

"A penny for your thoughts?"

"Thinking about the new car is all," I lied.

"You should be happy with it. I checked it out, and it has all the bells and whistles you could want, including a moon roof."

"Really? How about the hands-free Bluetooth feature so I can talk easily on my phone?"

"It's got it," he said grinning.

We pulled into the dealership and after two hours of looking, talking, and signing paperwork, I was out the door and into my brand-new red Jeep Cherokee.

I got into my vehicle and relished the new car smell; especially the leather. I buckled up, and suddenly, Paul was standing pointing at me to put the window down.

"Boy! You're sure into this new Jeep. I didn't realize you would get so excited."

"Been a while since I had a brand-new vehicle. I'm going to love this one. Paul, you did well. It will serve my needs perfectly. You were right; it has all the bells and whistles I will need."

"Follow me back to the hotel so we can catch up with Dean and Judy. It will soon be time for your walkthrough. I know you don't want to be late for that."

"You're so right. Enough fiddling around. I can play with all this later."

I followed him back to the hotel and carefully parked my new car in a space out by itself.

We walked in and spied Judy and Dean at a table in a secluded spot.

"Hi, you two lovebirds," I quipped.

"Back so soon?" commented Judy.

"It didn't take too long, and Paul had already given the salesperson a general idea of what I was looking for, so he had a car all picked out for me," I said as I noticed Paul over at the bar in a serious conversation with the bartender.

"Maggie, it's close to the time for your walkthrough. We don't want to keep Mac and Sara waiting, do we?"

"No, of course not."

Paul strode over, and I could tell there was a problem.

"Sorry, Maggie, but I need to stay here. There's a problem with my staff that I must clear up before any more time lapses."

"I understand perfectly. Besides your time is better spent here than with me on a boring ol' walkthrough."

"Maggie, maybe I should hang around here and let you and Dean go out and take care of your business," said Judy.

I could see the look of frustration on Paul's face, so I spoke up directly to Judy and said, "Not a chance. You were very instrumental in getting me to this juncture, so you have no choice."

"I'm with Maggie, Judy. You come with us. I'm sure she'll appreciate your input," remarked Dean.

"Judy, I would feel much better if you go with us. I can use your moral support and expertise."

"Okay. You guys have me convinced. I'm in."

Smiling, I said, "Paul, I'll catch up with you later."

"You better," he responded as he walked over to me and planted a kiss on my lips.

"Later, then. Come on, let's get started," I said linking arms with Dean and Judy as I steered them out to the parking lot.

"I'll drive," chimed in Dean. "Judy, you sit in the back and Maggie can sit up front with me."

With that settled, we were on our way.

CHAPTER TWENTY-ONE

D ean steered the car onto Kuhio Highway, and we drove north towards my new life without so much as a peep out of any of us. I know my mind was a flurry of excitement and some anxiety at the same time.

"Judy, any suggestions as to what I should look for during the walkthrough?"

"Oh, Maggie. Give me a break. You know what to look for. You just can't handle the silence, and I, for one, know that dragging me along was contrived."

"Judy, give Maggie a break. Besides, I was the one to drag you along with us. Keeps you out of trouble that way," Dean said with a laugh.

"Okay. Truce, please. This is a big day for me, and I don't want this sniping back and forth. Judy, if you don't want to contribute, you can stay in the car while Dean and I go in."

"Not on your life, Maggie. I plan to walk it with you and give you my expert opinion."

I sat thinking that she really can be a piece of work, but I love her anyway. She has been a good friend and someone I could depend on, so I will tolerate her until we are back at the hotel.

"Here we are, ladies," Dean piped up as he turned onto Alamihi Road.

Dean parked up under the shade of a large tree, and I took a deep breath as we got out of the car. As excited as I was, I was also nervous. *What if I'm a total flop at this?*

"Maggie, what's wrong?" asked Dean.

With tears forming in my eyes I looked at him and said, "I must admit that I worry about being a failure with this venture. Maybe I bit off more than I can chew?"

"A bit late for that now, don't you think? I think you're having a delayed case of buyer's remorse," said Dean as he put his arm around me to give me a comforting squeeze.

"Maggie, I'm confident you will be fine," said Judy.

Almost as if on cue, Mac and Sara appeared.

"Good afternoon. We were beginning to wonder if you were having second thoughts?" asked Mac.

"Oh, no. Just last-minute details that popped up. Sorry, Mac. I would have called you if there was a problem. Shall we get on with it?"

"Let's," said Sara and we began the walkthrough.

An hour and a half later after checking out the property for anything that needed attention and some questions, I was satisfied that all was well.

Mac and Sara introduced me to Keoki Opunui their handyman who would offer his services.

"Keoki, I am pleased to meet you. But you don't need to be concerned with me finding a replacement for you. From what I've heard from Mac and Sara, you are invaluable, and a trusted member of the inn, and I would like for you to stay on."

Keoki looked at me with tears welling up in his eyes.

"Ms. Langham, I'm happy you want me to stay on. My family depends on me to provide for them. This job has meant everything to me."

"Well, it's settled then. You will work for me as you have for Mac and Sara, although I may need your help with things that you haven't done for them, since I'm a single woman."

"No worry about that, Ms. Langham," said Keoki smiling.

Turning to Dean, I asked, "Before we leave, shouldn't we check out the house where I will be living?"

"Yes, we should, Maggie. Mac, would you like to lead the way?"

"It would be my pleasure."

Sara spoke up in a halting voice and said, "If you don't mind, I think I will hang back here."

"No problem, Sara," I said.

As I turned to wave goodbye to Sara, I caught a glimpse of her wiping a tear from her cheek.

"Mac, are you sure Sara is okay with all of this?"

"Maggie, she is, and she isn't. You submitted a low bid compared to the others, but we had our heart set on selling to you. We feel you are the one we want to leave The Inn with. She knows you will care for this property and safeguard it as much as we have. I'm not as emotional as Sara but still, I agree 100% with her."

"Thank you for entrusting me with your lifelong home. Rest assured that I will cherish this property."

"Thank you, Maggie," he said with tears in his eyes.

I walked back to where Sara was standing and, giving her a big hug, said, "I know this is hard for you, but trust that I will take care of the inn and you won't have to worry. I will carry on the tradition you and Mac have passed on to me."

She smiled half-heartedly and said, "I know you will, Maggie. It's so sad to leave after all this time here and our memories that will stay with me forever."

I strode back to where Dean was standing and said, let's check on my new residence. We started towards the cottage. Walking in, I saw the myriad boxes ready to be shipped out.

Dean took my elbow and whispered, "Let's get this wrapped up before someone changes their mind."

"You think?"

"Maybe."

"Okay, let's do it," I said as I pulled my clipboard out to make notes. I planned to have the rooms mapped out for the placement of my furniture.

As we walked around, I realized my furniture wouldn't do at all. This needed a different kind of furniture that lends itself to a feeling of the island and not reminders of my former life that I was working so hard to escape from.

We finished the walkthrough and started towards Dean's Land Rover.

"Thank you, Mac, for your hospitality. I suppose it's just a matter of closing the escrow, which should be tomorrow."

"We have movers coming in the morning to pick up our things," said Mac. "It's going to be bittersweet. Sara will be fine once we're on our way and she knows there's no turning back."

"I'm so excited but at the same time a little scared. But with Keoki and Ona, I know I will be fine."

I stepped forward to embrace Mac, who hugged me back. I pulled back and said, "All the best to you. I hope everything turns out well for you."

We got into Dean's Rover and waved goodbye to Mac. I caught a glimpse of Sara standing on the lanai upstairs and waved to her as we drove off, surprised at the tears welling up in my eyes.

Dean noticed and said, "Maggie, are you okay?"

"I am, but tender-hearted as my dad used to say."

CHAPTER TWENTY-TWO

Driving back to the hotel, I was having second thoughts that I had done the right thing. *What if I couldn't do this?*

Dean spoke up. "Maggie, having a second bout of buyer's remorse?"

"Well, you might say that. Only to the extent that I want to carry on what Mac and Sara worked so hard to establish. Being with them in their element makes me wonder if I'll be able to carry on their tradition. They have a following, and now I'm taking over. Only time will tell."

"I have an idea," said Judy. "Why don't you send out announcements that you are the new innkeeper and Mac and Sara have moved on?"

"I guess I could do that but not before I check with them. They may not want it put out there that they are no longer the innkeepers of their bed and breakfast."

"I know that they will be leaving you with their guest list for future reference. Keep in mind that past guests should know that they are no longer there," Dean commented.

I focused on watching the landscape feeling contentment and happiness I hadn't felt in years. Strange how a move like I have done could have such an impact. I should be patting myself on the back and not so unsure of myself. Even though I was anxious about taking over this business, I was ecstatic: a step forward in starting over.

Dean and Judy were very quiet on the way back to the hotel, which was fine with me. I had thoughts swirling in my head: a to-do list a mile long. I must get organized and focus on my tasks to get ready for the move. We pulled into the parking lot, and I saw Paul standing at the front desk, and I wondered if he was waiting for us to return. I got out of the Rover and dashed into the hotel as it had started to rain.

"Hi! Were you waiting for us to return?" I said to Paul.

"Yes, I was. I was getting concerned. If I had gone with you then I wouldn't have worried," he said to me, looking into my eyes with those bedroom eyes of his. "How about if you and I wander off and have dinner, just the two of us?"

"How do you think we can do that with Dean and Judy tagging along?"

"Leave it to me," he said as they walked up to where we were standing.

"Hi, Paul. Bet you're glad we're back. The walkthrough is all done, and everything looked great. The general contractor had already been out and cleared his part of the inspection. Mac and Sara have taken excellent care of the property," said Dean.

Judy was smiling like a Cheshire cat, and I wondered what could be on her mind.

Paul spoke up, "Maggie and I are going to have a quiet dinner – just the two of us. I hope you don't mind."

"Well, I do mind," declared Judy. "After all, I'll be leaving tomorrow. I wanted to have dinner with the four of us since it's my last night. You'll have her all to yourself when I leave this paradise."

"Oh, Judy. I forgot you were flying back tomorrow. I must apologize. The days have gone by so quickly," I said. "Paul, I think it best if the four of us have dinner tonight since Judy will be leaving tomorrow."

"Maggie, I agree with you. I think I can probably get us into

Gaylord's at the Kilohana Plantation," said Paul as he dialed up their number.

I stepped aside and asked Dean, "What time do you think I can move in?"

"I'll call you after I speak with escrow and they have confirmed everything has been completed," Dean said.

"That's fine. I know what I can do while I'm waiting. I'm sure I will be waking early in the morning. As soon as the stores are open for business, I'm going to look for some furniture that will fit nicely in my island home."

"A good use of your time, rather than standing around waiting for my call," replied Dean.

"Maggie, I can tag along since my flight doesn't leave until later in the afternoon?"

"Judy, good idea. I can always use another opinion."

"Opinion? Opinion about what?" asked Paul as he rejoined us.

"Judy has offered to go shopping with me in the morning while I wait for Dean's call. I've decided that I need some different furniture than what I had shipped over. It just won't work in my island home."

"Sounds good. You're probably right there," agreed Paul. "Our reservation is confirmed for 7. Does that work for everyone?"

We all chimed in "That works."

"In the meantime, I'm going back to my room to freshen up for dinner since we have an hour or so," I said starting to walk towards my room.

"Maggie, let me walk with you," said Paul.

"Sure, come on then."

Reaching my door, Paul said, "I'm going to miss the nearness of you when you move out to your new home."

"I won't be that far away," I said, leaning in to him kiss. "You're welcome anytime. Maybe then we can at least have some privacy."

Paul smiled and said, "I'm counting on it. See you in a bit."

I walked into my room and flung myself on the bed, relishing the soft, plush comforter. I had forgotten all about Mark but knew I must tell Paul about him before they met face to face.

I laid there looking at the ceiling and thought about the last time I saw Mark. It was before he went into the military, and we were both still in college. I remember him as boyish looking with that blond hair that always seemed like it had been kissed by the sun. What was I doing? Daydreaming about a man who probably won't know me after all this time, when I have Paul who I think has fallen for me? Enough of this! I got up, went into the bathroom, and turned on the shower to take a quick one before dinner. That should certainly give me a boost.

While in the shower, I heard my cell ringing and stepped out, grabbed the terry cloth robe, slipped it over my dripping body, and darted for my phone.

"Hello?"

"Maggie, it's Mac."

"Hi, Mac. Is everything okay?"

"Yes, dear. I just wanted to advise you we heard from Mark tonight and he's coming in a day early. As we speak, he's in Honolulu."

"So, what are you telling me?"

"Nothing except to make you aware and not to be surprised when he appears."

"Coming in a day early? That makes him arrive the day after I move in. That shouldn't be a problem. The only things that won't be organized will be my things, which won't be a problem."

"Sounds like you will handle this fine, Maggie."

"I will be fine, Mac. You and Sara take care and don't worry; all will be fine," I said not entirely convinced myself.

After I'd hung up, I walked to the closet and picked out a black maxi dress with spaghetti straps. It had a splash of beautiful tropical flowers around the hem, which I had purposely gotten for celebrating. Working on my makeup, I heard the hotel phone ring. I ran to answer it.

"Maggie, are you ready?" asked Paul.

"Almost, give me five, and I'll meet you in the lobby."

I finished getting myself dressed and put on lipstick and slipped my feet into black sandals.

I walked quickly to the lobby and saw I was the last one to arrive.

"Sorry it took me so long. I had a call from Mac."

"Everything okay?" asked Dean.

"Yes, for the time being."

CHAPTER TWENTY-THREE

Paul took my hand as the four of us walked out to his car and whispered in my ear, "You look beautiful." Once settled in, he steered the vehicle onto Kuhio Highway. While Gaylord's wasn't far, we had a bit of a drive. Fortunately, Judy and Dean were chattering away in the backseat until Judy asked, "Maggie, you're so quiet. Are you feeling all right?"

"I'm good. Just a bit tired but excited about my move."

"I'm glad to hear that," said Dean.

"Well, I have mixed feelings," said Paul. "I know Maggie can't stay indefinitely at the hotel and I knew that this day was going to come. Still, I'm going to miss having her around all the time."

"Paul, I won't be that far away and when we do see each other our time will most likely not be broken up with demands from the hotel."

"True I suppose," said Paul, "But then what about the demands of your guests?"

"We will just have to handle it as it comes, that's all," I said, reaching across the console to squeeze his hand.

I noticed we were on the Kaummualii Highway when Kilohana Plantation appeared sooner than I thought it would, and Paul turned the car into the long drive up to the front of the property. He parked, and we all got out and walked into Gaylord's in search of the dining room.

Paul walked up to the hostess and said, "We have a reservation, and I requested a table in a secluded area so we can talk."

"Let me see what we have." Checking her computer, she replied, "Okay, right this way."

She picked up four menus and led us to a perfect table with a lovely view of the mountains.

Looking over the menu, I noted several things that looked delicious. "Paul, I don't know what to have. I'm hungrier than I thought; everything looks scrumptious."

"I'll order us a nice bottle of chardonnay," said Paul. "That will at least get us started."

I kept perusing the menu not knowing what I was in the mood for until the server brought us our wine and, after pouring, asked what we would like for dinner. I finally decided on the Caprese salad with the seared scallops. Judy and Dean both ordered the Kilohana Caesar along with hoisin glazed pork spare-ribs while Paul ordered the shrimp & scallop spring rolls and the filet mignon.

"Paul, I'm surprised you ordered the spring rolls."

"I had an ulterior motive. I know you love shrimp and thought I could tempt you sharing them with me."

"No tempting required," I said, smiling.

I sat daydreaming about my new venture and what it would feel like to live out there all alone except for my guests when Paul spoke up.

"Penny for your thoughts?"

"Actually, much more. I'm thinking about what will be coming down the pipe for me with the bed and breakfast."

Judy spoke up and said, "Don't worry. You're going to be fine and do well. Your guests are going to love you, honey," she said, raising her glass for a toast.

Paul looked at me and said, "I agree. You will be great!"

Dean was the only one who remained quiet, and it alarmed me a bit. "Dean, is something wrong?"

"No, Maggie. I agree with Judy and Paul, but I'm selfish and will miss showing you around the island."

"No worries. You can come out anytime to visit. Consider it a home away from home."

"I like that you said that."

We finished eating our dinner, and all passed on dessert except each of us ordered a glass of Graham's Six Reserve Port.

Surprisingly, Dean reached for the check, and Paul said, "I was going to get that. How about if we split it?"

"Okay, if you insist."

Check paid; we were walking out when Paul grabbed hold of my hand and walked with me to the car.

On the drive back to the hotel, I said, "Tomorrow I'm going furniture shopping for my new place. I have a feeling what I have won't work."

Dean spoke up and said, "Maggie, I have a friend who has a furniture store, and I bet he would give you a good break. His name is Hoshino. Mind if I tag along with you tomorrow and assist?"

"That might be a good idea, Dean. Shall Judy and I meet up with you? Tell us where and we will be there."

Dean proceeded to rattle off some information, and I interrupted, "Maybe text me the address and whatever I need? I think that would be best."

On the way back to the hotel, Dean asked me what I thought I would need in the line of furniture.

I replied, "Definitely a dining room table and chairs, a bedroom set, including mattress with box springs and living room furniture. This is all to start, but I may need additional pieces. This will give me a sense of home."

"Sounds good, Maggie. I'll text Hoshino to give him an idea of what we will be looking for tomorrow so we won't be wasting time."

"Dean, you're on the ball. I'm getting excited and look forward to tomorrow. Shall we meet there at 10?"

"Fine. I'll be there to introduce you and get you started at least. I may have to bow out and return to the office."

"I'm the proverbial worry wart. I'm keeping positive thoughts that nothing is going south on my escrow."

"Oh, no. I have a couple of other ones I'm working on and have been spending so much time on yours the other ones have been a bit neglected."

"Dean, I don't like to hear that. Take all the time you need. I think Judy and I can handle purchasing some furniture."

"At the least, I'll meet you there."

The rest of the drive back to the hotel, we were all quiet with Paul holding my hand. He pulled into the parking lot and parked the car.

"Maggie, hold up a minute, would you?"

"Sure, Paul."

"Goodnight, you two," I said to Judy and Dean as they sauntered off into the hotel, headed to the bar area.

"Maggie, I hope you don't think I've gone too far into your business."

"Paul don't worry. It's been nice to have a man take an interest and look out for me. I will certainly need whatever assistance you can give me when I get out to the inn. I know you have obligations here so whatever time you can spare, I will appreciate," I said leaning over to kiss him.

"Let me walk you to your room," he said, getting out of the car.

He helped me out of the car, and we walked towards the hotel when one of the staff came running.

"Mr. Sinclair, we have a big problem in the kitchen. Need you to come right away."

Paul looked at me, and I said, "Go ahead, I can navigate to my room. See you in the morning?"

"Breakfast at 8?"

"See you then," I said, smiling.

Paul went one direction, and I went another, walking to my room before I caught Dean and Judy's attention. They were sitting at the bar deep in conversation, and I didn't want to have a drink but to go to bed.

Once in my room, I took care to prepare for bed, taking off my clothes and putting on a nightgown. I finished in the bathroom and was strolling to my bed when the hotel phone rang.

"Hello."

"Maggie, I'm finished with my kitchen snafu. May I come to your room?"

"Oh, Paul, I would like to say yes, but I was just getting into bed."

"Can't I at least tuck you in?"

"Not tonight. Maybe some other time?"

"You keep putting me off. One of these days, but until then I'll take a rain check."

"See you in the morning. Goodnight," I said, hanging up the phone.

Trying to get comfortable, my mind wandered to my conversation with Paul. I wondered why I was keeping him at arm's length. In the past, I wasn't always as reluctant to turn a man away. Maybe that was my problem, and I had finally learned my lesson. I drifted off as the brisk trade winds blew into my room and I smiled thinking of all I had to look forward to in the coming days with a slight trepidation named Mark Elliott.

CHAPTER TWENTY-FOUR

The next morning, I awakened before the alarm, disappointed my favorite rooster hadn't yet crowed. I smiled, wondering if I would have one out at the inn. I would miss this guy waking me every day. I stretched, flung back the covers, and got up to see what the weather was going to be. It looked a bit cloudy but with big patches of blue sky. I told myself it didn't matter as I was going to buy furniture for my new place today, regardless of the weather. I walked to the closet and pulled out a simple navy linen sheath and sandals. While in the bathroom taking care of my morning toilette, the phone rang. I ran to pick it up, and a familiar voice said gently, "Good morning."

"Good morning, Paul."

"Are you ready to get your day started? How about some breakfast?"

"Give me ten minutes, and I will meet you in the restaurant."

"I'll be here."

After I hung up and returned to the bathroom to finish my makeup, it occurred to me that generally, he doesn't call me this early. Could he have spent the night here at the hotel? Not that it matters but what's up with him?

Dressed, makeup nearly perfect, I left my room and sauntered to the restaurant to find Paul sitting at our usual table. As I approached, he got up and greeted me with a kiss.

"When you said ten minutes, you meant it."

"I try my best to be punctual."

I sat down and noticed that he had already gotten me coffee and juice.

"Did you spend the night here last night?"

"I did. I have one of the cottages here and thought if you needed me, I would be close by."

Smiling, I said, "Very nice, but you didn't have to. I'm a big girl, you know."

"Just say thank you and be grateful."

I replied, "Thank you," when Judy appeared all dressed for the day.

"I see you're already up and ready to go."

"Well, not quite. I need some food to fuel me for the day. After all I ate last night, you would think that I wouldn't be so hungry, but when I woke my stomach was grumbling for food."

"Maggie, Dean texted me the address of the furniture store where he suggested you go."

"Nice. As soon as we finish breakfast, let's go and see what I can find. I want to be done with it in time to see you off."

"You don't have to worry about me. I can go to the airport by myself."

"Oh, no. After spending this time with me and helping me out with the escrows, I want to give you a proper sendoff."

"I won't argue with you, and with that, I'll get myself some breakfast."

"I'll come with you."

We returned in a few minutes with plates heaped with papaya, pineapple, strawberries, cantaloupe, and honeydew melon.

Harmi, the server, came over to see if we wanted anything from the kitchen.

"I would love a couple of poached eggs, cottage cheese, and toast."

Judy piped up, "Same for me. Sounds good."

I noticed Paul was trying to restrain himself from laughing.

"I can certainly tell you two are friends. Each is eating virtually the same breakfast," he said winking at me.

As we finished, my cell rang, and I saw it was Dean.

"Good morning. I hope this early morning call brings me good news?"

"Yes, it does and the very best. You are now the owner of a bed and breakfast. Escrow closed, and I'm gathering the last of the paperwork for your files."

"Great news. I'm going to have to adjust when all this settles down. You all have been so attentive; it'll feel strange once I'm on my own."

"No worries there," Paul piped up. "You won't be getting rid of me anytime soon."

"What's my next step, Dean?"

"Nothing, just carry on and I will check with Mac and Sara as to when they will be out, and I'll let you know."

"Sounds good to me. Judy, let's get going to Hoshino's."

"Paul, I will let you know when we get back from our little expedition."

He leaned over to give me a quick kiss on the lips as Judy looked on.

Judy and I walked out to the parking lot to get into my new Jeep Cherokee.

I turned left from the Island Garden Inn onto Kuhio Highway to drive to Hoshino's.

"It looks like you and Paul have something going. I hope he'll make you happy," remarked Judy.

I couldn't help but detect a little sarcasm in her voice but decided to let it slide. No use in getting into a spat at this point.

"I'm going to wait and see what develops. If it works, I'll be happy, and if not, then we will each move on. I must take this attitude, or else I will be hurt again, and I don't want that."

Judy didn't comment, and as we pulled into Hoshino's parking lot, I noticed that Dean's Land Rover was parked right in front although he wasn't in his vehicle.

"Let's get out and take care of this," I said.

We got out, walked into a warehouse-size building, filled with furniture for any and every room in a person's home plus business furniture.

Suddenly, Dean was at my elbow. "Maggie, I would like to introduce Abia Hoshino."

"Hello, Ms. Langham," said this older Japanese gentleman of slight stature with twinkly brown eyes.

"Mr. Hoshino, it is a pleasure to meet you. Dean has told me a lot about your store, and I see looking around, you have nearly every kind of furniture suitable for island living."

"Based on what Dean described, I selected some pieces for you. If you follow me, I'll show them to you."

"Thank you. I appreciate you taking the time. You have gone beyond my expectations," I said as we followed him.

Mr. Hoshino had done an excellent job of selecting furniture based on what Dean had told him.

Judy and I looked each piece over carefully for quality and workmanship. The set that I was the most impressed with was for my office area. All of them would work. I ended up selecting a darker wood for my bedroom.

"Mr. Hoshino, you have done a great job with making these selections. Dean, I want to thank you as well. I can tell each piece was thoughtfully picked out. But, Mr. Hoshino, would you happen to have an outdoor papasan chair and a blue medallion hanging chair?"

"Ms. Langham, I don't think I have them here but possibly in our main warehouse. Would you like for me to have them brought in and perhaps delivered with the rest of your furniture? If they don't work out, you may return them."

"Mr. Hoshino, that would be fine. In the meantime, why don't you figure what I owe you and we can discuss delivery?"

"Ms. Langham, that will work."

Judy pulled me aside and said, "Maggie, don't you think he is a bit fast on this?"

"Well, he may be, but I like everything, and if the price is right, I'm going to go for it. Frankly, I love all the pieces."

We followed Mr. Hoshino into his private office where we sat, and a lovely young Hawaiian woman served us mango iced tea. After a few minutes, he presented me with an itemized printout of what I would be purchasing, and I was surprised.

"Mr. Hoshino, this reflects a 20% discount. Is that correct?"

"Yes, Ms. Langham. Dean is my nephew, and he asked if I could give you a bit of a break. It's my pleasure to do so."

"Thank you. I appreciate your generosity."

"Ms. Langham, may we deliver tomorrow?"

"Yes, that would be perfect."

We shook hands, and as we were walking out, I overheard Dean and Mr. Hoshino speaking in Japanese. Not wanting to worry, I just ignored it and thought I would ask Dean about it later.

Judy and I got into my Jeep and headed back to the hotel. She was subdued, which wasn't like her; it reminded me of how I used to feel when I would leave Hawaii to return to the mainland.

"You know, Maggie, since I have a car to return at the airport there is no reason you have to drive out to see me off. We can say our goodbyes at the hotel."

"Are you sure? I don't mind, and I feel bad thinking you will be departing all on your own."

"Maybe not entirely on my own," she replied. "Dean mentioned that he might go along with me."

"Good to know. I feel better knowing that he will be there to see you off."

We were quiet until we reached the hotel. I parked the car, got out, and walked with Judy into the lobby. She proceeded to the front desk to take care of checking out, and I watched as she continued to her room, presumably to pack for her return home.

"Maggie. Everything go okay with the furniture guy?" asked Paul who had walked up to me.

"Yes, everything was fine, actually better than fine. Dean had already spoken to Mr. Hoshino, and they had selected furniture for me to look at. It was all perfect, and I couldn't have done a better job myself."

"Doesn't that make you feel strange?"

"A bit, but I am just giving them, especially Dean, the benefit of the doubt and trying hard not to be suspicious."

"Suspicious?"

I didn't have a chance to respond as Judy had just walked up and I didn't want to get her started. That would be all I needed for her to cancel her flight home and stay to watch over me.

"Am I interrupting anything?" asked Judy.

"No, why do you say that?"

"You two looked like you were involved in a serious conversation."

"No, not at all. I think these last few days have been very stressful for me and some of that has rubbed off on Paul, for which I'm sorry."

"Maggie don't be sorry. It comes with the territory."

"Judy, are you all set to go to the airport?"

"Yes, I was just going to say aloha and wish you well with your new business venture."

"Thanks, Judy. I couldn't have pulled all this off without you!"

We exchanged hugs, and with tears welling up in my eyes, I said, "Have a safe trip and come back soon."

"Why are you crying?"

"Oh, you know me, I'm the sentimental type. I hate goodbyes. I'm a mess at airports."

"We will see each other again, my friend. I have enjoyed my time with you, Maggie. Stay well and take care," Judy said, walking off to join Dean in the parking lot.

Paul pulled me close with his arm around me and gave me a light kiss on the top of my head, "How about a cozy dinner, just the two of us. Will probably be the last time here in the hotel."

"Oh, that's right. Cozy dinner for two would be lovely. What time?"

"6 okay with you?"

"Sure, gives me some time to regroup and relax a bit," I said, giving him a quick kiss on the lips and walking towards my room.

I had a jumble of feelings in my head and heart. I would be glad to be out of here. Maybe then I could figure out where I'm going or not with Paul. I pulled out my room key, and as I walked into the room, I smelled the captivating scent before I saw the huge arrangement of stargazer lilies and tropical flowers. The card read 'Good luck, although you won't need it. Wishing you all the best. Much love, Paul, Judy, and Dean'.

I sat down on the bed, and the tears flowed. I couldn't believe I'd developed these relationships in such a short time. Tomorrow I'd move on and only time would tell what comes next. Since I had a few hours until dinner with Paul, I changed from my sandals into my walking shoes and went out the sliding door towards the beach. Walking along the surf, I felt elated but at the same time, sad. I'm finally here, doing what I set out to do, and tomorrow it all starts. I looked at my watch and saw I had one hour and had walked a good distance down to Lydgate Beach. I walked back to my room and started to get ready for dinner.

In the shower, my thoughts turned to Paul, and I wondered where we would go from here. I got out of the shower, donned the white terrycloth robe and started to apply fresh makeup. I had picked out a red strapless dress embellished with white plumeria flowers for our cozy dinner. I wondered what he had planned. I would soon find out.

Dressed, I applied my favorite fragrance, picked up my clutch bag, and started out the door towards the lobby. Paul was waiting for me and smiled as I approached.

CHAPTER TWENTY-FIVE

The next morning, waking to the sound of my favorite rooster, I laid in bed, thinking back to last night. We had dinner in the hotel restaurant consisting of sea bass, Caesar salad and, of course, a wine which was very low key from our dinner the night before. It was a bit of a letdown but good that it was easing me down from all the excitement from previous evenings. I was expecting Paul to make a move on me, but he didn't. I was disappointed and wanted to know why. But often some things are better left unsaid. I decided to get up, dress, and check out of the hotel quietly, without saying goodbye to him, as I wanted to avoid any emotion spewing forth from me. I thought I should be happy that he hadn't made any moves. But I'd been giving him the same signals and keeping him at arm's length. How long could I expect him to be patient?

I had arranged with the front desk late last night to settle my account and was surprised that it was much smaller than I expected. I wondered if Paul had anything to do with that.

Packed up, I did a double check of the room to make sure I wasn't leaving anything behind. I stopped and looked around the room that I had occupied since arriving in Kauai and realized how much I had accomplished but also felt wistful that this room had been my sanctuary, where I had come to decisions that I was surprised I could make on my own. I closed the door behind me and walked with my bags towards the lobby and a new chapter in my life. The lobby was quiet, virtually empty of anyone up at this hour. I stopped at the front desk and thanked the staff for all they had done for me while I stayed there and asked them to please remove the flowers from my room and place them on the counter for folks to enjoy.

I walked out to my car, dragging my bags, and taking deep breaths to fight back the tears. *I'm way too emotional about this. Gotta get a grip.* Once loaded up, I backed the car out and turned right onto Kuhio Highway and headed north to my new home.

I thought back to last night and the conversation I had with Paul. He confirmed to me what I had figured, and he was getting frustrated with me. He wants me, and I'm not so sure if I want him as much. Maybe it's too soon, after Jack passing away and my history that I've not forgotten. I don't know if I ever will, but hopefully, time will allow me to put all my memories to the back of my mind, and I can look forward to the future. I'll probably want a man in my life at some point but I'm not sure if Paul is the one. Then there's Mark to consider, not that he will remember me. In a way, I hope he doesn't, and he will be a guest at The Inn on Alamihi Road and nothing more.

The drive passed quickly, and I marveled at the lush landscape in the early morning as I drove, so happy to be here to enjoy this paradise and call it my home. I saw an arrow pointing to the sign for The Inn on Alamihi Road and felt a surge of pride. When I parked my Jeep in the area where Mac and Sara had parked, I felt reflective that they were gone but was still excited at the thought that I was now the innkeeper of this bed and breakfast.

Keoki and Ona approached with a breathtaking lei of pikake, the scent of which was intoxicating. "Welcome home," they said as I got out of my vehicle. They greeted me in Hawaiian style. Smiling, I said, "What a delightful way to greet me. I'm so happy you're here."

Keoki said, "We're happy you're here, Miss Maggie."

I turned to Ona and saw tears streaming down her cheeks.

"What's wrong, Ona?"

"I was so afraid you would not want me to stay and would bring your own person, and now I am so happy you didn't," she said tearfully.

"Ona don't worry – be happy, as I will be here with both of you. We'll be our own little family. I want you to know I will depend on you and if there is something that I'm not doing as I should, you must tell me."

"We will," said Keoki.

"Let's get my things out of the car and into the cottage so I can get settled in."

Each of us grabbed bags and headed off to my cottage. Walking in, I felt the absence of Mac and Sara but also felt contented with my new home.

As I walked around, Keoki came running and said a big truck was in the driveway. I followed him out to see which truck – my old stuff or my new furniture.

The truck was from the ship that had transported my things, and before I could approach the driver, three strapping Hawaiians had emerged from the back and were beginning to unload my boxes along with massive dollies. Before I knew it, they had pulled out my furniture that was carefully wrapped in bubble wrap.

The big guy who was apparently in charge asked, "Where do you want us to place your stuff?"

"If you could, please follow me." I proceeded to walk towards my cottage. It wasn't anytime at all before everything had been transferred from the truck to my new home. I tipped the guys generously and, smiling, they replied, "Mahalo."

After they left, Keoki, Ona and I stood looking at all I had to unpack. "If you have things you need to do, please, go ahead, and I will start putting things in order here."

I stood looking at the pieces of furniture which I had paid so dearly to have shipped, when really I should have given it more thought that they weren't going to work. I didn't know why I had even bothered to have them shipped when I was trying to start over. Perhaps I wanted to hold onto something of the past. But I was relieved Judy and I had gone shopping, and I could look forward to the new furniture which would fit in nicely.

I walked into the bedroom area and was thoughtfully arranging furniture in my mind when I heard Keoki calling me.

Back in the living room, Keoki had started taking off the plastic wrap from a piece of my furniture and exclaimed: "Ms. Langham, I don't want to hurt your feelings, but this furniture isn't what fits the island lifestyle."

"I'm not surprised you would say that. Exactly why I've purchased new furniture which will be delivered tomorrow. I want to fit into this new life, and shopping for traditional island furniture was at least a start. I'm going to donate all my old furniture to charity, except for the bookcases which I need for my book collection. Perhaps you could tell me who I should call?"

"Let me take care of that. I know of a group who can use these pieces," he replied.

"Perfect." As I said that I heard familiar voices and turned towards the kitchen and saw Dean and Paul walking in and, trailing behind them, were delivery people from Hoshino's.

"Hi, guys! What a surprise and you brought my new furniture with you."

"Yes, we did," piped up Paul grinning.

"Dean was able to work his magic with Mr. Hoshino and got your furniture out today, so at least you would have a proper bed to sleep in."

"That's great, but I have no idea where my bed linens are packed."

"Not to worry," Paul said, "I've taken care of that. Consider this an early housewarming gift." He handed me a huge shopping bag loaded with sheets and towels. I set them down and began to pull out what Paul had brought me.

"Paul, where did you go?" I yelled and heard grumbling coming from my bedroom.

I walked in and there he was with Dean and one of the delivery men attempting to assemble my new bed.

"Why in heaven's name did you buy a king-size bed? Are you planning on a slumber party?"

I couldn't contain myself and was laughing when he said: "Think you're funny, huh?"

Not wanting to lose the free labor, I said, "Not really, but the sight of you is so charming as you struggle to assemble my bed. I think I will leave you to it."

"Probably a good idea, Maggie. We don't need a sidewalk superintendent."

Smiling, I padded back out to the front of the cottage and continued to direct the delivery men on where to place the remaining furniture. When they finished, I glanced at my watch and saw it was almost dinner time.

I went looking for Keoki who was in the kitchen rustling around.

"Keoki, I forgot about dinner. Do you think it's too late to have Ona prepare something?"

"Miss Maggie, not to worry. She has been cooking and has prepared enough for everyone. I will go check and see when dinner will be ready."

"Mahalo, Keoki," I said, smiling gratefully to have these two helping me.

I noticed that Keoki had started rummaging through boxes, perhaps to sort through what he could help me put away, when Paul and Dean came into the kitchen.

"Well, where's our dinner?" asked Paul with a cocky smile on his lips.

"Very funny," I said. "You will be fed but in the main house. Ona has been cooking, and we should probably go up there and not keep her or her food waiting."

Once upstairs, I went into the kitchen to talk to Ona to make sure everything was under control.

"Miss Maggie, I have prepared Hawaiian food for your dinner tonight, as a welcome to your new home."

"Sounds lovely but I hope Keoki told you that Mr. Sinclair and Mr. Kalima would be joining us?"

"Yes, he did, and I prepared plenty for everyone, Miss Maggie."

"Thank you, Ona. I apologize for springing this on you so soon after I've just arrived."

"No problem," she said, smiling as she continued to finish up dinner.

I noticed Paul and Dean out on the lanai enjoying a cocktail provided by Keoki. Before joining them, I looked through the mail to see if there was anything requiring my immediate attention. Nothing seemed out of the ordinary, just the usual bills and junk mail.

I joined Paul and Dean and sat down at the table, where Keoki served us Rumaki Pupus and Prince Kuhio drinks.

"Thank you, Keoki. I can sure use this tonight."

Paul sat down next to me and asked if anything was wrong.

"No, just getting the feel of the place."

"Well, take it slow and easy. Nothing is so important that it can't wait. By the way, I understand you have your first guest arriving soon."

"Yes, the inn will be hosting a retired Marine Colonel. He's a nephew of Sara's. She and Mac had hoped to be here when he arrived, but schedules did not align for that to happen."

Ona started serving us the dinner she prepared, followed by Keoki who filled our water glasses. I could tell by the dishes she was setting on the table how labor intensive all this preparation must have been. As she placed the serving platters on the table, she described what they were.

"Miss Maggie, I have prepared for you, Mr. Sinclair and Mr. Kalimia Kauai, filet of sole, banana strips, Chinese peas and to start, papaya ginger udon salad."

"Ona, it looks delicious. This is a nice finish to my day moving in. After all the excitement, I need to adjust to daily living here."

"Maggie, I don't doubt you will be fine," said Dean.

Paul piped up with, "Maggie, you know how I feel and I know you will settle in nicely."

"I will have plenty to do here and of course adjusting to my new role," I added.

We finished eating dinner, and Paul said, "I need to get back to the hotel so Dean and I will be saying goodnight to you. Thank you, Ona, for dinner."

"I'll walk you out and will go on to my cottage. It will be an early night for me."

"Ona and Keoki, I will see you in the morning. Goodnight and thank you for the lovely meal."

Ona said, smiling broadly, "We're so happy to welcome you here, Miss Maggie."

The three of us went down in the elevator, and I could sense that Paul and Dean were wiped out.

"I couldn't have done today without you."

"Maggie," Paul said, "You don't have to say anything. We were happy to help. Dean and I are here for you."

Kissing me on the cheek, he turned to join Dean, getting in the Land Rover.

I stood thinking, *How did I get so lucky?*

CHAPTER TWENTY-SIX

The following day was spent organizing my possessions into my new living quarters. I planned on spending time each day getting accustomed to the business of running a bed and breakfast. There was more to learn than I had expected and while Mac and Sara had given me a detailed summary of what that entailed, I wished now that I could have spent more time with them. Not wanting to tire myself out, I planned on unpacking a few boxes each day, and as I did so, set aside things I didn't think I would have any use for. I had already purchased some Hawaiian dresses that I brought with me and figured I wouldn't need some of the clothes Judy shipped over for me. I certainly didn't plan on wearing any wool pants at present but thought it best to keep them packed away in the event I would ever need them when traveling to a colder climate.

While sorting through boxes, Keoki knocked on my back door with a look of concern on his face.

"What's wrong?" I asked.

"Nothing, Ms. Langham, except a man is asking for you," he said.

"Okay. We are prepared so nothing to worry about. Let me get my shoes on and I'll be right over."

Fortunately, I had already dressed and put on makeup. I slipped my sandals on, and we hustled over to the main building and, standing outside on the lanai looking out over the lush landscape stood a tall man with blond hair standing at least of 6'1. Tanned and dressed in khaki pants and a black polo shirt; he was irresistible. *I could be in trouble!*

"Good morning, I'm Maggie Langham. May I help you?"

"Yes," he said, turning towards me. Removing his sunglasses, he looked straight into my eyes with those baby blues I recalled, "I'm Mark Elliott."

Catching my breath, I said, "How do you do. Mac and Sara told me to expect you." Smiling, I extended my hand. "Welcome to The Inn on Alamihi Road."

He clutched my hand in his and looked into my eyes. "I apologize for being early – in fact, two days early. Is that going to be a problem?"

"No, not at all. Your room is ready, so that won't be a problem. Will you be eating any meals here besides breakfast?"

"Yes. Unless I decide to venture out, but then I may need a guide," Mark said, smiling at me.

"That could be arranged," I said, smiling back.

"Keoki, please assist Colonel Elliott with his luggage."

I looked at Mark and said, "I'm going to have you stay in the Hibiscus Suite. I hope you'll find it comfortable."

He looked at me with those steely blue eyes of his, "I'm sure it will be fine. My Aunt Sara told me you had purchased the property and would be expecting me, Ms. Langham. May I call you Maggie?"

"Sure, that will be fine. As I'm sure you are aware, we are informal here on the island."

"Good, then I insist you call me Mark and not Colonel."

"Oh, okay. I have family members who were Marines, so I always try and show proper respect."

"Maggie, I'm glad to hear that."

Oh, boy, I thought, this guy is going to give me a run for my money. Not so sure I will be able to handle him.

Keoki had brought up Mark's things, and the three of us headed over to the Hibiscus Suite. Out of the corner of my eye, I could tell that Mark was looking over everything, and I felt his eyes on me as we walked.

"Maggie, may I ask where you live?"

"Is there a reason why you ask?"

"No, only that my Aunt Sara and Mac lived in a cottage near the main building and I was wondering if it would be available to rent out if I should have guests?"

"It's the same cottage and unfortunately not available to rent. It's where I reside."

"You must show it to me sometime."

"I can do that, but after I have settled in. It's taking me more time than I anticipated." *Strange he would ask that.*

"If I can help in any way, I would be happy to do so. I'm very good at moving boxes around. On another subject, I have a rental car, since I'll have appointments at the local Veteran's Center. If you could give me the address and general directions? I'll be leaving early in the morning before you even get up."

"Sure. I can do that. I recall having passed it on my previous trips to the island and know where it is. I'm going to leave you to get settled. If there is anything at all you need that's not provided, please let me know."

"I certainly will," he replied, looking at me with those piercing blue eyes of his and grinning with that sexy smile I recalled.

"Keoki and Ona will be available in the kitchen area should you need anything before you head out in the morning, just let them know."

"I will probably grab something to eat on the way or when I get to the VA."

"No problem, I will see you when you return tomorrow?"

"You will. Maggie, if I didn't know better, I would swear that we have known each other before. You look very familiar to me."

Taken aback, I replied, "Could be, although I don't know where it could have been. I'll let you get settled in," I said, walking out of his room. I approached Keoki and Ona and told them I would be in my cottage if they needed me.

"No worries, Miss Maggie. We can take care of Colonel Elliott."

"Thank you. I appreciate that."

Walking back to my cottage, I was puzzled. *Did he remember?*

I spent the rest of the day, putting things in their proper places when the phone rang late in the afternoon.

"Hi, Maggie."

"Hi, Paul."

"How has your day been?"

"Busy, and I had a surprise. Colonel Elliott arrived early. Fortunately, we were prepared, so it wasn't a problem, but it still unnerved me somewhat."

"Sorry to hear that. I would suggest dinner, but I have the duty tonight at the hotel and have to hang around here."

"No problem. I am slowly running out of steam and will probably just grab something to eat."

"I'll call you tomorrow."

"That will be fine, Paul. Bye for now."

Well, that settles what I will be doing for dinner. I'll figure something out.

In my office, I felt satisfied that everything was in order, so it was good to get back to my writing. I looked out the window towards the beach at the beautiful sunset and realized my stomach was growling when there was a knock on the back door, and I could hear Keoki calling me.

I walked through to the kitchen and opened the door to a smiling Keoki. "Come in."

"Miss Maggie, Ona and I figured you would need to eat, so she prepared you a light dinner," he said, handing me a box covered with a couple of cloth napkins.

"Keoki, please tell Ona thank you. I hadn't planned on anything for dinner, so this is perfect."

Turning to leave, Keoki said, "Miss Maggie, so that you know,

Colonel Elliott left an hour ago. Didn't say where he was going or when he would return."

"That's fine. Thank you for informing me."

"Goodnight, Miss Maggie."

"Goodnight, Keoki."

I took the box outside to the porch area and set it on the small table. I removed the napkins and was surprised. Ona had prepared me a plate of fresh fruit and cheeses.

I took my time enjoying my alone time and realized this was the first opportunity I'd had to spend time taking in the beauty of Kauai as a new resident. I had looked forward to it and had been so busy moving here and getting into this property. I felt relief that I could sit back and enjoy the peace and tranquility of my new home. I removed the dishes and took them into my kitchen. Setting them in the sink, I felt that the day's activities had taken their toll on me, and I needed to retire early.

I went into my bathroom and prepared for bed but felt uneasy as if someone was lurking outside. I had locked all the doors, so no worries about someone just walking in. Still. . . Once in bed, I picked up my novel I had neglected since arriving in Kauai. I felt my eyes getting heavy and soon lulled into a deep sleep.

CHAPTER TWENTY-SEVEN

I smiled as I heard my resident rooster letting me know it was time to get up. I recalled reading that the chickens had been residents on the island since Hurricane Iniki. According to local residents the population of wild chickens increased after the Hurricane tore across Kauai in 1992. Chicken coops were destroyed, and domesticated hens were released along with roosters being bred for cockfighting. They now inhabit every part of the island, crowing at all hours of the day and night. While some were not happy with them, others like me were delighted to hear them.

From my bed, I could look out the window and see it was another beautiful day in Kauai with clear blue skies and bright sunshine. I recalled Mark telling me he was leaving early, to visit the Veteran's Center before I was up, so I wouldn't be playing hostess this morning. Not wanting to leave the comfort and coziness of my new bed, I dragged myself up and walked into the bathroom to start my morning routine. I finished applying makeup and hurried over to the closet and picked out one of my Hawaiian dresses, a blue floral print, and slipped it on. Looking at myself in the mirror, I reflected on the change I could see in myself since moving to Kauai. I certainly looked and felt less stressed and more relaxed. I searched for my sandals, and after looking under the bed, found them in the closet. As early as it was, I decided it would be an excellent time to sit at my desk and write a bit for the advertising I intended to run for the inn. I heard a knock at the back door and got up to answer it, grateful I had dressed for the day. Keoki was standing there holding a tray that included a pot of hot coffee and a covered plate that smelled divine. As an added treat for me, Ona had set a small dish of luscious pink papaya and breakfast muffins on the tray.

"Good morning, Keoki. How did you and Ona know I needed some coffee and food? Since my kitchen stuff hasn't been unpacked, this is a treat. Please tell her thank you for me."

"I will do that, Ms. Langham."

I looked at Keoki and smiling said, "Remember to call me Maggie. We don't have to be so formal."

"I will try and remember, Miss Maggie."

"That's better."

I sat at my desk, slipped off my sandals, and started to pen my advertisement:

Come stay at The Inn on Alamihi Road on Kauai's famous North Shore in the Hanalei area known as Wainiha. This lovely bed and breakfast, a mere 110 steps from the beach, features panoramic views of the nearby mountains, waterfalls, and pristine Wainiha Bay. Guests may hike in the nearby hills or walk the beach to the famous 'Tunnels' known as the finest snorkel beach on the island. Two world-class golf courses are a short ten-minute drive away, as are shops, restaurants, supermarkets, and two riding stables. Historic Hanalei, Lumahai Beach which featured in the classic film, South Pacific, is a scant few miles from the Inn. For relaxation visit the private and breathtaking 'natural saltwater jacuzzi Queen's Bath', named after the mother of Prince Albert. Retreat to the Inn for delightful wine, cheese, and fruit or cookies and tea.

After drafting what I could and reading it back, I thought maybe Paul could help me since he was in the hotel business and certainly would have an instinct for advertising to bring people in. Although I was hoping I would have some of Mac and Sara's guests return, I couldn't depend on that alone. If it meant going out and drawing people in, then I would do that. Whatever it would take, I was determined that I would make this a success despite being 'green' at it.

I was in deep thought, trying to make sure the wording for my ad was correct when I heard a knock at the front door.

I was pleasantly surprised to see Mark Elliott. I opened the door, smiled, and invited him in.

"Hi Maggie, may I speak with you?"

"Certainly. Let's go into the living room."

We walked into the living room, and as he looked around, he commented, "This is a lovely cottage. I can see you're adding your touches."

"Oh?"

"Yes, I remember it from when my Aunt Sara and Mac lived here."

"Oh, I see. Mark, please sit. May I get you coffee or iced tea?"

"No, thanks. This will be brief," he said, standing close to me, almost whispering. "I will be absent for a while as I need to return to the mainland to see one of my doctors. They haven't told me how long I will be there. But would it be too much to ask you to hold my room until I get back? I will call you when I know more."

"Of course. Too bad that you just got here and are leaving, even temporarily. When will you be leaving?"

"I'm leaving now. I have what I need packed and in the car. I'm sorry to be doing this to you, but I'll look forward to returning, soon," he said looking into my eyes with those sky blue eyes of his.

"So soon? How do you want me to handle what you have already paid?"

"Keep it. I trust you, and I expect to be back before you know it, to get to know you better."

Somewhat taken aback, I said, "All the best to you, and I'll see you when you return."

He turned to walk off but suddenly turned around and gave me a friendly hug. I watched him as he strode off and I felt that someone who I had once cared for was back in my life. I had my doubts that I would see him again, but there was always the chance I could be wrong, and he would return. His background and behavior gave me pause to consider that the mysterious Colonel Mark Elliott was holding something back.

I kept working at my desk on the advertisement when I heard Keoki calling from the porch.

I got up from my desk and walked quickly towards the front of the cottage, concerned that something could be wrong.

Upon seeing me, he said, "Miss Maggie, I knocked on your back door, and when I didn't get an answer, I went around to the front door worried that something was wrong."

"No, Keoki. I'm fine, just concentrating on some work, and I didn't even hear you."

"Are you okay, Miss Maggie? Ona and I haven't seen much of you today."

"Keoki, only after a week or so you have come to read me pretty well."

"May I bring you some food? Ona cooked all day, and there is plenty of food in the refrigerator."

"Better yet, I think I could use a change of scenery, and I'll come up to the house and eat on the lanai. See you in a few minutes. Thanks for checking on me, Keoki."

I looked in my bathroom mirror and, satisfied that I didn't need a touchup, started my walk over to the big house. I took the stairs this time and felt a bit breathless but somewhat invigorated. Maybe that's what I needed, some exercise. Now that I'd moved in, I should have some time for walks along the beach.

I walked into the kitchen and saw Ona and Keoki were busy setting up dinner.

"Good evening. The food smells scrumptious. I appreciate your efforts and want you both to join me on the lanai. I hate to eat alone, and with no one here, it's a bit lonely."

"Miss Maggie, that's kind of you," replied Ona.

I strolled out to the lanai, sat down, and thought about the guests arriving next week. *I'm looking forward to playing innkeeper. This downtime will allow me to tighten up my duties, and I can figure out how to best represent the inn.*

Ona and Keoki came out with plates heaped with food. It looked like she had been working all day. Too bad there wasn't anyone else here to enjoy it.

As if out of the blue, I heard a familiar voice in the kitchen: Paul.

"Good evening, Maggie. I thought I would surprise you. I spoke with Keoki earlier, and he said you were closed up in your cottage. Didn't want you to think I had forgotten about you."

"No, not at all. You do have a hotel to run, after all. It's nice to see you. Please sit down."

I noticed he had brought a bottle of wine which he handed to Keoki to open.

Ona brought out another place setting for Paul, who sat across from me, looking into my eyes, expressing a message that only I would recognize.

Keoki spoke up, "Miss Maggie, since Mr. Sinclair is here, maybe just the two of you eat dinner?"

"Oh, no. You're both welcome, and I had planned on you eating, so please sit down."

Paul looked at Keoki and asked him to pour the wine. "I would like to offer a toast. To Maggie and The Inn on Alamihi Road. May she be successful and find her happiness here."

"Thank you, Paul. I appreciate your thoughtfulness."

The four of us proceeded to enjoy the food Ona had labored over all day. We started with Portuguese egg soup followed by papaya ginger udon salad and then Chinese peas, garlic chicken, and rice.

"Miss Maggie, we haven't talked about what I should cook for your guests, so this is a practice dinner."

"Ona, this is all delicious. We can talk tomorrow about the food preparation. I'm not sure what I'll need you to do since it depends on each guest. Some may choose to eat dinner away from the inn, and for those who prefer to stay here, we will figure out how to accommodate them."

Smiling, Ona said, "Mac and Sara did the same, so you will be following what their guests have come to expect."

Paul spoke up, "If this meal is any indication of how Ona cooks, your guests will be well fed and happy."

The four of us finished dinner and enjoyed a pleasant conversation. It allowed me time to get to know my two employees. I could feel Paul's eyes on me, and as Keoki and Ona began to clear dishes from the table, he came over to help me with my chair, and said: "How about a walk on the beach?"

"I would love that, Mr. Sinclair," I responded, smiling. "Keoki and Ona thank you for the delicious meal. Goodnight and I will see you tomorrow."

They both smiled proudly and proceeded into the kitchen to leave Paul and me alone.

Paul took my hand and led me down the back stairs, and we walked to the beautiful white sand adjacent to Wainiha Bay. I slipped off my sandals, and Paul slipped off his deck shoes as we strolled down the beach.

"Beautiful sunset, isn't it?" I said.

"Yes, but not as beautiful as you."

"I think it's time we had a serious talk, Paul."

"I agree with you. Here or inside?"

"We can do it here. Maybe better – neutral territory, you know. Let's sit."

We sat down on the wicker loveseat that had been left by Mac and Sara.

"Paul, I know you have been very patient with me, to the extent that most men would have walked away. I came to Kauai to start my life over, and I have come to a decision that I'm ready to move on with my life, and that may include having a relationship with you, if that's what you want."

"Maggie, only if you're ready. I've felt a strong attraction to you since we met, and I have wanted only you since you arrived in Kauai. I've put aside other potential relationships because I felt that one day, you would be ready to be close to me, and we could explore a relationship. But I don't want to put you in a position that you're not comfortable with for the sake of making me happy. I realize that we haven't known each other that long, but at our age, we can't afford to wait and play games."

"Oh, Paul, I know what I want and when I want it. I don't want to play games either, and you are correct that for us we can't or shouldn't delay the inevitable. I only want to make sure that we're on the same page. I'm not ready for a long-term relationship, yet, but want to work towards that step by step, and I want it to be with you."

Paul placed his arm around my shoulders and drew me close and kissed me fully and passionately.

I pulled away with my hands on his arms and whispered, "Shall we go inside?"

He replied, smiling, "Yes."

We got up, arm in arm, and with my head resting on his shoulder we strolled back to my cottage. Stopping on the porch, Paul said, "Are you sure?"

"Yes, I'm sure. I even have one of the robes we provide for guests, and I believe I have an extra toothbrush for you."

CHAPTER TWENTY-EIGHT

The next morning, I was awakened by a rooster crowing and smiled to myself thinking of my old pal at the Island Garden Inn and remembered I wasn't alone. I turned over to face a sleeping Paul. Last night went beyond my expectations for he was a very gentle and tender lover. He was passionate and attentive to my needs but didn't take anything for granted. I felt fortunate that I'd found him and happy that our relationship had moved on to this level.

Not knowing when he needed to be at the hotel, I murmured in his ear, "Good morning, sleepyhead."

He opened his eyes and smiled at me. "Good morning to you too, gorgeous. How are you this morning?"

"So far, I would say great. How are you?"

"Better than ever," he said.

"Really? Did I surprise you?"

"More or less."

"Can you elaborate on that?"

"I didn't expect to stay the night. You took me off guard and yes, you surprised me."

"Don't you like surprises?"

"Sometimes," he said inching closer, kissing me fervently.

Coming up for air, I said, "I left you a towel and washcloth, so you are welcome to use the shower, and then, how about some breakfast or at least coffee?"

"Coffee would be good, and I will take a quick shower. I do need to get to the hotel."

I slipped out from under the covers and put on my robe that I had left on the bedside chair. I turned around and saw that Paul was looking at me intently.

"What's wrong? You seem so serious?"

"This is almost too good to be true. I hope I'm not dreaming."

"No, you're not dreaming, and all is good," I said, leaning over the bed to kiss him. He pulled me down onto his chest and were it not for the phone ringing, we would have had a repeat of last night. I ignored the phone and asked, "Say, how about that coffee?"

"Sounds good. But aren't you going to answer the phone?"

I got up, looked down at him, and said, "No. Whoever it is will call back, I'm sure."

I walked into the kitchen and was happy it was reasonably organized. For now, I could at least fix coffee. I pulled out the coffee canister filled with my precious Kona coffee and made a large pot, knowing that it would be consumed after Paul left and I went back to my writing. I stood waiting for the coffee to finish brewing, thinking back to last night. I took a tray out to the porch and was glad I had the small table and chairs that Sara and Mac had left. They were going to come in handy. Paul strode out and put his arms around my waist from behind me and nuzzled my neck.

"How was the shower?"

"Great! It was a bit lonesome. The shower was certainly designed for two. Maybe you could join me next time," Paul said, sitting down at the table.

"I think that can be arranged, I replied smiling. I poured us coffee, and Paul asked, "Tell me about this Mark Elliott. Should I be jealous?"

"Jealous? Why would you say that?"

"Since he left, you seem down. Is that an accurate statement?"

"Oh, I don't know about that. I would say disappointed would be more like it. I'd been looking forward to having guests, and now there will be a break before the next ones arrive."

"When will that be?"

"By the end of the week."

"Let's see. Today is Wednesday, so you have two days."

"I certainly have enough to do around here. Getting used to my new role as an innkeeper is going to take some time. But I'll be fine. I need to get back to my writing as it is. The area adjacent to my bedroom is perfect. Looking out at the lush landscape will be inspiring to me."

Paul looked at his watch and got up. "I had better get going."

He kissed me and whispered, "I would like to stay, but duty calls."

"I know. We'll have more time later, I promise."

He walked back to the big house, and I watched until he had reached his car and drove out of sight.

I sat back down at the table and poured a refill. I felt like I would need more coffee to get me going after last night. Paul had surpassed what I expected. He was an artful lover. My house phone rang and as I got up to answer it, I spied my rooster on the porch. "Checking up on me, are you?"

I answered the phone. "Hello."

"Good morning, it's Mark."

Surprised, I replied, "Good morning, Mark. Where are you?"

"Back on the mainland. I had to call and wanted to apologize for leaving so abruptly."

"No need to do that. But I appreciate your thoughtfulness."

"I wanted to hear your voice."

Surprised again, I said, "Nice to hear from you. I look forward to your return."

"As do I. I'd better cut this short. I'll try and stay in touch."

"Okay," I said, and click went the phone.

Stunned and not sure what to think, I walked into my bedroom to make the bed and sat staring at the rumpled bedcovers. Paul had just left, and Mark calls me. A wave of sadness came over me, and I wasn't sure why. Could there be something yet to happen that I sensed from Mark? *Never mind. Get on with your work and forget about him. Damn it. He isn't worth it. Better get dressed before you start on anything else.*

I padded over to the closet and pulled out a colorful Hawaiian print dress in blue with splashes of white plumerias. Maybe it would cheer me up. I must shake off this feeling, whatever it is. Best way to do that is to go for a drive. I hadn't been away from the inn in several days. When I walked into the bathroom to put on makeup, I looked in the mirror, *Who do you think you are fooling? You are more attracted to Mark than Paul. Better resolve this before you make a mess of it.*

I finished up, grabbed my tote bag and walked over to the big house.

"Keoki!" I called out, "I'm going into Lihue for a bit. I have a couple of errands to run; please tell Ona, if you would?"

"Yes, Miss Maggie."

"Thanks, Keoki. See you later. Oh, one other thing. You have my cell number, so if something comes up, you can call me."

"I will do that," he replied.

I went to my car and smiled at the new car smell. I loved leather and this Jeep Cherokee was a beauty, although I shouldn't have spent so much money. But Paul's advice was well taken. It will come in handy when I'm out and about. As I drove onto Kuhio Highway from Alamihi Road, I had a feeling of peace, serenity, and independence. I was so happy with where I was and what I was doing. Smiling, I continued the drive, and suddenly, I realized I had driven to the Veteran's Center in Lihue! *Why have I driven here, this is crazy!* I pulled into the parking lot to turn around and saw in my rearview mirror, a man standing outside the Center talking to a man dressed in Marine fatigues. The man in fatigues resembled Mark! Could it be? He said he was on the mainland. I sat stunned and crouched down in my seat but managed to keep an eye on them. Soon, the man resembling Mark shook the other man's hand and walked over to his vehicle, a white convertible just like the one he had and got in. It was Mark! He pulled out, and I followed him as he turned out onto Kuhio Highway heading towards Waimea Canyon.

I kept a safe distance behind Mark's car. I didn't want him to be suspicious and think I was following him. I checked my odometer and made a mental note of the mileage. Fortunately, I was familiar with the road and had an idea of where I was going, so I wasn't nervous about driving. Mark turned on his left turn indicator and made a sudden turn into the Waimea Plantation Cottages. I maintained a discreet distance behind him and watched as he drove towards the rear of the property. I followed him, and in the blink of an eye, he disappeared. *Where in the hell did he go?*

I stopped to turn around and heard a voice yell, "Stop!"

I complied and looked up to see Mark running towards my car.

Taking a deep breath, I had to think fast. There was no question as to what I was going to say to him. I was going to tell him the truth.

Suddenly he stopped and when he recognized me, ambled over to the car.

"Hello, Mark."

"What are you doing here, Maggie?"

"I'm not sure," I responded.

"Maggie, please get out and follow me," he demanded turning and walking towards one of the cottages.

Crap! What had I gotten myself into?

I did as he asked and grabbed my bag.

I followed him and entered one of the cottages. I expected it to be lacking maintenance and also lacking as to furnishings, but it was spotless and nicely decorated although hot and stifling.

"If you want to know more, follow me."

Mark walked into the living room area, turned on the overhead fan, and stood to look at me.

"Please sit down," he ordered.

I was nervous and scared at the same time but did as he said.

"Would you like something to drink? How about bottled water?"

"Okay."

Mark walked into the kitchen area and brought out two bottles of water, handing me one, our fingers touched, and he looked at me with those sky blue eyes, shaking his head, he sat down.

"Maggie, why did you follow me, or rather, how did you follow me?"

I described my driving and ending up at the Veteran's Center and seeing him.

"Mark, I wasn't following you. It just happened. I went out for a drive, and before I knew it, I was in the parking lot of the Veteran's Center. Don't ask me how. I know I've intruded. Why don't we forget this ever happened? I'll drive back to Hanalei, and you can go about doing what you are doing. I promise I won't tell anyone I saw you today. But answer one question: what are you doing in fatigues?"

"Maggie, for your safety, I don't want to involve you in my affairs. I can say that I am here doing some work for the Marines and let's leave it at that."

"Are you recovering from whatever it was that got you medically retired? Can you tell me that much at least?"

"You mean my post-traumatic stress disorder? I'll always have that. I'll probably always have to have some treatment, but this project I'm working on is separate from that."

"Okay. Thanks for the water," I said, standing up, "I really must be getting back. Keoki will be sending out a search party if I'm gone too long."

"You could call him and say you are shopping or whatever."

"Why would I do that? Best I leave now before I get into more trouble."

Mark approached me, placed his hands on my arms, looked me in the eyes, and said with a straight face, "Please don't be afraid. I'm not going to hurt you. You're safe with me."

"Well, I would hope so."

Mark pulled me towards him and kissed me tenderly. I didn't resist and kissed him back until I realized what was happening.

Pulling away, I said, "Mark, you're moving too fast. It's been too many years. Don't you remember me? I remember you, but this Mark standing in front of me isn't the one I knew all those years ago. You've changed. I don't know who you are, and now I'm being drawn into this mystery of yours. You told me you were going to the mainland and I find you still here on the island."

"Maggie. I remembered you when I arrived at your bed and breakfast. People change."

"Yes, Mark, I remember what you were years ago, and that's where the problem is. I don't want to relive history and be hurt again. At this point in our lives, you and I have experienced a lot of living, and I'm sure not all of it is pleasant. But that's how we mature and grow – by living life. Yours has been much different than mine. No matter how I feel about you – and seeing you has stirred up a lot of old feelings. I'm not sure I want to go there."

"May I ask a question about you and Paul?"

"How do you know about Paul? Have you been stalking me?"

"No, but I drove out to the inn last night to talk to you. I looked for you and saw you walking with him."

"How do you know his name?"

"Trust me. I have my ways. I'm concerned for your welfare and wanted to make sure you hadn't fallen in with an undesirable character. I took a picture and ran it through some intel."

"I guess you do have your ways. Rest assured, Paul is a reputable man, and I trust him. We are friends and haven't known each other for long, so we are taking it slow and there is nothing serious between us."

"So, if I hadn't arrived on the scene, would you be further along? What I mean to say is, has seeing me given you pause to have second thoughts about where you want to go with Paul?"

"I'm not sure at this point. My feelings are conflicted. I look at you, and I feel the same spark as I did all those years ago. I don't want to be hurt like that again, ever. I've suffered enough at the hands of the men in my life and want to move forward away from my past."

Mark pulled me into his arms and kissed me tenderly. I didn't resist and clung to him. I enjoyed the closeness of him and the way his lips felt on mine. We continued kissing. I suddenly realized what I was doing and pulled away.

"Mark, I can't do this. Please try and understand," I said, walking towards the front door when suddenly I felt his arms around my waist, and his lips kissing my neck sent shivers up my spine. I took a deep breath, enjoying the sensation but feeling tears starting to well up in my eyes; I said: "Can you give me time to think this through?"

"Maggie, I can only give you so much time. I'm not sure how long I'll be on the island. The project I'm working on is time-sensitive, and we're nearing the culmination of what we set out to do."

"Mark, I don't want the details but can you tell me if you have been here all along and only recently surfaced to satisfy Mac and Sara?"

"More or less. I didn't want to worry either of them. They know how I have loved the military life and given myself to it at the risk of losing other things. You know I was married. My wife wanted me to put her first, and I couldn't sacrifice my career and work as a Marine at the time. Now, as time has gone on, I've realized that there are other things in this life and I don't want to live the rest of my life alone. Seeing you has given me hope that I do have someone I can spend the rest of my life with: if you will have me."

"Mark," I said choking back tears that were starting to flow.

"Maggie," he said, wiping my tears gently with his fingertip, and pulling me close, he whispered, "Please don't cry. Trust me. I love you and always have. We were just too young back then, and it wouldn't have worked. Now, I think it can."

I pulled back and looked into his baby blues and said, "The best I can do is to tell you that I won't say no; I can't say no to you. I have a lot to think about. It's complicated and let's leave it at that."

"Fair enough. I plan to return to Hanalei in a few days. Will it be awkward for you?"

"No, but you have to give me some space."

"Only if you tell me when you have made up your mind about us."

"Can you let me know when you plan to return?"

"No, I can't."

"I guess that has to do with your work?"

"Yes, it does, regretfully. It's just the way it has to be right now."

"Can you answer me another question?"

"I'll try."

"Does the work you are doing have anything to do with the Pacific Missile Range Facility?"

"You would have made a good spy at the very least. What have you been doing? Are you digging for information? I think your imagination has run away from you."

"Oh, no! Maybe I'm just going to put it out there. I'm firmly convinced that you're involved in a hush-hush project, and you're hoping I don't stumble onto what you're doing."

"You need to return to Hanalei now and forget you saw me. Forget we had this conversation. I want you to stay out of this, for your sake. I will see you in a few days. Maybe we can start over."

"Maybe being the operative word?"

"More rather than less."

"You're making this difficult, but I'll do as you say and return to Hanalei. Goodbye, Mark."

I strode out to my car and could sense Mark on my heels running after me. As I placed my hand on the car door to open it, he grabbed me from behind, spun me around, and kissed me hard. I pulled back and got into my car. Tears welling up, I rolled down the window and said: "Until I see you again, please stay safe and out of harm's way."

He leaned into the car and looked into my eyes and said, "Always. You stay safe too. Now go on and get out of here before I change my mind and keep you as my prisoner," he said with a devilish look on his handsome face.

Seatbelt fastened, the car in gear, I backed out carefully and turned to leave but not before I looked into my rearview mirror and saw Mark standing, staring at me as I drove off. Tears started to fall as I made my way to Kaumualii Highway. I made a hard right and sped away from Mark. Not wanting to risk a ticket, I reduced my speed, but all the while, tears continued to flow. Why now after all these years have I run into him, which only complicates my life?

CHAPTER TWENTY-NINE

As I neared Lihue, my cell phone rang. I answered it, and said with my voice wavering, "Hello."

"Hello, Maggie."

"Hi, Keoki, is everything all right?"

"Well, yes, it is, but you have a visitor. She is inquiring about a room."

"Okay, please offer her snacks and a drink and I will be there very soon."

I hung up and thought, *my business must be picking up. This will give me something to think about besides Mark and Paul.*

I was intent on getting back to Hanalei without any further emotional interruptions. If I stopped to see Paul at the hotel, he would sense something was wrong, although I could use his comfort to pull me back into reality. I felt like I was in a dream spiraling downward; not quite believing where I had been or who I had been with. Mark Elliott had caused me to feel confused. Hopefully, Paul would bring me back to where I needed to be. But then, if he saw me now, would he suspect I had feelings for this man from my past who had suddenly appeared? How could I not have realized who Mark was when he arrived at the inn? Had he changed that much or had he had some plastic surgery? Okay. Get a hold of yourself and drive back to your bed and breakfast and busy yourself with the tasks at hand.

Fighting back the tears, as I drove, I didn't know if I would ever see Mark again, but then again maybe it would be for the best if I didn't. Turning onto Alamihi Road, I breathed a sigh of relief that I had made it safely back. I was still feeling shaken and wanting to hunker down and regroup. After discovering Mark had lied to me, I told myself that he didn't deserve another thought.

I got out of my car and decided to walk directly to my cottage to avoid running into Keoki and Ona, at least for now. But I couldn't push Mark out of my mind, and then my thoughts ran to Paul. Oh damn. What had I gotten myself into? To start my life over was my mantra, but here I was again letting a man take over my heart and head. Maybe I needed a shrink?

"Miss Maggie, where have you been? We were so worried about you."

I turned to see Keoki rushing up to me with his arms extended wildly in the air. Behind him came Ona trying to keep up with him.

"Keoki, I'm sorry that I didn't tell you where I was going, but I had to run an important errand, and it came up rather suddenly. I wasn't gone that long. My goodness, back on the mainland I could take the whole day to shop, but here it's another story. I'm fine. You and Ona don't have to worry about me."

"But we do, Miss Maggie. You're more than our boss, you have become like family, even though you're new here."

"Thank you, Keoki. That means a lot to me. Let me change, and I will come up to the big house and welcome our new guest."

"Okay, Miss Maggie," he said, turning and leading Ona in the direction of the big house.

Walking back to my cottage, I felt an overwhelming sadness that I had said goodbye to Mark. It was almost too much to bear. I was still fighting the tears when my cell rang.

Paul's number. "Hello?"

"Hi, Maggie. I know this is short notice but would you like to have dinner with me tonight?"

"Oh, no, it is not too late at all."

"Great, I will swing by to pick you up at 7, and we will eat in your area. I think you will like what I have picked out."

"I'll look forward to it. Thanks, Paul."

"See you, Maggie."

I wanted to look like the hostess of this bed and breakfast. I pulled out from my closet a casual Hawaiian dress, a plumeria pink cotton long muumuu dress. I changed quickly and walked over to the big house to meet my new guest.

It was starting to rain, so I hurried, not wanting to get wet. I walked into the kitchen and found them both busy looking in the recipe book that Mac and Sara had left for me.

"I'm back. Where's my unexpected guest?"

"She's in the great room," replied Keoki as Ona stood with a worried expression on her face.

"Ona, what's wrong?"

"Nothing, Miss Maggie."

"Okay, if you say so. After checking my guest in, I'll come back, and we can discuss the menu."

Nodding they turned back to what they had been doing.

I walked into the great room and, reclining on the plush off-white sofa, was my daughter Brooke.

I quietly walked over, sat down, gently tapped her shoulder, "Brooke, it's Mom."

Opening her eyes, she looked up with a sleepy look on her face.

"Oh, hi, Mom!"

I said quietly, "Brooke, what are you doing here?"

Brooke sat up and said, "Thought I would surprise you."

"Well, you certainly did that. I wish you had let me know so I could have properly prepared for your arrival," I said, taking her hand.

"That's okay. All I want to do is hang out here and enjoy the peace and quiet after all the craziness in New York City. I've been working too hard and need a vacay. This was the first place I thought of going. To be honest, I miss you. We haven't had an ideal mother-daughter relationship."

"I am happy you would want to come and stay here with me. I take a great deal of responsibility for our mother-daughter relationship. I wasn't always there for you and not having a father figure didn't help you either. If there had been a 'dad' in our lives, things might have been different. But then again maybe not?"

Brooke, smiling through tears welling in her eyes, said: "Can't we catch up for all the time wasted?"

"Sure," I replied. "I have heard that mothers and daughters often have better relationships as adults."

"True. Our magazine recently ran a series of articles on mothers and daughters. I think those articles may have been what I needed to get my butt over here to see you. I haven't shown interest in what you have been trying to do, and I know what miserable experiences you have had with men in your life. I often wonder if that affected our relationship."

"In some ways, I think it did. I never felt I had the 'proper' family for you growing up."

"I know now you did the best you could."

"Thanks for that. But I know I could have done more, like providing you with a dad."

"Mom, can we talk about my father? We never really have. Don't you think it's time?"

"It's never too late, I guess. But can this wait until tomorrow when you are rested and settled in?"

"Sure. I think a good night's sleep is what I need. Don't fix me anything for dinner. I'll grab something from the fridge, if that's okay."

"Make yourself at home. Ona, will help you and make you anything you want. She's a great cook."

"What are you going to do about dinner?"

"I have plans for dinner tonight with a friend."

"Would it be a male friend?"

"Yes, as a matter of fact, it is," I said, smiling.

"No problem there. I am exhausted from traveling and my heavy workload. It will be good to stay in, relax, and sleep. Maybe tomorrow we can catch up?"

"Sure. Sounds good. Think about what you might like to do while you're here; I can give you a tour of our beautiful island."

"Frankly, I would like to spend time with you. It has been a while since we have spent time together."

Taken somewhat aback, I said, "Thank you for thinking like that. I take it you haven't been given a room yet?"

"No, Keoki said I would have to wait until you returned. He seems to look out for you."

"He does, even though I haven't been the innkeeper for that long. It's nice to know that he's keeping an eye on things."

Thinking of which room to assign to her, I decided that the Pikake Suite would be ideal – not close to the Hibiscus Suite. Since Mark would be coming back at some point, I didn't want to give them an opportunity to get acquainted until I was ready.

"Brooke, I am going to have you stay in the Pikake Suite. It's quiet on that side of the house, and I think you will like it."

While happy to have my daughter here but not sure how this was all going to play out, I should be patient and not worry about our 'dad' discussion. I would have to wait and see.

She grabbed her one bag and followed me down the hall. *I envy her, she sure travels light. Wish I could.*

I showed her to the Pikake Suite with creamy yellow walls, a queen-sized bed with white quilt adorned with appliqued pikake flowers, and the adjoining bathroom with a similar theme. Upon entering, she exclaimed, "This is so much nicer than I expected. I'd say you've invested wisely in this property. From what I've seen, it's lovely."

"Thank you, Brooke. I have a cottage adjacent to this building. I would have you stay with me, but I don't have an extra room. But I think you will be comfortable here. If you need anything, Ona and Keoki will be here to help you, and I always have my cell phone on if you need me."

Not having been an affectionate child nor adult, surprisingly, Brooke walked over to me, put her arms around me and said, "I'm happy that I came to see you. You enjoy your evening out. I'm going to unpack and rest. I've been traveling since early this morning having left JFK in the wee dawn hours. I'll probably call it an early night."

"You should have everything you need, but if there is something that we have not provided for you, please let us know."

Brooke gave me a hug which felt warm and loving. "Mom, this is lovely. I'm sure I'll be comfortable."

I hugged her back and kissed her on the cheek. Stepping back, I remarked, "I'm so proud of the young woman you have become."

"Mom, I had a good teacher. You taught me everything I know."

Walking out of the room, I turned and said, smiling, "See you in the morning."

I walked back to the kitchen area and asked Ona, "What do we have for breakfast tomorrow?"

"Miss Maggie, I have a recipe for Hawaiian pineapple pancakes that we can serve with Portagee sausage and fresh fruit."

"Ona, that sounds delicious! Do you need anything to prepare for tomorrow?"

"I will work with Ona and take care to grocery shop," piped up Keoki.

"Perfect. Oh, please let's make sure we always have a selection of fresh fruit and juices to serve. Now, what do you need me to do?"

"We will take care of everything. You want to keep the same way that Miss Sara and Mr. Mac treated their guests?"

"Yes, that would be fine. I will be out for the evening. If you need to reach me, I will keep my cell on. You and Ona can go on home after you have finished for the day. My daughter will be fine."

"We will do that, Miss Maggie. Have a lovely evening."

"I hope to, Keoki."

I walked back to my cottage to get ready for my date with Paul. I unlocked the front door but felt uneasy, as if someone was there. *But how could that be? I always lock the doors; I haven't taken on the Hawaiian way of leaving them unlocked.* I approached my bedroom but stopped to turn on a light. Looking around, all seemed as I had left it. I pulled out a black full-length dress with a splash of colorful flowers on the bottom of the skirt. Sandals would work. I loved the freedom of fewer clothes on the island. Grabbing a quick shower, I had thoughts of Mark running through my mind. Why oh why did he have to reappear in my life now? But I would be taking control, and I chose not to let him back in. Too much heartache. Stepping out of the shower, I pulled a bath sheet off the towel rack and wrapped it around myself. Still, the feeling persisted that I was not alone. A shiver ran up my spine as I stood in front of the bathroom mirror applying fresh makeup and heard a familiar voice: "Maggie, don't be alarmed. I didn't come here to scare you."

I turned and saw Mark sitting at the desk in my office still dressed in his military uniform, appraising me with a look that made me feel uncomfortable.

"How in the hell did you get in here?" I said with clenched fists.

"It wasn't hard. You should get some new locks that are more secure. If I can get in, I'm sure others can too."

"Stay right where you are while I put on some clothes."

Closing the bathroom door to afford myself some privacy, I

quickly slipped on the dress for my dinner with Paul and stepped out of the bathroom.

"You look great! Have a date tonight?"

I approached Mark and said, "Would you mind telling me what's going on, and it's none of your business if I have a date tonight."

"I didn't like how we left things this afternoon and felt it best to clear the air between us."

"You are deluding yourself. Why? I don't seem to see any reason why you should do that."

"Maggie, regardless of what has happened in the past, I still love you and will always want to be with you. I regret that you don't feel the same."

"You can regret all you want. I won't play second chair to anyone, even if it is your wife. I find it odd that you were not going to reappear for a few days, or at least that's what you said earlier this afternoon, yet here you are."

"Yes, I did say that, but my plans have changed, and I will be out of touch for a while."

"Oh! Here we go again. Now, what is it?"

"I can't tell you now but will be able to later. All I ask is that you trust me to come back to you – no strings attached," Mark answered.

"I can't give you an answer right this minute. I need time to think carefully about this. I take it you aren't staying here tonight?"

"No. I should leave. I wish I could stay here, but we'll have other times."

"You're sure about that?"

"Yes, I feel confident that we can work things out."

Mark approached me, placed his hands on my hips and pulled me to him. He kissed me gently.

"I'll be in touch," he said and quietly walked out.

I stood holding my ground, unsure how to respond. Thoughts were racing through my head. Brooke is here. Do I tell him about her or just hope they don't connect?

CHAPTER THIRTY

After Mark left, I finished getting myself together for my dinner date with Paul. Satisfied that I had done all I could do to make myself look presentable while feeling I was emotionally spent, I poured myself a glass of chardonnay and sat out on my lanai overlooking the blue Pacific. I struggled with my feelings for Mark and Paul. I had decided that I was finished with men when I left the mainland, and now? *I must pull myself together before Paul arrives or he is going to sense something is wrong, so what do I say? Best not to say anything unless he asks.* Finishing my wine, I heard a car door slam and almost immediately, I heard a familiar voice.

"Hi, Maggie."

"Hi, Paul. I've been looking forward to having dinner with you tonight," I said, standing up from my sofa.

Walking in, he came over to me, "You look beautiful, as always." he said, brushing my lips with a brief kiss. "Wasn't sure when or if we would see each other again."

"Why do you say that? Do you know something, I don't know?" I asked.

"Only that I sense you are struggling and won't tell me what it's about."

Taking a deep breath, I said, "It's passed, and I'm good. No worries. Would you like a glass of wine?"

"No thanks, I'll wait until we get to the restaurant."

"Okay, sounds good. Let me grab my bag and put this glass in the kitchen."

I stepped back inside and took a deep breath. *I think I have convinced him that all is okay. At least I hope so. I must get past this. Paul has become an important part of my life, and I don't want to jeopardize our relationship.* I placed my empty glass in the sink and picked up my clutch bag from the dining room table.

"I'm all set to go."

"Let's do it," he said, taking my hand and leading the way to his car.

Ever the gentleman, Paul helped me settle into his car, and once he was behind the wheel, I asked, "Where are we going? You know I'm always curious."

"Sometimes too much so. You're going to have to wait."

We drove out to Kuhio Highway. With the Beemer's top down, I sat back and enjoyed the ride, reveling in all the luscious green foliage and taking in the fragrant plumeria blossoms.

I was enjoying the ride and scenery. I don't think I will ever get tired of this tropical paradise. After a day like today, it's nice to sit back and relax.

"In that case, relax all you want. I was just concerned something was wrong."

"No, nothing. I feel perfectly at ease going to dinner with you – just the two of us for a change. It's been a little crowded, if you know what I mean."

"Yes, I understand what you're saying."

Paul eased the car onto the road to Princeville.

"What I'm saying is, that Judy and Dean have been with us constantly since she arrived. I don't think we're attached at the hip. Why couldn't she and Dean have done their own thing instead of tagging along with us?"

"I guess they could have, but I thought Judy was such a good friend of yours?"

"She has been, but since I found out about your history with her, it's clouded my perception of her as my friend."

"Could we just put that aside and enjoy our evening?"

"Yes, we can do that. Besides, Judy has returned to the mainland, and Dean is back to hustling real estate."

"You know I have a good ear for whatever that's bothering you, so please don't hesitate," he said, taking my hand.

"Thanks, Paul. I will keep that in mind."

We continued to the restaurant with me deep in thought. I could see out of the corner of my eye that Paul kept glancing at me. *Guess I had better engage and not be so remote.*

"I forgot to ask you, but how's the hotel doing? I miss being there and the interaction with everyone."

"It's doing very well. I feel comfortable leaving it for a few hours, even during dinner time. I have reliable staff that I can count on. They are good people."

"That's good. I feel the same way with Keoki and Ona, although I've only been with them a very short time."

"You are fortunate that they stayed on to work with you. I can't imagine taking on a new business and not have anyone to back me up."

"I have a comfort level I wasn't expecting and feel secure with them on the property although, I can't imagine anyone bothering me, at least not here. I feel the islands are rather benign."

"Don't get cocky. You still need to be situationally aware at all times. You are a woman on her own, don't forget."

"Oh, I won't. Still, in all, I feel better and happier here than I have in a long time." Then I recalled Mark. *Well, I'm going to have to tell Paul one of these days about Mark. While I'm not afraid of him, he unexpectedly showed up tonight, which reminded me of my vulnerability. It gave me chills. I must look into having those locks changed.*

"Earth to Maggie."

"Sorry, my mind must have drifted back to the inn. Did I miss something you were trying to say?"

"Only that we're driving into Princeville and dining at the St. Regis Hotel. They have a great restaurant, Makana Terrace, and it overlooks Hanalei Bay. It comes highly recommended by a friend."

Paul slowed the vehicle and turned into the parking lot of the Makana Terrace. I was instantly charmed by the outside appearance of the restaurant and, as he said, it overlooked Hanalei Bay. *I hope the food is as good as the outdoor ambiance.*

"Cat got your tongue?" Paul quipped.

"Well, maybe just a bit. This restaurant looks wonderful, at least from the outside. The view is breathtaking."

"I thought you would like it. Shall we go have dinner?" Paul said, getting out of the car.

Always the gentleman, he came over to help me out of the car; taking my hand we strolled into the restaurant.

After being shown to an outside table overlooking the bay, the waiter, whose name tag read Aka, handed us menus, and Paul asked if he could order for me. Somewhat relieved, I said, "Of course you may order for me. Everything looks scrumptious. With so many choices I may have a hard time deciding on what to order. Besides I think by now you know what I like and what I don't like."

Smiling, he said, "Great. I appreciate you trusting my judgment."

Aka reappeared, and Paul, with his usual expertise, gave him our order including drinks.

"You need to tell me about your day. But I'm concerned."

The waiter arrived with our Lilikoi sangrias, and Paul ordered the roast beet Kunana goat cheese and Kailani greens with local cucumber and hearts of palm, with hibiscus honey lime vinaigrette for starters. For our entrees, he said to the waiter, "The lady would like the tamarind glazed mahi mahi with coconut rice, sautéed kale, and spiced mango sauce and I would like the pan seared ahi black pepper ginger crust, wasabi potatoes, soy lime vinaigrette. We would also like a side of grilled asparagus for us to share."

The waiter walked away, and Paul proceeded to quiz me about what was wrong. "Maggie, I know you have had a lot of changes recently. You have impressed me with how well you have adapted and taken everything in your stride."

I took a deep breath and said, "There are some things I can do and other things that affect me deeply. I have trouble coming to terms with them."

"Can you elaborate? But only if you want to," he said as the waiter approached with our starters.

Setting them down in front of us, I remarked, "The presentation is lovely, and I hope they taste as good as they look."

Aka said, "If for some reason you don't find them to your taste, please let me know, and I can get you something else."

"Thank you, Aka."

We started eating, and I said to Paul, "So far, this food is amazing. Although I don't think that Ona is set up to prepare food that looks to be this labor intensive."

Paul replied, "Perhaps, but she might surprise you."

We finished our starters and Aka brought our entrees and grilled asparagus which looked every bit as appetizing as the starters had.

Not wanting to get involved in a discussion about my daughter until we finished our meal, we ate and exchanged small talk about the Island Garden Inn.

Aka approached our table and asked if we wanted dessert.

"No, thank you. I don't think I can eat another thing," I said, smiling.

Paul asked for the check and suggested we go outside and sit on the terrace.

"I would like that," I replied nervously.

We got up and walked to the tables, set up for cocktails, and sat down.

"How about a nonalcoholic spritzer?" Paul asked.

"Sounds refreshing after all we ate."

A waiter came over handed us drink menus. I asked for a Lilikoi Mint Cooler, and Paul ordered for himself the Melon Spritz.

Paul reached across and took my hand and said, looking into my eyes, "Are you going to tell me what is troubling you?"

"Yes. Today I had an unexpected visitor. My daughter Brooke flew in from New York."

Looking surprised, Paul asked, "I didn't know you had a daughter. But then we haven't discussed if you had children."

"I didn't think I needed to at this point, not knowing where our relationship was going."

Paul looked at me, and I wasn't sure what his reaction was other than perplexed.

"Why don't do you tell me about her?"

"What would you like to know?"

"How old is she?"

"Brooke is thirty-two. She lives in New York and is the consummate career woman. She is an editor for a high-profile fashion magazine in New York. I'm very proud of what she has accomplished. She isn't married although she has had several boyfriends. She doesn't seem interested, although she has had a couple of proposals."

"Mind me asking about her father?"

"No, not at all. I told her years ago that he was killed in an automobile accident before we could be married."

"I take it that's a stretch of the truth?"

"Why do you say that?"

"I have come to know you and your facial expressions, and when you are uncomfortable telling me something, it's obvious. This is one of those times. It seems like there is more."

"Brooke's father and I were young. I was just out of high school and working, and he was working a summer job when we met. He lived in another town, and his parents had his life all mapped out for him. He committed to going into the Marines. Sadly, for me, they had a young woman they wanted him to marry. They were Catholic and friends with her parents, and all was set for them to marry. While I knew he loved me, I also knew that there was no way he would go against his parents. I couldn't understand how he could go into the Marines and yet be so weak in other areas of his life. After he had gone back to resume his life, I found out I was pregnant.

"My mother was furious and ordered me to leave town. She sent me to live with an aunt who was much more understanding than my mother. I had the baby, and my aunt wanted to raise her. Later, when I was on my own, and Brooke was eight years old, my aunt became very ill and died. She had left instructions that I was to take Brooke, and when she was a young teen, I was to tell her I was her mother. By that time, I had married, and my husband was barely tolerant of her and jealous that I had a child with another man. Unfortunately, we were mismatched, had our problems and soon divorced, leaving Brooke and me on our own."

"So, what happened to Brooke?"

"I sent her to private schools and wanted her to have advantages that I did not have. I worked hard to provide for her, and she went on to college and started a life of her own. We were never very close, and whenever we were together, I could feel the tension and rightly so. Putting myself in her position, I would probably have felt the same way. But I feel things are changing with her. Hopefully, we can de-velop a relationship – as late as it is."

"Have you had any contact with her father, or do you know what became of him?"

Startled by Paul's question, I practically choked on my mint cooler.

"Did I say something wrong?"

"I'm surprised you asked about her father. Why would that even matter at this point?"

"Well, if you knew he was alive, wouldn't you want her to get to know him?"

"I do know that he's alive and I've recently seen him."

"You have?" Paul asked with an alarmed look on his face.

"Yes, I have. I might as well tell you now. If you recall; the nephew of Sara and Mac's who arrived as my first guest, Mark Elliott? He's Brooke's father but doesn't know it."

"Oh, Maggie! This gets more convoluted. Is there anything else that you want to tell me or is this all, for now?"

"You make it sound like I'm a criminal. I only made the mistake of having a child when I wasn't married."

"And not telling the father!"

"How could I when he had his life mapped out for him? Me telling him then would have only been a disaster."

"That's assuming a lot, don't you think?"

"In light of his strict Catholic upbringing, abortion was out of the question. I doubt his parents would have been welcoming to their impending grandchild or me. It has been so long ago, and if Mark had not popped up now, I probably would not have ever told her. I'm confused and feel like I'm stuck in a vice. I'm trying not to panic and stay calm about this."

"Putting this off will only cause you more anxiety and inevitably grief if either one of them finds out first."

"I know what you're saying, but I keep vacillating, and one minute I think I should let it all stay as it has been. If only Brooke hadn't surprised me with this visit. Things would be much easier."

"However, I must tell her at some point that her father isn't dead but alive. I fear that will ruin whatever chance we have of developing a relationship."

"Then why tell them?"

"I fear they will run into each other and start to question who the other one is? I don't think I can lie anymore. I'm getting too old."

Paul looking grim, asked, "Is your mother still alive?"

"No. She passed away several years ago and was still the same miserable, spiteful woman she always was. At the time, I was too young to understand what she had gone through in life and only knew she was coerced into marrying a man set up by my grandmother. Back in the day, women didn't have the confidence or self-esteem they do today. My grandmother had convinced my mother she couldn't get a job nor take care of me on her own. The days of helping my mother out had long passed, but she had forgotten how instrumental she had been in forcing my mother to divorce my father, which is how this miserable scenario started.

"If we could just look into a crystal ball and see what direction our lives will take, I'm sure we would make different decisions. But then we learn from our mistakes, and there were plenty to go around in my family. Why am I going on about all this? I should let things take their natural progression and see what happens. If I don't like what happens, then, I will have to take the drastic steps to tell the father and daughter of their relationship. I would like to avoid that. I'm struggling with all this. I wish it would all go away."

Paul took my hand and said, "I want you to know that I will help you in any way I can. This hasn't changed my feelings for you. We all make mistakes."

"I have made a ton of them," I said.

"But not everyone has the opportunity of turning them into positives. Maybe you will be one of the lucky ones," Paul added.

CHAPTER THIRTY-ONE

We left the restaurant and started the drive back. Paul was very quiet, looking straight ahead as he drove. There was a lump in my stomach. I was hoping he had something to say, even if it was "goodbye, see you around." *I hate the silent treatment. I don't know what he's thinking. Why do I care? He's just another guy! No, really. He's someone I have come to care about, and I care about what he is thinking.*

"Cat got your tongue?" I asked.

"You haven't exactly been chatty Cathy either; sorry for the sarcasm. I don't know what to say at this point. You've given me a lot to think about. You have your daughter who has paid you an unexpected visit and a former lover who doesn't know he has a daughter. That's a lot to handle for one night."

"I agree. To be honest, I'm not sure how I'd handle the situation if you told me about your old lover and a daughter or son you had kept in the background. I don't blame you a bit. Nor would I blame you if you decided you didn't want a relationship with me and walked away."

Paul pulled over to the side of the road, released his seatbelt and turned to me, placing his hand on my chin, he looked me straight in the eye and said, "I don't want to go there yet. You know I told you how I felt from the first time I met you. But then I had no idea you came with all this baggage. I'm not sure how I would have handled it. Maybe walk away. Maybe keep our relationship as strictly friends. I don't know. But I do know that I have deep feelings for you. I would like to see how this all plays out. I'm going to take a gamble and see what my odds are. What about you?"

"At this point, I can't even begin to wonder what's going to happen. This can go sideways, and my daughter may leave, angry, and Mark may walk away furious with me, but as far as he's concerned, I have good reasons why I didn't tell him. For that matter, the same goes for Brooke. All I know is that I would miss you if you walked away."

"I'm happy to hear that," he said and leaned in to kiss me.

I kissed him back and whispered, "Hope we don't attract attention and an officer of the law stops and asks us what we're doing. At our age, he would probably wonder why we're here and not somewhere more private."

"I agree," he responded as he refastened his seatbelt, started up the car and pulled onto the roadway. He took my hand and held it as we drove back to the inn.

Pulling into the parking area, Paul came around and helped me out of the car. "You know as dark as it gets out here, maybe you should think about putting up some motion lights. It would be a good safety precaution," he said.

I reached for his hand, and we started walking to my cottage. "I don't know why I didn't ask Mac and Sara about whether they had motion lights out here. I know for my own safety's sake, and that of my guests' it would be a good thing to do. I'll have to check into it. I don't want to become complacent although I feel safe out here. You want to sit out on the porch?"

"Sure, although I don't know what we have to talk about except for one thing."

"What's that?"

"I would assume you won't want me spending the night here while Brooke is visiting?"

"I hadn't thought about it. But then I wouldn't think she imagines I'm living a celibate life. What are you comfortable with? I don't want to put you in a spot."

"No, you won't, but maybe it's better that you break our relationship to Brooke when I'm not around."

"You have a point there. Although I don't want to be sneaking around like I'm a teenager."

Paul laughed and said, "Hardly, but you don't look much more than an older teen."

"Flattery will get you everywhere," I said, smiling as I planted a light kiss on his lips. Firmly pulling me towards him, his gaze being drawn to my lips, I sensed his desire and need as he kissed me deeply, tasting and gently playing with my tongue.

"Whoops, what if Brooke sees us necking out here on the porch?"

I replied, "When I left her earlier, she was going to call it an early night since she'd been traveling all day."

"Regardless, I want to err on the side of caution and will wait for the appropriate time to meet your daughter."

"I appreciate your understanding," I said.

"Besides, if you and I are to have a future, I would think it best I remain in the shadows until the dust has settled."

"My goodness," I exclaimed. "You're assuming I'm going to tell her about Mark?"

"Why wouldn't you? He's practically on your doorstep. Wouldn't it be a wasted opportunity not to take advantage of bringing them together?"

"So says you? I'm sorry for sounding sarcastic, but I'm disconcerted about Brooke arriving unexpectedly and, knowing Mark is on the island, somewhere, I'm not sure what to do. Maybe leave sleeping dogs lie?"

Paul added, "I know if it were me, I would want to know if I had a daughter, or son for that matter. Put yourself in his place."

"That's you, and I can't do that, and for that matter, you and Mark are different people. Not having been around him all these years, I can't say that I know him, at least not like when we were kids. We have both experienced life in different ways, and when it comes down to it, perhaps a teenage summer romance was just that and nothing more. We are not the same people. The more I talk about it, the more confused I become. I need to find out about who he is now."

"I think that's my cue to say goodnight. I wouldn't want to take advantage of you in your confused state of mind," Paul said, not smiling although there was a look of sadness in his eyes.

"Paul, I'm not confused, and I know who I want, and it's you. I'm sorry for subjecting you to all this. Maybe I'm naïve, but when I came here, I never imagined the past would catch up to me. It was the last thing I thought would happen. I wanted to start over and hopefully lead a happier life and maybe find someone to share it with if fate would smile down on me."

"Maggie, you haven't subjected me to anything. I'd think you could figure it out that when people reach a certain age, their past might come back, to haunt them, shall I say. If you don't take a chance on love when you find it then maybe it will elude you. I'm starting to sound maudlin. Time for me to go."

"Shall I walk you to your car?"

"No, I don't think it's a good idea this late at night and as dark as it is. Are you worried I won't be back?"

"The thought had occurred to me."

"Don't worry about it because you can't get rid of me that easily."

We stood up, and Paul drew me to him, pressing himself against me, kissing me deeply and passionately.

"Goodnight, Maggie."

"Goodnight, Paul. Safe driving back to the hotel," I said, chin trembling and my voice breaking feeling the oncoming tears.

I watched him walk down the steps and towards his car. *This evening wasn't what I expected. I didn't intend to dump all this history on him either. Maybe I was using the time with him as an escape from my reality? What am I going to do?*

I took a deep breath, and as I turned to go inside, I heard a familiar voice, "Mom, who was that man you were kissing?"

"Brooke, were you spying on me?" I snapped.

"No, I wasn't. I was having a hard time falling asleep and decided to take a walk on the beach and, coming back, I saw this cottage and was curious if it was yours. Thought I would check it out and got a surprise. You weren't exactly hiding in the shadows; you were right out here in plain sight. Anyone could have been watching you."

"So what if the whole world was watching. I've nothing to hide. The people who know us wouldn't be surprised if we were kissing. Isn't it a natural thing for two people to do when they have feelings for each other?"

"True, but aren't you going to tell me who he is?"

"His name is Paul Sinclair. I met him when I arrived here. He's the manager of the hotel where I stayed upon first arriving. We hit it off and have been seeing each other. He helped me get settled here in my cottage and has become a good friend."

"Are you sleeping with him?"

"Young lady, show me some respect! I don't think it's any of your business. At my age, I can do what I want and with whom I want. Have I asked you who you have been sleeping with? It's your business, not mine. That changes only if you ask me for advice," I said.

"Mom, I apologize for overstepping your boundaries. Still, I would like to meet him."

"Are you saying you want to put your seal of approval on him?"

"Indirectly, I suppose. After all you have been through I think I can look at him more objectively. At this stage in your life, I want you to be happy," Brooke said with tears welling up in her eyes.

"Now, why are you crying?" I said, stepping forward to embrace my daughter.

"I don't know. Maybe because at my age, I have come to realize how fleeting happiness can be."

"Oh! You sound much wiser than your years. I'm proud of you. Now I would like to know what you were doing out here at this time of the night all by yourself?"

"Like I said, I couldn't sleep and thought a walk would slow down my mind when I come across you and a man in a lip lock. So much for settling my mind. Guess this is my cue to go back to my room and turn in."

"I think that's a good idea, but since you're here, let me show you around. It isn't real big but perfect for me." I led the way towards the bedroom and my writing office.

"Gee, Mom. This is really nice. You mean you moved in here without having to do anything?"

"I did buy all new furniture. Interestingly, I hadn't even thought of painting the place but looking around when I moved in, I noticed they'd had it painted recently; I guess for the new buyer. Mac and Sara are lovely people. I hope you can meet them someday."

Looking in my office, Brooke said, "Are you using this room for your writing?"

"Yes, I am."

"I bet you love this big window looking to the outside."

"Yes, I do. Although, I haven't been spending too much time out here but hope to in the future."

"Are you writing anything now?"

"I'm happy you asked. I'm working on a historical novel set here in Hawaii."

"That sounds interesting. How far have you gotten?"

"Just started, and I'm spending a lot of time doing research when I can."

"I'm glad you're continuing with your writing."

"Me too."

Showing her the bathroom, I could tell by the look on her face she had questions.

"Go ahead and ask," I said.

"Is this set up as a he and she bathroom? Sure looks like it."

"I bought it the way it was, so I would guess so."

"From what I've seen, it's nice. What's the kitchen like?"

She followed me into the kitchen and commented that everything was in order.

"Oh, yes. That was the first thing I wanted, and Keoki and Ona helped me get everything settled."

"It's lovely, Mom. Time to turn in. See you in the morning?"

"Of course. We can have breakfast together. Ona is a great cook."

"With that, I'll say goodnight," Brooke said, stepping forward to kiss me on the cheek and hugging me.

"Same to you, my dear daughter. You are, you know. I just don't say it often enough."

Smiling, Brooke went out the front door and walked quickly over to the main building.

Securing the doors, I turned off the lights and walked back to my bedroom to get ready for bed. Watching her walk towards the main building, I said out loud, "Paul is right. I need some motion lights out there."

After doing my nightly ritual and slipping on a white cotton nightgown, I called Paul to find out if he had gotten back to the hotel safely.

He answered after one ring.

"Hi, gorgeous."

"I wanted to call and see if you arrived back at the hotel in one piece. I know you're a big boy. Just checking after our heavy conversation tonight."

"I like that you're concerned about my welfare. A lot of women don't think that deeply. They're in it for a good time. But I'm not a good time Charlie kind of guy."

"Interesting. I didn't know that. I won't forget. In the meantime, I'll keep this short as I need a good night's sleep for tomorrow and I'm sure you do too."

"Tomorrow? Sounds ominous. Are you okay?"

"I mean I've had an eventful day and need to get a good night's sleep to be prepared for tomorrow. Just the usual and, of course, I need to check on arrival dates for incoming guests for I need to start making some money with my inn. Then spend time with Brooke and come to a resolution about whether I tell her father."

"Don't dwell on it for too long, or you'll never get to sleep."

"I try to compartmentalize and will set that aside so I can sleep."

"Do you have a compartment for me?" he asked with a chuckle.

"I do," I replied, trying to sound playful but not sure if I was succeeding.

"I need to turn in as well, so I'll call you tomorrow. Maybe dinner with Brooke?"

"I'll see how the day goes."

"Until tomorrow, goodnight, Maggie."

"Sleep well, Paul."

Setting the phone down on the night table, I turned back the comforter and laid down, not wanting to cover with anything since it was so warm. With the windows open and the ceiling fan going, it was staying reasonably comfortable. But then I had a weird thought. *Maybe I should close the windows in case Mark comes back, although I don't think he will. Oh damn! What a mess this is!* Erring on the side of caution I got up and went around closing windows and flipped on the air conditioner. Now I would have to get under the sheet at least. Drifting off, I kept thinking back to the look on Paul's face when I told him about Brooke and her father. Practice what you preach, I told myself as I slowly felt sleep coming on.

CHAPTER THIRTY-TWO

The next morning, my resident rooster woke me crowing at his best. I opened my eyes to bright sunlight streaming in through the French doors. I laid there, thinking, why do I feel like there's a cloud over my head? Oh, that's right. Brooke and Mark – how could I forget? I threw back the covers and walked into the bathroom. I turned on the shower for the water to warm up and looked outside. *I am so thankful for this beautiful property. Wish I didn't have these two wrinkles I must smooth out. Enough! This doesn't get the day started.* Shedding my gown, I stepped into the shower and stood under the showerhead, letting the water run over me, as I reached for the shampoo. *Showers are an excellent place to think things through. I wish there were a magic bullet to solve this dilemma I'm faced with.* I heard the phone ringing. Should I let it go to voicemail or attempt to answer the call? Deciding on the latter, I stepped out of the shower, grabbed a shower robe, and walked into the bedroom and picked up my phone.

"Hello."

"Good morning, Mom. Did I wake you?"

"Oh, hi, Brooke. No not at all, sweetie. Just out of the shower."

"Are you about ready for breakfast? Ona is cooking up a great smelling dish. When can you come over?"

"Give me ten minutes, and I'll be right over."

"I'll wait to have breakfast with you."

"Sounds good to me."

So much for my leisurely shower. At least I was almost finished! Now what to wear?

I did my usual morning toilette and dried my hair with the blow dryer. Walking over to the closet, I pulled out a black and white striped t-shirt dress and slipped on sandals. Makeup all done, and I was good to go. *It has been a long time since this mother and daughter spent quality time together.*

Walking over to the big house, my mind was focused on telling Brooke about her father. More specifically, if I should tell her and, if I decide to tell her, when? Entering the kitchen, I smelled Ona's divine Hawaiian pineapple pancakes and Portagee sausage that she had told me about.

"Ona, this breakfast smells terrific. I didn't realize it, but I'm hungry."

"Miss Maggie, your daughter is out on the lanai waiting for you. She and I talked this morning. Just general things about the bed and breakfast. Go sit with her, and I will bring out the food to you."

"Okay. I'll pour myself some coffee first and then join her."

I watched my daughter drinking her coffee. She looked so lovely and even at thirty-two seemed innocent. Telling her about her father would probably shake her to her core.

"Looks like Ona has taken care of you this morning," I said walking out onto the lanai.

"Yes, she has, Mom. You're lucky to have her and not to have to worry about cooking for everyone."

Sitting down across from Brooke, I said, "She's a jewel. I'm sure one of these days I'll have my turn at the stove! I don't think I will mind at all. I always liked to cook."

"Yes, you did. I remember the holiday meals we had even though my dad wasn't present. I always wondered about him. You never had much to say."

"At the time, there wasn't much to say. He and I weren't together that long. You didn't say how long you'll be staying?"

"True. I wasn't sure how you would react with me showing up unannounced. The day I leave isn't set in stone. I have unused vacation time and an open ticket," Brooke replied.

"Okay, that's fair. But in the meantime, what would you like to do: drive around the island, seeing the sights, relaxing on the beach? You need to tell me."

My cell phone rang just at the right time.

"Brooke, excuse me while I answer this."

"Sure, Mom. No problem."

Stepping away from the table, I answered.

"Hello."

"Good morning."

"Hi, Paul. I saw your number come up. How are you this morning?"

"I'm great. How are things going with Brooke?"

"At this point, fine so far. We were just getting ready to start on one of Ona's delicious breakfasts."

"So, you haven't told her anything yet?"

"No, I haven't. The time must be right before I can just spring it on her. But it's something I must do."

"The sooner the better. You wouldn't want Mark showing up and springing it on her."

"Since he doesn't know, I'm not afraid of him appearing."

"Aren't you being naïve?"

"Perhaps. I'm still not sure that I shouldn't let sleeping dogs lie."

"You don't want to wake up that sleeping dog!"

"Granted."

"What are you girls doing today?"

"Not sure. We haven't discussed it. My head is so full of what may happen when I tell Brooke about her father... if I decide to tell her, that is."

"It's good that you're taking it one day at a time."

"At this rate, I'm taking it one hour at a time. I feel like a cat on a hot tin roof! Stepping carefully around Brooke is more than I can handle at this time. She saw us kissing last night."

"She did?"

"Yes, she did and was quite curious. It was one of those who's the mother and who's the daughter moments. I did tell her about you, and she would like to meet you."

"Oh."

"Is that all you can say?"

"It does put me in a spot, but maybe it would be a good idea, so she knows you're in good hands. At least I will have appeared on her landscape."

"So, it's settled then. When would you like for me to set something up?"

"Tonight? Would that work for you?"

"I'll check with Brooke and ask her what she would like to do. Not sure if she is ready for a face to face with you. I think she is still getting used to me having a man in my life."

"I think you're a bit old and she is too to be concerned about that. You're both adults and have your own lives."

"Thank you for reminding me of that. Sometimes it takes another person to see what's going on and offer their perspective. It's like reining me back in to face the realization that we are both independent women. I'll give you a call a bit later about tonight after I have spoken to her."

"Fair enough."

"Thanks, Paul, for understanding. Talk to you later. Bye for now."

"Bye, Maggie."

I walked back to where Brooke was sitting eating her breakfast. She had made good headway on the Hawaiian Benedict and was now working on the papaya, pineapple, and melon.

Sitting down, I said, "That was Paul."

"I kinda figured that," she replied, a bit on the sarcastic side.

Oh, brother! Here we go. May as well jump in and set her straight.

"Brooke, remember you are my daughter, not my keeper, and I want you to keep an open mind. Paul is not Jack the Ripper!"

"Could have fooled me!" she snapped.

"That is enough. You are an adult, and I wouldn't have expected that reaction from you. I thought you had grown up."

"Well someone has to look out for your best interests and, let's face it, your choices when it comes to men have not been good. You have made some lousy decisions!"

I sat stunned that my daughter would speak to me like that. Taking a deep breath, I said, "That may be true, but I have moved on. Besides what if I visited you unexpectedly and you were with someone, how would you react?"

"Good question. But that's only a 'what if'. This is now."

"I had hoped we could get back on an even keel while you're here, but you are making it difficult!"

"It takes two, and you're not making it easy either. I thought when you moved here you were starting over and declared you were finished with men?"

"That's what I thought, but often as you will learn, situations present themselves. When I met Paul, I hadn't planned on anything more than being just friends. I didn't want anything more, but it's evolved. We are close friends, and he has been helpful to me, and I am comfortable with having someone here that I can trust and count on."

"Sleeping with too?" she quipped.

"That's none of your business. Again, I haven't asked you who you are sleeping with."

"Good thing. I don't have the track record you do."

"I don't need a watchdog. For now, let's drop this and plan our day. What would you like to do while you are here?"

"I didn't come here to argue with you. I agree to a truce."

"Good!" I responded, smiling at my daughter, older than her years, although at times, she acted like a spoiled child and not her age.

"I hadn't thought much about sightseeing and was looking forward to spending quality time with you. Since you have a great beach that's right here outside your door, I would like to spend time relaxing today, and maybe you can show me around tomorrow?"

"That's fine. But I need to spend some time here in the office taking care of business for the inn."

"No problem. I can get my beach things together, and when you're finished, you can join me. Are there beach chairs available?"

"Yes, Keoki will help you with that. Paul called and would like the three of us to have dinner but was fine if you decide you aren't comfortable with that?"

I could see in Brooke's expression that she was considering it, but her hesitation gave me pause.

"Mom, I'm not sure if it's a good idea right now. I came here to rekindle our relationship and don't want anyone or anything getting in the way!"

"Paul wouldn't be getting in the way. He would like to meet you and reassure you that he is not the bogey man but a good friend to me. Besides you may not have a say so in when you meet people."

"That brings me to a hidden agenda that I have."

I took a deep breath.

"Oh, what is that?"

"I would like to know about my father. You haven't shared very much with me, and I think it's time."

"Are you sure? It's been so long ago, and you've built a good life for yourself with responsibilities. I would think this would be the last thing you would want to have to think about."

"In some respects, it is, but I need you to tell me about his background. In case I have children, it would be good if I knew what I'm dealing with genetically."

I had been waiting for this shoe to drop. Although I hoped she had far more important things on her mind.

Ona appeared and told me I had a phone call. *Talk about saved by the bell.*

"Thanks, Ona."

She walked back into the kitchen, and I felt on edge, knowing I had to take the call but also that I couldn't ignore Brooke and walk out on her.

Turning back to Brooke, I said, "I'm sorry, but we need to wait till later when we can talk about this privately. I need to take this call. Can I catch up with you a bit later?"

With a look of disdain, she responded: "As usual you're avoiding me!"

"Brooke, I have a business to run, and I want you to understand that. I'm not avoiding you but saying we need to continue our conversation later, in private. Isn't that fair?"

"Putting it like that, you are right. Later then. I'm heading off to the beach," she said, standing up.

I approached and hugged her and said, "I promise to catch up with you later."

Brooke left the lanai in a huff and started back to her room, acting like a petulant child.

Whew! Got out of that one. At least for now.

"Ona, thanks," I said, walking into the office and taking the call.

Hanging up, I felt some relief that it was a guest confirming their reservation for next week. *Would be nice if I could get this settled so that by the time the guest arrives, I will be able to focus on being the innkeeper.*

I walked back into the kitchen where Ona and Keoki were working at the sink cleaning produce.

"Sorry to interrupt but I want to let you know that a guest arriving late next week has confirmed. His name is Francis Reagan and he'll be flying in from New York. I understand he is a retired chief of police and will be staying as long as it takes him to find a place to live. He is relocating from the East Coast. Another transplant for the island!"

"Miss Maggie, do you know which room he will be in?" asked Keoki.

"Not sure yet. It will depend on whether Colonel Elliott and my daughter have departed. But I will look at what we have available and figure out the best location for him. I'll let you know."

"Thank you," replied Keoki.

"What about food, Miss Maggie? Will I be preparing anything special for him? Does he have any specific things he cannot eat?"

"We'll figure that out the closer it gets to his arrival date. In the meantime, I need to go down to the beach and sit with my daughter for a while. If you need me, I'll have my phone with me."

Smiling they both acknowledged with a shake of their heads yes.

I looked at them and said, "I consider myself lucky to have you both here to assist me. I don't think I could have handled the turnover without you. I just wanted you to know that. See you later," I said, walking out to join Brooke.

"Thanks, Miss Maggie."

CHAPTER THIRTY-THREE

Taking a detour to my cottage, I quickly changed into my beach sandals. Sunglasses and straw hat on, I made sure I had my cell phone in my pocket and started towards the beach, wondering how I would approach the subject of her father. Maybe I should let her bring it up first? Approaching the beach, I saw my daughter in a red bikini sprawled out on a large beach towel. Slipping off my sandals, I grabbed one of the beach chairs and walked over to where she was basking under the warm Hawaiian sun.

Setting the beach chair down next to Brooke's towel, I said, "I see you're all settled, but you didn't want to use one of these beach chairs?"

"Hi, Mom. No, I don't, but a suggestion to the innkeeper if I may?"

"Sure," I replied.

"Might be a good idea to invest in some beach umbrellas. I'm surprised that the people you bought the inn from didn't have them."

"I agree with you. It never occurred to me, maybe because I had so many other things on my mind. I'll look into that and purchase some. I hope you're using a good sunblock; the sun here can be brutal if you lay out too long without sunscreen."

"Always the mom," she replied, smiling. "Yes, I have an excellent sunscreen on."

"Brooke, what would you like to do today?"

"I'm perfectly contented to lay here on the beach, and maybe we can catch up later today, and you will tell me about my father?"

"I suppose we can do that, but I thought you wanted to see some of the island?"

"Oh, we can do that another day," Brooke replied. "I really want to learn about him. To be honest, that's my primary reason for my visit."

"Really! I thought you wanted to see me? It's been so long since we last saw each other."

"It's only been a couple of years, Mom."

"Brooke, that's a long time for me."

"Are you trying to avoid talking about him?"

"Why do you say that?"

"Maybe because… there's something you don't want me to know?"

My cell went off and, reaching into my pocket, I saw it was Keoki calling me. "Hello, Keoki."

"Miss Maggie, I think you should come here quick."

Alarmed, I said to "Brooke, apparently there's an emergency. We'll continue this conversation when I get back." I sensed she wasn't happy with that and I got up and started walking quickly back to the inn.

"Mom, wait. Maybe since we're staying around here today, we can have dinner with your friend?"

Smiling, I said, "Sure, Brooke. I'll let Paul know."

As I walked back to the big house, I kept thinking about what it could be that Keoki was calling me about. *Could Mark be back? No, I didn't think so. At least I hoped not.*

"Hi, Keoki. What's the problem?"

"Maggie," he said, "you got another call for a reservation."

"Okay. We can handle that. I don't understand what the problem is."

"The lady who called said her name is Patricia Elliott!"

I don't believe it. What would she be doing traveling all this way and making her own reservation? Why wouldn't she have just said she was Colonel Elliott's wife and that she would be joining him?

"Keoki, you and I should sit down and talk about this," I said, grabbing a notebook from the office and leading the way out to the lanai area, which had become my favorite go-to place.

Ona appeared and asked, "Can I get you both something to drink?"

"Sure, that would be fine. How about some of your mango iced tea? Keoki, is that okay with you?"

"Yes, Miss Maggie."

Ona turned and walked back into the kitchen, and I could hear her clanking around fixing our tea.

"Let's start from the beginning, Keoki."

"Miss Maggie, the phone in your office rang, and I went to answer it. A lady asked to speak with the innkeeper. I told her you weren't here right now. She said she wanted to make a reservation. I told her we have rooms available."

"Okay, then what?"

I could see Keoki was concerned; something was very wrong, and I asked him, "Why are you so upset?"

"I asked for her name, and she said, Patricia Elliott." *I could only imagine the connection that Keoki was making to Colonel Elliott. How many Patricia Elliotts could there be and wanting to stay here?*

"Go on."

"She said her husband Colonel Mark Elliott has been staying here and she would like to book a room for a short stay."

Oh, brother! Short stay sounds like it is ultimatum time for Mark and his wife. Unless I was imagining things or maybe she hoped that she could talk him into going home with her. I could then avoid a confrontation between Mark and Brooke. Damn. I don't know how I can orchestrate that. Wishful thinking?

Ona came out to the lanai and brought our tea.

"Ona, why don't you join us?"

She meekly sat down and looked from Keoki to me with her hands folded in her lap.

"First off, Keoki why are you so anxious?"

"Miss Maggie, please excuse me, but I could see something was going on between you and the Colonel the last time he was here."

"Let me stop you right there. I want you to know that Colonel Elliott and I knew each other a long time ago when we were very young. We were both surprised to see each other, and that's the end of the story. There is not any need for you to be concerned. What else did she say?"

"She asked for her own room."

"I take it she didn't elaborate as to why?"

"No. Mac and Sara always said I wasn't to ask too many questions when people called to make reservations."

"That's excellent advice, Keoki. Did she say when she would be arriving?"

"Mrs. Elliott said she would be here in two days."

"Okay, I think we can be ready for her arrival without any problem. Let's get busy preparing her room."

"Did she mention what time she will arrive?"

"Yes. She said her plane lands at 1:11 in the afternoon."

She sounded very precise, but then what would I expect from a woman who had been married to a career Marine.

Ona and Keoki got up and walked back into the kitchen where I could hear them chatting. I got up and followed them to the kitchen.

"Ona, please double check the Anthurium Suite. We have Mrs. Elliott arriving in two days, and I want to make sure it's PERFECT."

"I will take care of that right away," she replied.

"Keoki, did Mac and Sara ever have beach umbrellas?"

"No, not at least while I've been here."

"That's what I thought. I couldn't remember them telling me about them, only the chairs. I'm going to run a few errands and be back in a while. If my daughter asks, just tell her I had business to do for the inn."

"Will do," replied Ona.

I quickly walked back to my cottage for my handbag and keys. I decided to put on my white sneakers since I might be walking around the local Home Depot. All set to go, I strode to my car to find Keoki standing like he was waiting for me.

"Miss Maggie, try Home Depot for those umbrellas."

"Thanks, Keoki. You read my mind. I'll map it on my GPS. See you later."

Before backing my car out, I mapped the location of the Home Depot on Nuhou Street. My GPS showed I would drive to Kaumualii Highway and Nuhou was close by. I drove out to the highway and, making a left turn, headed for Home Depot. Thoughts preoccupied with the arrival of Mark's wife, I struggled with whether to tell Mark or not. *Do I even know how to reach him? I could drive out to the Waimea Plantation Cottages and see if he's there. I don't want to break this news to him over the phone.* Fortunately, at this time of day, traffic was light. I noticed from the GPS I was close to my destination when my cell rang. "Hello."

"Hi, Maggie, Paul here."

"How are you this fine day?"

"Do I detect a bit of sarcasm?" he replied.

"You could say that. I'm glad you called. I talked to Brooke, and she's fine with the three of us having dinner tonight. You pick the place and time, and we can meet you there."

"I would rather you stop by the hotel, and I can drive us there."

"Okay, we can do that. I must tell you we had an interesting call for a reservation today. Mark's wife called to arrange for a room. She will be arriving in two days."

"Wow! That's certainly something you didn't need."

"You can say that again. It may sound trite, but it's the way I'm feeling. If I don't have enough on my plate with Brooke here and Mark somewhere on the island."

"What are you going to do?"

"I think I should warn him but then on second thought let him be surprised."

"If it were you, would you want a surprise like that?" Paul responded.

"You have a point. No, I wouldn't want to be surprised like that. I have some thinking to do. Right now, I'm on the way to Home Depot to buy umbrellas for the beach. Brooke asked me why I didn't have any, and I told her it was because there weren't any when I took over."

"Good luck with your umbrella shopping. Can you be here at 5:00 p.m.?"

"That early? You must have something special planned?"

"I do. No more questions now. See you gals at 5."

"Thanks, Paul," I said as I hung up.

Arriving at Home Depot, I walked as fast as I could into the store to the customer service desk to inquire about beach umbrellas. The clerk was helpful and asked me how many I wanted; thinking a moment I said, "Six."

Glancing up from his computer, he said: "I have solid colors in red and blue and also a multicolor stripe."

"The multicolor will be fine."

After arranging to have them delivered the next day, I thanked him and hurriedly walked to my Jeep making a mental note to drive out to the Waimea Plantation Cottages to face Mark with the news of the impending arrival of his wife... or do I call her his ex? Fortunately, I was on the right highway heading for the cottages. *I'm dreading seeing Mark, alone. Still extremely attracted to him but I don't want my life complicated any more than it already is. Fortunately for me, with the arrival of his wife, her visit should deter any impulse I may have to be with him. I'm curious, however, about her. I always wondered what she would be like. Damn! It would be so much easier if she weren't coming. I can only juggle so many things at a time.*

I drove to the cottage where Mark was staying and parked. Taking a deep breath, I got out and walked to the front of the cottage. I knocked and, getting no answer, turned around to leave and saw him dressed in bathing trunks walking from the pool area, towel in hand. The sight of him took my breath away. *Oh, why couldn't he be dressed in his fatigues or at least covered up?*

"Maggie, what a surprise to see you," he said smiling broadly as he walked towards me, dripping from his swim and, the closer he got, the more I wished I hadn't come out here.

"Hi, Mark. I only came to tell you that I got a call from your wife today and she made a reservation."

"Really? So what. She and I are over!" he said, trotting up the steps into the cottage.

I stood there feeling awkward, afraid to follow him inside. *I don't want to risk a compromising situation.*

"Maggie, please come in," he said, holding the screen door open.

I guess if we are to carry on this conversation I had better go in and get this over with.

"When's she arriving?"

"She will be here in two days," I said brushing past him as I entered the cottage.

"Please sit down, Maggie. I won't bite!"

Sitting down, I took a deep breath and said, "Not knowing when you would be back at the inn, I thought it best to drive out here and warn you."

He stared at me with those crystal-clear blue eyes of his and said, "I was planning on coming back this evening."

"Really? Were you going to call me and let me know?"

"I didn't think it was necessary. I thought the arrangement was that I would come and go as I please. Why do you need a warning?"

"Not a warning," I said, trying to sound calm but not sure it was coming across that way.

"What is it then? You didn't need to drive out here to tell me Patricia's coming to Kauai."

"True but I wanted to do it face to face to see your reaction. Besides, I had purchased some beach umbrellas at Home Depot and since I was on this side of the island decided I would come out to tell you rather than call you."

"You wanted to see my reaction?"

"Maybe that's the wrong word. Yes. I thought that if I told you in person, I could see how you felt about her coming here."

"I have always been straight with you, Maggie," he said, approaching me.

I quickly stood up to leave and realized we were nose to nose. I responded in a whisper, "Yes, you have. I always knew where I stood with you."

He put his arms around me and drew me to him. Kissing me fully, I felt overwhelmed by his manliness. Suddenly, with his muscular tanned arms around me, I sensed we were moving into another room.

Breaking away from his embrace, I said, "Mark, what are you doing?"

"You want me just as much as I want you. You just won't admit it."

"How can you be so sure of yourself? Don't you think you are presumptuous?"

"Admit it! Damnit!"

"All right! I am and will always be attracted to you, but when I feel myself getting pulled in, I recall how you hurt me and chose someone else. Maybe you didn't love me like I loved you and certainly not the way you loved Patricia and desired your parents' approval! I'm glad I drove out here and not because I needed to warn you about Patricia but because I wanted to put my feelings out in the open. I never thought you fully understood how deeply I felt for you. To you, I was one of those quick summer romances, but you meant so much more to me than that. I was willing to sacrifice anything for you and commit to you to the exclusion of all others, and I did. Well, let me tell you! You have a daughter!" I was in tears.

Wrenching away from him to walk out of the room, I felt his strong hands on my arms pulling me back into his embrace.

Looking me straight in the eyes he said with choking emotion, "Daughter? What are you talking about?"

"That summer we met and fell in love, I got pregnant. My mother insisted that I have an abortion, but I wouldn't hear of it, so she shipped me out of state to stay with her sister until I gave birth. My aunt, never having had children of her own, wanted to raise Brooke as her own although she never formally adopted her. I remained her mother on the birth certificate."

"Who is named as her father? You must have someone's name on the birth certificate. It couldn't be left blank."

"You're correct. Your name is on the birth certificate: Mark Elliott – father of a healthy 8-pound 6-ounce baby girl with ten fingers and toes. Perfect in every way except she was missing a father."

Mark stood there with tears pooling in his stormy blue eyes. *The big fearsome Marine Colonel shows he does have feelings. Now what do I do?*

"Maggie, I don't know what to say except why tell me now?"

"You big lug, can't you figure it out?" I cried at him, "Because she wants to know about her father!"

CHAPTER THIRTY-FOUR

"Why now?"

"I don't know. I suspect she wants to have a child and wants to check out your gene pool! If that is the case, I'll be surprised."

"Why is that?"

"Brooke lives in New York City. She has a career as a successful editor for a high-fashion magazine. To say she has worked hard to get where she is an understatement. She has never seemed to be mommy material."

"Is she married?"

"No. I don't even know if she has anyone in her life she's serious about. We haven't been close; not like I'd hoped. I always kept her at arm's length because I didn't want her to be so comfortable with me, she would ask about you."

"Maggie, why are you telling me after all this time?"

"Because we were never in touch and you show up out of the blue. I felt that for whatever reason, call it fate, you were back in my life, even for a short time and should know, especially since Brooke has wanted to know about you. I have been weighing, in my mind, all the eventualities that could arise from telling you, but since she's asking, I know in my heart it's time she knew about you and you her. I hope you have it in your heart to accept her and want to get to know your daughter."

"I understand perfectly what you're saying," he said, looking crestfallen. "You don't know, but Patricia and I couldn't have children. She miscarried several times, and we gave up. Adoption was out of the question for either of us. She didn't want another woman's child, and I didn't feel secure in our relationship. Our marriage wasn't sustained out of love but necessity. She made a good officer's wife, and I provided for her. But now at this time in our lives, she has found someone else, and I want something more than what she and I had. Sad that we remained together all those years for the sake of appearances. Ironic that I find out now I have a daughter."

"I bet your parents were happy."

"Yes, until they realized that we weren't the happily married couple they had planned for me."

"I don't know what to say about that except good riddance when I think back to all those letters that were never answered and phone calls never returned. They kept us apart for their selfish reasons."

He stepped closer to me and said quietly, "Where do we go from here?"

"Where do WE go? I'm not sure. I need to think this through. I hadn't planned on telling you today, but it just slipped out," I said looking at those piercing blue eyes I had fallen in love with all those years ago.

Mark pulled me to him in a hug, and I returned the hug, crying quietly. *What have I done? Am I crazy? What do I do about Paul?*

"Maggie, don't cry."

"Easy for you to say," I sniveled choking back my tears and pushing away from him. "I had better leave now and go back to the inn." *I didn't want to succumb to temptation.*

"Must you leave now? I would like us to spend some time hashing this out," Mark said, speaking tenderly.

"Do you think that if I stay, we can resolve this? Are you sure that's the only reason why you want me to stay?"

"I would like to but realize you may not want to now."

"Why do you say that? We should resolve this but on neutral ground."

"Why not here?" he asked smirking.

"Because I don't trust either one of us to avoid a compromising situation which I'm not ready for. I have experienced too much to put myself in that position, which could result in only hurting me."

"You're worried about being hurt?"

"Yes, I am. I'm getting too old for these games."

"I admit I have the same hesitation. I don't want to be hurt either, but if there's any way we could be happy, I'm willing to give it a go."

"Mark, I can agree with you to a point, but how do we get to that point? It seems to me we have a couple of obstacles to overcome. The first one being your wife Patricia, who will be here in a couple of days. The second one is our daughter."

"You don't have to worry about Patricia. I have an easy fix for that one."

"Really! What on earth are you talking about?"

"I suspect if I convince her that our divorce is set in stone and then she still balks, I can offer to pay her off. I have the means to do that. Patricia has very expensive tastes, and our property settlement was fair and equitable to both of us. She has told me on more than one occasion that she's unhappy with it but agreed to it anyway."

"If she was unhappy with it, why would she agree?" It doesn't compute to me."

"Patricia wasn't exactly the most faithful wife. With all my various deployments, she was lonely. We didn't have children for her to focus on, and she found other means with which to occupy her time and provide her with companionship."

"If I get your drift, I presume she fooled around?"

"You can do more than presume. She was an out and out hussy. Patricia can't hold her alcohol and got loose when she visited the officers' club. It didn't take long until I received word that she'd taken up with other men. Of course, when I confronted her, she gave me the excuse she missed me and couldn't deal with being alone. So, I insisted on a divorce so that she could have her freedom, and I wouldn't have to face ridicule. At my rank, I needed to save my reputation and thought it best if we went our separate ways."

"What a shame that after all the years you were married it would end that way. I can't be the one to criticize or cast aspersions as my life hasn't been what I wanted it to be either," I said, looking at him with tears welling in my eyes.

Mark extended his arms, and I walked into his embrace. Feeling his arms around me gave me what I needed at that moment but pulling away, I said, "Look, let's agree. What we each need is to move forward, whether it is together or apart. We can't live our lives on this precipice of emotion. Everyone deserves love and happiness, even at our age and maybe more so. My first step will be to go back to the inn and talk to Brooke."

Taking hold of my arms, he said, "Do you mean to tell me she is on the island now?"

"Yes, she is," I admitted with apprehension, not knowing how he was going to react.

Sitting down on the bed, Mark placed his hands on his face and mumbled, "When can I see her?" Placing his hands on his knees, he looked up at me with tears in his eyes, "Having a daughter even at my age means a lot. I would like to connect with her. I think it's only fair that you give me that."

"Fair? For who? Now you want to play daddy dearest? If I want to be fair, it will be for Brooke because she has asked about her father. I don't know how she will react after I have deceived her all these years but whether she sees you or not will be up to her. I don't think I owe you fairness after the way I was dumped, but I'm willing to let that go."

"Maggie, for what it's worth after all these years, I'm sorry for hurting you. But I thought you understood. If it weren't for my parents, pushing me into marrying Patricia, things might have been different for us."

"Oh, how I wish you had said that all those years ago. I was hurt, sure, but when I found out I was pregnant and alone, hurt doesn't even cover it. I felt abandoned!"

"Again, I'm sorry. Could you see it in your heart to forgive me?"

"I'm not sure. It may be too late. As for Brooke, I can't say."

"Maggie, if she doesn't want to meet me, could I at least see her without telling her who I am?"

"I would need to think about that, but first let me talk to her," I said, walking towards the door.

"Okay, let me walk you to your car."

"Fine," I replied, walking out the door, and down the front steps, I felt his hand reach for mine. I took his hand, and we walked quietly to my car.

"Maggie, I plan on telling Patricia about Brooke one way or the other. It may be the last straw. I hope it will be the last I see of her."

Getting into my Jeep, I rolled the window down, and he bent down, kissing me on the lips. I looked at him and said, "I hope that regardless of how this all turns out, we can at least be friends and not enemies."

Standing back from the Jeep, he said, "Yes, I would like that, but I would hope for more."

"We'll have to see about that," I said as I started to back out.

I heard him yell for me to stop as he ran to catch up with me.

"Maggie, will you let me know?"

"Sure, but will you let me know when you expect to make an appearance at the inn, so I can at least be prepared?"

"I can do that," he replied with a somber look on his face.

"I'll call you later, Mark."

"Thanks, Maggie."

As I pulled out onto the highway with my thoughts swirling about what I had just done, I breathed a sigh of relief that I was working my way towards resolving this predicament one way or the other. Trying to maintain a sensible speed, I eventually pulled into the parking lot of the Garden Inn to see Paul.

I walked quickly into the open-air lobby and to the front desk, I asked for Paul.

I heard a familiar voice and turned as Paul approached me.

"This is a surprise. I wasn't expecting to see you until tonight."

"I need to talk to you and get some advice, if you have any, for what I've just done."

"Okay, let's go sit out by the pool where we can have some privacy. There aren't any people out there," he said, taking my hand. *The feel of his hand in mine was comforting. I welcomed his touch and realized that even with Mark here on the island and about to meet his daughter that I couldn't see a future with Mark. If things work out with Brooke so much the better, but I don't think it would work with us.*

"It's very peaceful out here, which is what I need right now. I had so hoped to have that at my bed and breakfast, but I don't think that is going to be possible or at least until I get Brooke and Mark resolved."

"Here we are," he said, pulling out a chair for me under a private cabana. "Now tell me what's going on."

"I hope you're ready for this. After I purchased the umbrellas for the beach, I drove out to where Mark is staying at the Waimea Plantation Cottages."

"You didn't!" he said.

"Yes, I did. I felt there were things I needed to discuss with him. One is that his wife or ex-wife or whatever, called and reserved a room. She's coming in this weekend and, I wanted him to be aware, not that I really could give a damn. Then there's Brooke. She's asked me about her father. I didn't give her any information other than what she already knows. As for Mark, if he should return to the inn, I wanted to forewarn him about Brooke in case she gets suspicious. They do resemble each other. It's my best guess that Brooke has been asking me about her father because she's planning on having a baby and is concerned about any unknown genetic problems."

Paul sat looking out towards the beach when he stood up and said somberly, "This is a surprise. I don't want you to worry about how I feel."

"Well, I do. I consider you more than a good friend and don't want to ruin the relationship we have so far. I know we've had our ups and downs but this…"

"Let me stop you right there," he interrupted. He sat back down and reached across for my hand. He looked me in the eye, with such tenderness, and said, "While to some men this may cause a serious roadblock in a relationship, to me it doesn't. We each have our histories and cannot change where we've come from or what we've experienced. I would be the last one to criticize or cut you off just when you need me for support. Consider me in for the long haul or whenever you have had enough."

"After this bombshell, I would expect you to have second thoughts, but as for me, I want you in my life and I was worried about how you were going to handle this news. Now I can say with certainty that you have stepped up and for that I'm grateful. With Mark's wife arriving this entire situation could blow up. He didn't indicate when he would be returning to the inn, but he does want to meet Brooke and face Patricia with the truth," I said.

"If I were him, I would return to face the music with Patricia and unite with Brooke. But then that's me," declared Paul.

Looking at him, I could see that he was being sincere and honest with me. "Paul, I appreciate you giving me your opinion and being so candid with me. I wouldn't have expected this to come from you, and this confirms what I felt upon our first meeting that you are a person who understands, and I can depend on."

"At this point, what do you expect to happen when you tell her, or maybe I should retract that question?"

"Oh, no. My thoughts exactly. To be perfectly honest with you, I'm not sure how she'll react. We haven't been close, and I'm not in tune with her or her emotions. Do you still want to have dinner with us? I don't plan to say anything to her until later."

"As far as I'm concerned, we are a go for dinner."

"Good. I must head back to the inn, and before I know, it will be time to drive back down here."

"Change of plans. Rather than have you come down here to the hotel, I will pick you girls up for dinner."

"But I thought you had a place already picked out and made a reservation."

"I did, but I can change it and know of the perfect place in Hanalei to take you to. Then it's settled. Let me walk you out to your car," he said, standing up.

I stood up and, taking his arm, we walked back to the hotel lobby where the desk clerk stopped us and told Paul he had a page.

"Let me take this, and I will walk you to your car," he said.

"Paul, that's okay. You take care of whatever it is, and we will see you later," I said turning to walk out to the parking lot when he pulled me to him and delivered a kiss to my lips. "Don't worry, Maggie, it will turn out all right and the way it is supposed to," he said.

"Thanks. I'll try and count on the best outcome," I replied, struggling to smile.

Walking out to my car it came to mind *Could Paul be the man for me? Not that I planned to ever get involved with one again, but I'll take it as it comes, and whatever happens I'll look at the bright side and be happy. How could I not be, living on this beautiful, tropical island, a paradise all of its own and meant for me.*

Looking up at the clear, vivid blue sky with a hint of clouds appearing over the mountains, I backed my car out and headed for Kuhio Highway. Driving the picturesque route to my new home, I felt better having spoken to Paul. *Surprisingly he had provided me with the support and encouragement I had hoped for. This should resolve itself one way or the other. Maybe I underestimated him!*

As I approached the turn off to The Inn on Alamihi Road, I felt my anxiety return. *Maggie, get a hold of yourself. Remember what Paul said and what you were saying to yourself. You must keep a clear, steady head so that when you speak with Brooke, you will exude confidence and not worry whether she rejects you or not. It won't be anything new, and life will be what it was, only here on Kauai.* I parked my Jeep in the usual spot and went up to check in with Keoki and Ona. *Hope all is quiet on the home front and Brooke hasn't pulled her princess attitude on my staff.*

"Hello, Ona, Keoki, I'm back," I called out.

Keoki came running from the kitchen as I walked into my office. "Miss Maggie, so glad you are back!"

"Oh, dear! I hope you weren't worried? Anything new happen while I was out?" I asked with mounting anxiety.

"No, nothing happened that we couldn't handle. Miss Brooke kept asking when you would be back."

"Oh! Is that all. I was concerned something had happened."

"No. We served her lunch because she said she was hungry."

"That's good. Thank you for doing that. I know you and Ona don't normally serve lunch."

"It was fine. She didn't eat a lot but enjoyed the papaya and melon we served her."

"Since we won't be here tonight, if you want to take the night off, it's fine with me."

"We would like that. Nice to be home with our family."

"See you in the morning," I said, walking towards Brooke's room, not sure what kind of reception I would receive.

Her door was ajar, and I poked my head in calling, "Brooke, I'm back."

Suddenly she appeared from her bathroom, her head wrapped in a towel and she was wearing one of the inn's terry cloth bathrobes.

"Hi, Mom."

"Hi, Brooke. I understand you were asking Keoki about me."

"I thought you would be back earlier since you hadn't said what time you would return. I was worried."

"Rest assured if something had happened, I would have called.

No worries," I said, not sure if she could hear the tension in my voice. I'm going back to my cottage to get ready for our dinner with Paul. Do you need anything?"

"No. I would like to resume our conversation about my father, though."

"We'll get back to it. I promise," I said, turning to walk out of her room.

"Mom, do you know where Paul is taking us for dinner?"

"No, I don't, but it will be someplace I'm sure you will enjoy. He knows his restaurants. Why did you ask?"

"I wanted to know what I should wear."

Hesitating, trying to focus on what she was saying I answered, "Dressy casual will work. See you in a bit."

I know I was abrupt but didn't want to let anything slip at this point. I must think this through.

CHAPTER THIRTY-FIVE

Walking to my cottage, my heart was heavy, knowing I was about to change my daughter's life forever and probably mine as well. What's particularly worrisome was that I didn't know if Brooke would understand why she was told that her father wasn't alive. I worried she would want nothing more to do with me; I've heard of adult children disowning parents for less. But I wasn't going to say anything about it until after we had dinner with Paul tonight. I didn't want to spoil the evening, and I wasn't quite ready to tell her. Also, I was gambling that Mark wouldn't appear until Patricia arrived which gave me a couple of days. I grappled with the thought that it would be best to get it over with before she got here.

Once in my cottage, I felt happy to be back in my space. At least I'd created an environment in which I could escape and mull over what I must do. *First: shower and dress for dinner.*

Stepping into the shower, I kept thinking about how I would tell my daughter about her father. After several minutes, I concluded I would do it tonight after returning from dinner with Paul. Satisfied I had that resolved at least for the time being, I stepped out of the shower and donned a white terrycloth shower robe. I looked in my closet for something that would be comfortable and yet give me confidence tonight. I chose a maxi black print halter dress splashed with red hibiscus and white plumeria flowers. Looking at it, I thought this dress would certainly change my mood.

I looked in the bathroom mirror and could see the heaviness my heart was feeling. *Being torn between telling my daughter the truth and allowing Mark to enter her life is wearing on me. Damn! I would never have thought in a million years that Mark would resurface after all this time – he could have been deceased for all I knew. No one had shared any information with me, and I certainly hadn't any contact with his parents. I had never met them, but I'm sure they must have known about me, having returned my letters I had written to Mark. No sense in dwelling on this but take one step at a time. The first step is to have dinner with Brooke and Paul tonight. I will give it my best to make it a positive evening.*

I finished applying my makeup and added extra concealer to cover the dark circles under my eyes. *I wish there was a magic elixir to make me feel better.* I slipped into my dress and, looking in the full-length mirror, was satisfied with how I looked – on the outside! Adding black patent leather sandals, I was all set to meet the evening head-on. As I was about to step out onto my porch to start the walk over to the big house, my cell rang. *Mark! Damn, why now, of all times?* If I don't answer it, he will keep pestering, and if I do, I must sound convincing that we have other plans for the evening.

"Hello."

"Hello, Maggie. Have you had a chance to talk to Brooke yet?"

"No, Mark. We're going out this evening, and I've been occupied with getting ready."

"Oh, just the two of you?"

"No, why do you ask?"

"I thought maybe I could join you."

"I don't think that's a good idea. I won't spring this on her in a public place. Best to give her time to adjust to the knowledge that she does have a father who is alive."

"You're probably right. Admittedly, I am anxious to meet her and to get to know her."

I stood holding the cell phone and was tongue-tied. *Now that I have opened this can of worms, it'll be up to me to do what I can to make it as easy for Brooke as possible. Feeling a sense of doom and gloom for not knowing how my adult daughter was going to handle this revelation,* I said, "Mark, give me a little time, at least until tomorrow. I need to prepare myself before I just blurt it out that her father isn't dead after all," I said imploringly. Silence. "Mark are you still on the line?"

"Yes, Maggie. Okay. Have it your way. You know what's best for our daughter."

Hearing him say those two words, "our daughter" gave me pause.

"Well?" he asked.

"I'm surprised you're so cooperative."

"Why not. It's the least I can do under the circumstances."

"Thanks, Mark. I'll call you tomorrow after I have spoken with her."

After I'd hung up the phone, I switched it to silent mode. *I don't trust that he won't call again while we're having dinner. That wouldn't be a good thing.*

"Maggie."

I looked up to see Paul standing at the bottom of the steps with his hand extended. I stepped down to greet him with a kiss on the lips and grasped his hand like it was a life preserver. I felt his arms encircle me and felt a great sense of relief to have him to turn to.

"That's quite the greeting," he said, looking into my eyes with tenderness.

"I'm just happy to see you, and looking forward to our dinner tonight."

"I am too although I can see a worried look on your face. I take it you haven't told Brooke yet?"

"No, I haven't and to add to my consternation, Mark just called and wanted to know if I told her and I told him no. I want this evening to be free of turmoil and drama. By tomorrow she will know she has a living and breathing father and I will have to deal with the fallout then. I'm curious though, where are you taking us for dinner?" I asked, linking my arm with his as we walked toward the main house.

"I picked out a place that I think you both will like. It isn't far from here. It's the Kalypso Island Bar & Grill."

"Sounds like fun," I answered.

"Should be. I've only been there once, but I enjoyed it. Shall we get Brooke and head out?"

"Yes, let's."

Upstairs, waiting for us on the lanai was Brooke engaged in conversation with Keoki. I was pleased to see her dressed in a shocking pink linen sheath with white sandals.

"Hi. Ready to go to dinner?" I asked.

"Sure. I'm starving. Haven't had much to eat today in anticipation of tonight."

Paul stepped forward, extended his hand and said, "Hi, I'm Paul. Nice to meet you."

"Hope you won't be disappointed with the restaurant." Paul said.

"Don't worry about it. I'm sure we will have a good time," she responded, looking at us.

"Keoki, we will see you in the morning. Have a good evening," I said smiling.

Downstairs, Paul led the way to his Beemer as Brooke remarked, "I like your car. Did you have it shipped from the mainland?"

"I did. I hadn't had it too long when I decided to take this job and knew I would need wheels once over here, so it was easy enough but not cheap! Hope you don't mind the top down."

"Oh, no, I love it," she said.

Settled in the car, Paul deftly backed it out and turned towards Kuhio Highway. We were quiet enjoying the drive through the lush tropical foliage. Paul was right; the restaurant wasn't that far from the inn, which was a good thing. My stomach was telling me it was past time to eat. Parking in the front of the Kalypso, Paul helped us out and took my hand as we walked up the steps to the outdoor patio area.

"Paul, you did well. I love this type of place," my daughter commented.

Settled at our table, we looked over the menu while the waiter whose name tag read Mano brought us our table settings.

"Well, ladies, what will it be?" Paul asked.

"I'll have the Kalypso's Seafood Pasta," I replied, "with a glass of the merlot."

Brooke piped up with "I'll have the Coconut Shrimp and a Kauai Tai."

"I'm going with the Huli Huli Chicken with Mango Teriyaki," Paul added.

The waiter approached, and Paul said, "I think we're ready to order." He gave the waiter our order and asked for waters all around, adding a bottle of the merlot for us to share.

"Brooke, how long will you be staying?" asked Paul.

"Why do you ask?" she replied.

"I just thought maybe there would be time to show you around the island," he responded, smiling.

"Are you suggesting you and I tour Kauai?" she asked coyly with a smirk on her face.

"No, not at all. What I meant was, your mother and I would like to show you around," he answered.

"Oh," she replied with a touch a sarcasm.

"Paul, Brooke and I are taking this visit a day at a time. I know she wants to relax before heading back to New York and her job," I chimed in.

"Mom, it's okay, you don't have to put in your two cents', although you are accurate. Not sure how much of the island I care to see, at least on this trip."

I didn't want to fuel her fire and let the comment slide but maybe remind her later that I don't approve of her sarcasm.

Fortunately, the waiter appeared with our drinks and interrupted this exchange.

Tasting the wine, Paul addressed the waiter, "Very nice."

"Thank you. It's one of our most popular wines. Your food will be here soon. I'll go check on it."

Taking a sip of the wine, I said, "Paul, this is a lovely merlot. You have good taste."

An awkward silence followed with Brooke downing her Kauai Tai, which was heavily laced with gold and dark rum. "This is a delicious drink. I think I'll order another."

I looked at Paul, and he answered with, "Sure, when the waiter returns, I'll get you one."

"Thanks. That will be my limit. I don't want to get tipsy," Brooke said.

Smiling and trying not to appear nervous and on edge, I said, "Here's our food. Don't know about you two but I'm starving."

Brooke and Paul both responded with, "Me too."

Our dinners were served, and I watched Brooke for any reaction. She was smiling and eagerly digging into her dinner, so I could relax at least for the time being.

"Paul, your choice of restaurant, as always, is spot on," I said.

"Mom, do you and Paul dine out often?" my daughter asked.

Looking at Paul, I said, "We've had dinner on occasion and especially when I was staying at his hotel and looking at properties. He's made my transition easier than I expected and has been a gracious host."

"Brooke, your mother and I have a lot in common and have developed a close friendship. If you are wondering where this is going, I can't tell you. It's too soon." Taking my hand that had been resting on my lap, he said, looking in my eyes with tenderness, "We have had relationships that didn't turn out well, so we are taking it slow."

"Paul," Brooke replied, "Glad to hear it. I want my mother to be happy, and if that is with you, then I'm all for it."

"Thanks, Brooke," he responded.

"Now that you two have come to this resolution, let me say I'm pleased to get your concerns out of the way and would like to finish dinner, if that's okay," I said with an edge to my voice. *I'm feeling like the pressure is building to tell Brooke about her father. I thought I could put that aside for tonight, but I can't.*

"Excuse me, ladies, I'll be right back," said Paul as he excused himself from the table.

Smiling, Brooke said, "Mom, I like Paul and would like to get to know him better."

"I'm sure you will have the opportunity to do just that," I said.

Paul returned to the table, and we continued eating our dinner, and the waiter appeared asking, "Will there be anything else?"

"Well, ladies, what will it be?" Paul asked.

"I, for one, couldn't eat another thing. I'm stuffed."

"Paul, thank you for a lovely dinner, but I'm good. No dessert for me tonight," replied Brooke.

"I'll bring you the check then," Mano said.

Paul paid the check and, walking out the door to the car, he assisted us with getting into the car. We were all quiet driving back to the inn, *although I wasn't sure if it was from having had a satisfying meal or avoiding what hadn't been said.* Car parked, Paul walked us up into the main house and said, "Goodnight, Brooke. Maggie, I'll call you later," kissing me lightly on the lips before he made his way down to his car.

"Goodnight, Paul," we replied in unison.

"Brooke, you want to talk for a while?"

"Sure."

"Let's go sit out on the lanai. It looks like Keoki and Ona are gone for the evening. Can I get you something to drink?"

"Water is fine."

I walked into the kitchen and poured two glasses of water for us and returned to the lanai.

"You seem to have enjoyed your evening."

"Mom, it was fine. I do like Paul and think he'll be a good friend for you."

"Is that all you want for me?"

"I thought you were finished with men?" Brooke queried.

"But certainly, if one appears on my doorstep that I like and can see a future with, I won't walk the other way. I don't want to live the rest of my life alone. But I'm not sure if I'll ever marry again. I'm sure you would feel the same way. Right or wrong?"

"I didn't think we were talking about me," Brooke replied curtly.

"I'm speaking generally. Do you have a significant other?" I asked.

"Actually, no. From what I've seen, I'm not sure if I want one, but I do want a child and will probably use a sperm donor."

I was taken aback by her candor and didn't know how to respond.

"Brooke, please don't judge all relationships because you don't want to close yourself off. You have only one life, and you should be happy."

"Mom, I'm happy, but don't think a man will make it any better. Do I need a man to have a child and raise it? You certainly didn't, nor did my aunt."

"Not necessarily, but it does make it easier. It isn't what I wanted at the time, but I had no choice. I mean the family unit is a mother and a father. I think it is better to bring a child into the world with two parents. But that's my opinion, and I realize your generation has its own ideas."

"Yes, we do, but what I'm trying to get at is, I didn't have a father figure growing up, it was just Auntie and me."

"So true, but don't think that's the norm, and if I could have done it differently, I would have."

"I know, but so far I don't have anyone nor am I looking for someone to make my life complete. But I do know a child would complete me."

"Are you sure? A child is a huge responsibility. I never once forgot about you or failed to worry about how you would turn out. I had faith that between your aunt and me, we would see to it that you grew up with the right ideals and could live a happy life."

"I know you did, but you are skirting the inevitable."

"What do you mean?"

"You said you were going to tell me about my father."

"I will but not tonight."

"Then, when? You keep putting me off."

"I'll tell you tomorrow, and with that, I'm off to bed."

"Goodnight, Mom."

"Goodnight to you too, and I'm happy you're here," I said, kissing her on the cheek.

"Me too."

CHAPTER THIRTY-SIX

I awoke to the sound of my resident rooster crowing. I often wondered if he knew just when I needed him to wake me up, for this of all days was the one I needed to be up and prepared for. As I stretched under my bedclothes, my thoughts turned to Mark's wife, ex-wife, or whatever she calls herself, who would be arriving this afternoon. Mark doesn't seem to be overly concerned about her arrival and has yet to make an appearance. I would give a good guess that he's still hunkered down at the Waimea Plantation Cottages. Knowing how spineless men can be, he's probably not eager to confront Patricia and is likely waiting for the ax to fall on his handsome neck. My cell phone rang, and I turned towards the nightstand – it was Paul. Not wanting to ignore him, I answered it. He'd been so supportive and never made any demands.

"Good morning," I said, trying to sound cheerful.

"Good morning to you too, Maggie. Hope you don't mind me calling so early, but I wanted to catch you before your day starts."

"No, Paul it isn't too early at all. My resident rooster, my alarm clock, woke me up a few minutes ago. I've been lying here in bed, thinking about Mark's wife arriving today and not wanting to give up the sanctuary of my home."

"You know, you should name your rooster. You and he have a relationship. Have you ever gone out to feed him?"

"No, but I know that Keoki has fed him and that's probably why he stays here, knowing his tummy will be taken care of," I said trying to sound jovial.

"Okay, I sense you don't want to talk about Patricia's arrival, and I won't push you on that. What about Mark? Have you seen him?"

"No, not since the other day when I told him about Brooke."

"You mean, he hasn't even called?"

"Not a word."

"He has most likely settled down in his man cave, hoping to avoid the inevitable. Plus, he has a lot of explaining to do when Patricia becomes aware of Brooke's existence. Do you think he'll admit to having a daughter?"

"I would hope so. Today I must deal with Patricia."

"I won't keep you, but wanted you to know I have your back; whichever way it goes. I'm in your corner."

"Thanks, Paul. I appreciate that. Right now, I'm on edge and nervous about the whole situation: Mark, Brooke, and Patricia. I can't possibly begin to anticipate what my future will be. But living here and having you in my life takes the edge off. If I were on the mainland, I think I would feel different."

"You will have to explain what you mean, but that is a discussion for another time. I don't want to help you put off what you need to do, which is to get up and face the day!"

"Paul, you are spot on. Uh oh, I hear a knock on my front door. I'll talk to you later."

"Go get 'em, tiger."

"Bye," I said, smiling.

I threw back the covers and stepped into my slippers, grabbing a robe from behind the bathroom door. Padding my way out to the front room, I saw Keoki pacing the porch.

Opening the door, I said, "Good morning!"

"Miss Maggie, Colonel Elliott has arrived and gone to his room. I wanted you to know."

"Thanks, Keoki. I appreciate you giving me a heads-up. I will dress and come over to the big house."

"What should I do in the meantime, before you get there?"

"Give him coffee. I will join Mark and Brooke for breakfast so anything you and Ona can put together will be fine."

With that, he turned and hustled back to the big house.

Crap, why did Mark have to show up so early? Couldn't he at least have given us time to start the day, on Hawaiian time?

I walked to the bathroom, turned on the water, and jumped into the shower. *Can't dilly dally this morning. My day has already begun, and I can only hope that I can avoid the inevitable with Brooke.* I finished my shower and had a thought, what if Mark decided to come over here and pay me a visit? *Better hurry, dress, and get myself over there.* I chose a casual Hawaiian print sundress in a blue flower pattern. Finishing my makeup, I slipped on my dress and, taking one last look in the mirror, murmured, "Good to go."

Walking over to the big house, I wondered if Brooke was awake or if she was going to avoid me today? *Whatever will be will be!*

I quietly slipped into the kitchen where Keoki and Ona were busy preparing breakfast. "Good morning!"

I smelled the heavenly aroma of Kona coffee and reached for a cup.

"Miss Maggie, your daughter is on the lanai with Colonel Elliott," Keoki piped up.

Terrific! First thing in the morning! I walked out tentatively to where father and daughter sat talking and having coffee, although I wanted to run the other way.

"Good morning, Mom."

"Good morning, you two," I said, trying to sound cheerful.

Mark rose and said, "Good morning, Maggie. Would you care to join us? Your daughter and I have been getting acquainted."

"I will if I'm not interrupting anything," I responded.

Brooke looked up and said, "Please, Mom. Join us."

"I will but for a bit. I have some work to do in my office," which was partly true. *How could I concentrate while my daughter and her father were talking?*

Mark pulled out a chair for me and, almost immediately, Keoki came out with another place setting and a cup for me in the newly arrived dishes I had ordered from a local vendor.

"Mom, I love these new dishes. The dark blue and white plumeria blossoms are beautiful."

"Thanks, Brooke. I had picked these out on a prior visit and knew I had to have them for the inn. It does add some color." *Why am I going on about these dishes when there is another discussion looming that could alter my life?*

"What are you two having for breakfast?"

"Keoki said he and Ona were going to surprise us."

"Maggie, please stay and join us," added Mark.

I sat, stomach churning, looking at Mark, wondering how I was going to handle what was coming. *He looks so smug and self-assured just as he did all those years ago. Even at his age, he is a hunk! Damn him!* As I looked at father and daughter having an amiable conversation, Mark turned to me and said, "Brooke has been telling me about her life in New York. It sounds exciting!"

"Yes, I suppose it is," I replied looking into those blue eyes and trying to keep my voice from quivering, so nervous, waiting for the other shoe to drop, I was hoping he could tell that I wasn't pleased he had gone ahead and met Brooke on his own.

Fortunately, there was a break in the conversation as Keoki placed a bowl of papaya and pineapple along with cantaloupe on the table. Ona followed with plates full of her delicious Hawaiian French toast and Portagee sausage.

"You have outdone yourselves," I said to Keoki and Ona, "this all looks delicious."

Mark added, "I'm ravenous, and this is great!"

"My diet has just been abandoned," replied Brooke, starting to dig into her breakfast.

"Brooke, you don't look like you need to diet," complimented her father.

"It does take some effort on my part – a constant struggle every time I put a bite into my mouth," she replied, smiling as if she thought he could be flirting with her.

I see I'm going to have to step this up before it goes any further, just wait for the right moment.

Breakfast finished, I took a deep breath, looked at Brooke and placed my hand on hers. I said, "Brooke, there is no easy way to say this. Colonel Elliott is your father."

"Mom, you've confirmed my suspicions. I caught a glimpse of him last night when he arrived, and it occurred to me that he and I resemble each other. I didn't think it was possible," she said her voice breaking.

"This isn't easy to admit to you, but since you asked me about him and by coincidence he is here on the island, I felt that it was time. I hadn't seen Mark since all those years ago, and you can't begin to imagine how I felt when he arrived here as my first guest. I want the two of you to get acquainted and will leave you to it. There isn't much more I can say except I won't apologize. What happened all those years ago – happened and can't be undone. It is the way it is. I wish it could have been different, but our lives went in different directions."

Brooke interrupted and asked, "What do you mean different directions?"

I went on to explain to her how Mark and I met and how his life had been all planned out and didn't include our baby or me. "You have to understand that as hard as I tried, I couldn't reach him. All my letters were returned to me – unopened." As I spoke, I glanced at Mark and surprisingly for a tough Marine, he had tears welling in his eyes.

Mark broke in with, "Brooke, my parents were very controlling and had a girl from our Catholic church picked out for me. Strange as it may sound, there were arranged marriages in those days."

"At least you two are on the same page," Brooke quipped. "Sorry I didn't mean to sound sarcastic, and I do believe you, but until I get my head wrapped around this scenario, it's going to take me a while to adjust. Mark, are you married?"

"My wife and I have been separated for some time. Our relationship was strained from the start and complicated in that we couldn't have a family. It was a difficult time. Now to find out I have a daughter, is like a miracle to me and one I am thankful for."

"You said, separated? Are you going to divorce?"

"That's been the plan, but it's very complicated, and Patricia isn't an easy person to negotiate with."

I sat listening and felt like a fifth wheel in the conversation.

"If you were divorced, would there be any chance for you and my mother?" Brooke questioned.

Startled by her question, I looked at Mark. He looked at me, taking my hand and said, "I can't say. It's something your mother and I would have to discuss."

"Brooke," I interjected, "It isn't that simple. I'm building a life here and have no idea what Mark's plan is. With Patricia arriving, it would seem there is a lot of talking that must be done."

"Mom, do you have feelings for him?"

"Brooke, I will always have feelings for him, but we are different people now. We have led very different lives, and his marital status is in the way."

"Brooke, I still have feelings for your mother and didn't realize it until I saw her when I arrived here at the bed and breakfast. Before I can plan for the future, I must dissolve my marriage before I can move on. But to put your mind at rest, I have no intention of remaining married to my wife. We don't love each other and haven't for a long time. She will want to get as much out of me as she can before she moves on. I know she has had other relationships, so I know she doesn't love me nor want to be married, which is fine by me."

I added, "Brooke, this can't be resolved overnight. It's going to take some time, and Mark and I must explore our feelings if there is a future for us. Until then..."

"I understand, but then I don't. You always seemed like you wanted to be part of a couple, and God knows you tried. Unfortunately, the men you chose weren't always what I would have thought were right for you. Maybe this is karma, and you and Mark are destined to be together. Who knows?"

"Brooke, your words are well taken, and I appreciate how well you have taken this revelation about Mark. All I can say is that time will tell. It sounds like a cliché, but it's true. I'm going into my office to do some work. I want the two of you to have some time together to get to know one another," I said quietly and stood up from the table.

Mark stood up and brushed my cheek lightly with a kiss and said, "Maggie, I appreciate this time I can spend with our daughter."

"Our daughter! Has a nice ring to it, doesn't it?" he said.

"Do you think you can get used to it?"

"No question," he said, reaching out for Brooke's hand.

"I'll see you two later," I said, standing up and walking towards my office. I walked in and stood looking out the window at the Pacific Ocean. *I'm getting out of here and going for a walk along the beach to clear my head. A walk is always good and gives me a positive perspective. Whichever way this goes, I will accept it and not regret what I have done.*

I closed my office door and stopped to speak with Keoki, who was sweeping the floor in the great room. "Keoki, I'm stepping out for a bit. No need to tell anyone I'm going for a walk."

"Okay, Miss Maggie. You all right?"

"I'll be fine. Just need to clear my head."

Once downstairs, I avoided being seen from the lanai. I didn't want any company on my walk and needed to be alone. Slipping my sandals off, I dropped them on one of the beach chairs and walked along the shore, the waves splashing at my feet, and I gazed off into the vast blue Pacific. My toes sank into the moist sand, and I stepped up to where the sand was dry and warm. Unaware of how long I had been gone when suddenly I stepped on something sharp and yelled, "Damn!" I looked down and saw I had stepped on a sharp piece of coral shell and blood was oozing from the bottom of my foot. Almost instantly, I felt arms lifting me and carrying me back toward the beach chairs where Mark set me down. He looked at my foot and said, "Maggie, you're bleeding! Keep your foot elevated and stay here until I get some antiseptic and cloths." *Mark to the rescue! He must have finished his conversation with Brooke and decided to look for me. So much for my alone time!* I sat looking out at the ocean and listening to the waves lapping onto the shore when he was back in no time with Keoki in tow.

"That was fast! What did you do, run?"

"Maggie, it was part of my training to react quickly when someone was injured. When I went into the big house and asked Keoki for a first-aid kit, he insisted on coming with me."

"Keoki, thank you for coming back with Mark, but I think we can handle my cut foot."

"Okay, Miss Maggie. If you think you'll be all right; I'm going back to finish my work."

"Sure, that's fine, Keoki."

Mark was gently applying the antiseptic, and I watched as he tended my foot, focusing on the cut. Placing a bandage on the wound, he said: "I should help you back to your cottage."

"That's a good idea, but I don't think you need to carry me. I can hobble along and lean on you."

"Let's do it," he said and, helping me to my feet, we managed to stumble back to my cottage where I dropped onto one of the rattan chairs on the porch. Mark sat on an adjacent chair and looked like he was inclined to stay awhile.

"Mark, I appreciate you coming to my rescue, but I think I'll lie down for a while and rest this foot. Since I'm stuck here, and if I feel up to it, I may work on my book, which has been lacking my attention. I may even take a nap. So far, this day has me wiped."

"Sorry, Maggie," he said.

"Please don't take it the wrong way. I'm taking full responsibility for this situation."

"You don't need to. Don't forget, there's two of us now, and we can work this out together."

"I appreciate your willingness, but how was Brooke when you finished talking?"

"She seemed all right and went to her room. Then I came to look for you."

"Why? I can take care of myself."

"That's fine, but considering you cut your foot and would have had trouble walking I'm glad I was there. But I intended to talk to you about where we go from here."

"Good question," I replied, feeling unsure of what I was getting myself into. "With Patricia arriving tomorrow, I'm not sure if we have anywhere to go except to stay where we are. Can you honestly tell me what you plan to do?"

"I know what I would like to do."

"Let's not go there. Patricia sounds like a woman on a mission and very tenacious."

"She is to a point, but for the right price, I can get her to go away."

"You think so? I'm not so sure, at least at this point in her life she may want to hold on to you."

"Patricia has her agenda, and I know from reliable sources that she has someone in the wings waiting for her to be free."

"Really? Are you sure, or do you think this is a ploy for her to win you back?"

"Maggie, there's no ploy, nor does she want me back."

"Let's wait and see. Women can be fickle and change their minds on a dime. I wouldn't be surprised if she does just that."

Mark looked at me, shaking his head, and said, "You're pretty sure of yourself, aren't you?"

"No, not at all. It's just that I have more life experiences than when I knew you when we were young. Let's wait and see what develops. Are you going to tell her about Brooke?"

"Yes, although she might take it as rubbing her nose in it. She will have to accept it one way or the other. I don't care at this point."

"Well, if you wouldn't mind, I'm going to go in and rest for a while. My foot is throbbing, and I need to elevate it."

"Maggie, what are your plans for dinner?"

"I don't know yet. It's only a little after two. Maybe in a couple of hours, I'll have an idea of what I want to do."

"Keep in mind; I would like to take you and Brooke to dinner."

"I'll do that," I said with some apprehension.

Mark stood up to go and asked me, "Do you need me to help you inside?"

"No, I can make it. It isn't far, and I'll just lie down on my bed for a while."

"Not a good idea," he said, lifting me into his arms, he started to carry me to my bedroom. He set me on the bed and smiled. "I can give you a good back rub if you like?"

"No, thank you, not today," *and not ever if I have my way, but Brooke may have other ideas. Damn, why does life have to be so complicated?*

He bent down and kissed me lightly on the cheek and said, "I'll check on you later."

"That will be fine," I replied, gritting my teeth. "One other thing, please don't come into my bedroom or surprise me like you did the last time."

"Okay, I understand, and I won't come over until you have invited me."

"I would appreciate that," I said as he turned and walked out.

I propped my foot up on a pillow and tried to relax, thinking of my conversation with Mark. *I don't want to build up my hopes and plan on a future with him. I'm not sure if I would even want one.*

After dropping off to sleep, I heard a knock on my front door. Not wanting to get up and struggle to answer it, I yelled out, "Who is it?"

CHAPTER THIRTY-SEVEN

"Maggie, it's Paul, may I come in?"

"Sure, I'm in my bedroom."

Paul appeared, bent down to kiss me and exclaimed, "What happened to you?"

Feeling sheepish, I replied, "I was walking on the beach and stepped on a piece of coral that sliced my foot open. Mark appeared and helped me back here. He left, and I've been snoozing ever since."

"Do you want me to leave?"

"No, not at all. Please sit. We need to talk."

"Okay. Can I get you something to drink?"

"Water would be good."

He returned with chilled bottles of water for us, and I struggled to sit up.

"Brooke and Mark met this morning. The three of us had breakfast together and talked. Then I left to give them some time to get acquainted. After they finished talking, he tracked me down to the beach. He's still pushing for us to be together, but I insisted that it's too soon to plan anything."

"I thought we had talked about a future together?"

"Yes, we did. Rest assured I would like for him to leave when his wife returns to the mainland. To have him in my life would only complicate what I've set out for myself. Even though I fell in love with him all those years ago, now I don't feel the same. Maybe because of all I've been through?"

"What about Brooke? Do you think she would want you together?"

"I'm not sure. It isn't like she's a child and wants her mommy and daddy together. She's a grown woman and planning on having a child of her own. At the very least, I would like for her to think of us as her parents but accept that we live separate lives. I haven't had a chance to speak to her yet and need to find out what she's thinking. I hope she's mature about this."

"Sounds like you two have some talking to do. But before you do that, you need to have that foot looked at. You may need a stitch or two."

"You think so? Maybe just let it heal like it is?"

"I have a good friend who's a doctor here on Kauai. I can call him, and I know he'll come out to see you."

"Paul, that's very kind of you, but do you really think it's necessary?"

"Yes. Do you recall when you had your last tetanus shot? At the very least, you may need one."

"True. Okay. Go ahead and call your doctor friend."

He pulled out his phone from his pocket and dialed up a number just as my cell rang.

"Hello, Mom, Mark told me you cut your foot. Do you need anything?"

"No. Paul is here and calling a friend who's a doctor. He thinks I need a tetanus shot."

"Okay, then. I'll check on you later. Mom, thank you for introducing me to my father."

"You're welcome, sweetie. I've been worried about how you were going to take it."

"I'm quite happy about it."

"Good. I'll let you know what happens to my foot."

Paul reported, "Dr. Sugino will be here in an hour or so. I caught him at the right time."

"Good. In the meantime, we should plan on doing something for dinner."

"Let's wait until the doctor comes."

"All right. I do think you are making this a bigger deal than it is."

"Maybe, maybe not. Let's wait."

Then I heard a male voice from the front of the cottage.

"Maggie, how are you doing? Are you okay?" asked Mark walking into my bedroom.

"You don't have a very good memory. Didn't I ask you not to come walking into my bedroom?"

"Yes, you did, and I apologize."

"To answer your question. I'm okay. A doctor is coming out to check my foot."

"Anything I can do?"

Paul broke in and said, "No, I have it handled."

"Do you now?"

"Yes, I do. You may as well go back to the big house and spend time with Brooke."

"Is that what you want?" Mark asked.

"Yes, it is, and I'll be fine. The fewer people here, the better. You need to get further acquainted with your daughter."

"I'll check on you later then," and with that, he left in a huff, slamming the door behind him.

I laid my head down, took a deep breath, and listened as Paul dialed to check on the hotel.

"Everything okay?" I asked as he disconnected the call.

"Yes. I'm free to stay here with you for as long as you need me," he said, taking my hand.

I smiled.

I heard a knock coming from the front door. Paul went out to answer it.

They came back to my bedroom, and Paul introduced us.

"Dr. Sugino, I'm happy you could take the time to come out here."

"No problem, Ms. Langham," he said, removing the makeshift bandage. Looking at the wound, he remarked, "That is a bad cut." After cleaning the wound, he rebandaged it and said, "No stitches, but you need to be careful and keep walking at a minimum. When was the last time you had a tetanus shot?"

"Please call me Maggie. I can't recall when I had a tetanus shot."

"I had better give you one," and with that, he pulled out a syringe and quickly gave me the nasty shot.

"Your foot may be sore for a few days, but otherwise I think you'll be fine."

"See, Paul. I told you."

"It's a good thing Paul called because the island has some nasty critters and I understand you stepped on some coral. It could have been loaded with harmful bacteria but for now you don't need an antibiotic."

"Thank you for taking care of this. What do I owe you?"

"Paul has taken care of the charge since I'm on a retainer at the hotel. Please let me know if anything changes."

"Dr. Sugino, could you leave me a card? Since arriving here, I haven't acquired a doctor and probably should."

Handing me a business card, he said, "Goodbye, Ms. Langham," as Paul walked him out.

"Mahalo."

This couldn't have happened at a worse time. With Patricia Elliott arriving tomorrow I need to be ambulatory. Damn!

"You look grumpy," Paul said, walking back into the bedroom.

"I am! This is not a good time to be gimping around!"

"Don't worry. Dr. Sugino left you this cane," he said, laying a generic looking brown wooden cane next to the bed. "He said this should help you but not to get overconfident and walk around too much. Tell you what, I'll check with Keoki and Ona and see if they can prepare dinner for all of us. If not, I can get something ordered in."

"Sounds like a plan. I won't argue with you this time. Maybe if I rest this foot tonight, tomorrow I can be up and around."

"Don't push your luck," he said, walking out.

I wonder how this is going to work with both Paul and Mark with me at the same time. Maybe Mark won't show? I will have to wait and see.

I dozed for a bit and awoke as Paul sat down at the foot of the bed and gently said, "Maggie, wake up. Dinner will be ready in thirty minutes."

Sitting up, I looked at Paul and said: "Thank you for helping out."

"I think you know me by now. I plan to be here for you until you kick me to the curb."

I smiled and said, "May I remind you I don't have a curb to kick you to!"

"You're right. Well, you know what I mean. Keoki gave me this cane for you in case you need it to hobble around with."

"Oh, goody! Now I have two, one for each hand," I said, looking at the flashy cane decorated with exotic birds.

"At least you haven't lost your sense of humor, but as Dr. Sugino advised, stay off the foot as much as you can."

"I cut it in the right place, didn't I? I guess though anywhere on my foot, it wouldn't matter."

"No, probably not. Here let me help you get up," he said as I struggled to get up. "How does that feel?"

"I must admit I'm a bit lightheaded so it might take me a bit to get going."

"Just take your time," he said, handing me one of the canes.

"I'll do that. I don't want to fall," I said as I took the cane and made my way to the bathroom. I stood looking in the mirror and saw how bedraggled I looked. *Oh boy, I need to fix this face and at least look cheerful even if I don't feel that way.* After refreshing my makeup and using the facilities, I went back out to the bedroom but didn't see Paul. I hobbled out into the living room, and he was staring out the bay window. "See anything interesting out there?"

"Nothing, really. I'm just thinking that maybe I should go back to the hotel and leave you, Mark and Brooke alone tonight."

"No, please don't do that. Mark needs to accept that you and I are together, and he must move on. He can't assume I'll want to take up with him after all these years just because he and I have a daughter!"

"True. But stranger things have been known to happen."

My phone buzzed, and I saw a text message from Keoki that dinner was ready.

"Let's head on over to the big house; dinner's ready."

Offering me his arm, Paul assisted me down the front steps, and we walked slowly over to the big house. Fortunately, with the elevator, I didn't have to struggle going up the stairs. Walking into the great room, I heard voices on the lanai.

"Here goes," I said to Paul taking his arm and leading him out to join the others.

"Good evening," I said, trying to sound cheerful as Mark and Brooke broke their conversation and looked up at me.

"Hi, Paul," said Brooke while Mark sat looking glum.

"Hi to you too," he replied smiling.

"Dinner will be served now," said Keoki as Paul helped me with my chair.

"It's a beautiful evening," I commented trying to break the silence.

"Yes, it is," replied Mark not smiling but staring daggers at me.

Paul said, "Maggie, would you like a glass of wine?"

"Sure; chardonnay please," I replied as he stood to get us glasses of wine.

I noticed that Mark and Brooke had been drinking something tropical and when Paul returned, he handed me my glass of wine and I sipped hoping it would relax my jangled nerves. *Damn, I didn't think this encounter of the four of us would be this stressful.*

Keoki placed piping hot serving dishes of orange chicken, steamed white rice and braised string beans on the table. I didn't feel hungry, but the aroma had awakened my taste buds.

After we had served ourselves ample amounts of Ona's home cooking, we ate quietly.

"Mark, have you heard from Patricia? I want to make sure we have her room ready."

Paul spoke up and asked, "Won't she be staying with Mark?"

"No," I replied, "She specifically asked for her own room, but maybe she'll change her mind and stay with Mark."

"She can change her mind, but I will not want her staying with me," Mark replied with a bite in his tone.

"Whatever she decides we'll do our best to accommodate her," I said with a strong emphasis on best.

All too soon Keoki came out, cleared our plates and said, "Ona has prepared her special dessert, French pineapple cake."

Ona followed and set the cake down, cutting slices.

"Ona," Brooke asked, "Do you ever share your recipes?"

"Sorry, I don't because they are all up here," she replied pointing to her head.

"That's okay. My auntie used to tell me the same thing when I wanted her to share her recipes with me."

"The beauty of Ona's cooking is that it is authentically Hawaiian and always delicious. She never disappoints me," I said smiling at my cook.

After finishing the cake, I said, "Please excuse me, but I need to go down to my cottage and elevate my foot – it's throbbing, and I'm feeling tired."

"Mom, do you want me to come with you?"

"No, Brooke but thank you. Paul can walk me down, and I'll go straight to bed or maybe read awhile. You stay here and visit with your father."

"Okay, if you're sure?"

"Yes, I'm sure," I said standing up.

Paul stood and said, "I'll make sure she gets settled in for the night, and then I'll take off for my hotel," directing his remark to Mark.

"Goodnight and see you in the morning."

"Maggie," Mark piped up. "Would you like company for a while?"

"No, Mark, she doesn't want or need company, she needs to rest," retorted Paul.

I stood stunned and wondered if these two were going to have a confrontation.

"Let Maggie speak for herself," countered a gruff Mark.

"Mark, I'm tired and need to get a good night's sleep for tomorrow. The way my foot is feeling, I'm not so sure how much sleep I'll get, but I'll give it a shot."

"Okay, if you're sure. If you need anything after Paul leaves, you have my cell number."

"Thanks, Mark," I replied.

I took Paul's arm, grabbed my hideous cane and hobbled to the elevator. Walking to the cottage, he said, "I may have spoken out of turn, but that guy bugs the hell out of me. Why can't he leave you alone?"

"I can't answer that except I think he hopes I'll encourage him to stay. If not for Brooke's sake, then for his own unrequited need to pick up where we left off."

"How do you feel about that?"

"Paul, I thought when I first saw him that if we could have a second chance, I would jump at it. After some soul searching, I've come to realize that I can't go back but want a fresh relationship without the baggage."

"If you're sure?"

"Oh, yes! I want to start over and not go backward, which is what a relationship with Mark would mean."

"I hope you know your decision makes me a very happy man, Ms.

Langham," Paul said stepping forward; embracing, he placed his lips on mine and kissed me tenderly.

I kissed him back with as much fervor as there was in my body and then stepped back. "I think we should stop before you end up spending the night."

"Would that be so wrong?" he asked.

"Well, not as far as I'm concerned but I'm not sure how Brooke would feel. After all, she still has hopes for a reconciliation between her newfound father and me. But let's not forget my injured foot."

"Don't you think that, at her age, she may be more inclined to want you to move on. She isn't a child but a mature adult."

"True. But when all is said and done, deep down she may have wanted her father and I together."

"What do you want?" he asked.

"Frankly, I want you. When I left my home in Pasadena, I left with the intention that I would be starting over, and at that time I didn't plan on there being a new man in my life. But as I've settled here, my feelings have changed, and I like what I've found with you."

Paul replied smiling and said, "Me too."

"Listen, I need to get into bed, would you mind staying a few minutes until I get settled for the night?"

"Sure, no problem. I will wait out in the living room while you change. Don't want to encourage any temptation on either of our parts if I stay in here."

"Thank you," I said.

I turned to go into the bathroom, and Paul walked back towards the front of the house. *I'm relieved he'll stay until I turn in and, with any luck, his being here will discourage Mark from visiting me.* I finished my usual nighttime toilette and put on a white cotton nightgown and hobbled out into the bedroom. Paul was sitting at the foot of the bed looking at his phone and looked up when I appeared.

"All ready?" he asked, standing up and offering me his hand as I made my way to the bed.

"I'm all set for the night. Thank you for staying. I think you can leave anytime now."

"No, I'll stay for a while until you have dropped off to sleep," he said, handing me a pill and a glass of water.

"What's this for?" I asked him.

"Dr. Sugino left it in case you had a hard time going to sleep. No worries, he said it was very mild, and you wouldn't wake up hungover."

"Good." I took the pill and once in bed under my covers, Paul laid down on the opposite side and leaned over to kiss me goodnight.

"Have a good night's sleep," he said as I nestled into my pillows.

"You too," I mumbled drifting off to sleep snuggling into his arms.

CHAPTER THIRTY-EIGHT

I awoke to the sound of my ever-faithful rooster. For now, I'll call him Herman after Bishop Herman Koeckmann who served as a Roman Catholic Bishop in Hawaii from 1828-1892. Somehow, I felt Herman was an appropriate name for my number one resident rooster. Looking at the clock, I saw it was 7 a.m. Earlier than I would like to get up. But today, Patricia, Mark's ex-wife, wife, or whoever she is would be arriving. I must be on hand to greet her. From my bed, I could see that the day had dawned bright and beautiful, and hopefully it would stay that way without storm clouds. Those I would take as an omen.

I recalled falling asleep while snuggling with Paul, but when did he leave? *Best to get on with the day.* I threw back my covers and, remembering I had an injured foot, gently placed it on the floor, testing it to see if I could walk on it. Still sore, I opted for my cane to get me into my bathroom. Hobbling, I recalled not sleeping that well and having thrashed around most of the night; I didn't feel rested. But it is what it is, and maybe if all goes well and quietly, I could nap later. I washed up the best I could, not wanting to get my sore foot in the shower yet. Maybe later, if I can. Finishing my morning toilette, I hobbled over to the closet and looked at what I could wear. Best I wear something not too long – don't want to risk getting tangled up and falling. "For today this will be perfect," I said as I grabbed a knee length white dress splashed with red hibiscus. *Not too bright and flashy but just right for meeting Mark's wife; not that I care, but I want to feel good in whatever I pick out to wear. I bet she will look like the typical officer's wife: not a hair out of place, she'll be perfectly groomed and wearing a suitable outfit for traveling. What a pain in the butt!* I went back into the bathroom to apply my makeup and primp a bit when I heard a knock on the door. I yelled, "Who's there?"

"Mom, it's just me. Thought I would see if you needed any help getting dressed."

"Oh, sure, thanks. Come on in. I'm just finishing up. Could you hand me the white sandals from the closet?"

"Sure, you look great. You don't even look like you had that horrible time with your foot yesterday."

"Thanks, but I feel like it inside. I would rather the arrival of Mrs. Elliott wasn't happening, but I'll have to step up to it. With the appearance of Patricia Elliott today, I can't even begin to anticipate how the day is going to unfold. I've decided that Mark and I are going nowhere. I hope you're not disappointed?"

"If I were a little kid, I would certainly want my mother and father together. But I'm not, and frankly, all I want for both of you is to be happy. You especially."

"I appreciate that, Brooke. I was worried you were pulling for your dad and me to get together. I think too many years have passed although I'll always have a place for him in my heart."

"Mom, what about Paul? How late did he stay last night?"

"Frankly, I don't know."

Brooke gave me a worried look. "I dropped off as soon as my head hit the pillow. I recall him snuggling with me and then nothing. I woke up this morning, and he was gone."

"You don't know how long he stayed?" Brooke asked.

"No, I don't, but I trust him, so he probably left once he was sure I was secure for the night. Paul and I are good friends, and he's important to me, but I can't predict what our future holds either. Who knows what may happen? He's had previous relationships, so it's all a wait and see. I wish it were more straightforward than that, but when you're dealing with human emotions, it's not so easy. Besides, I need to think very carefully about both Mark and Paul before any commitments can be made. Shall we walk over and have some breakfast?"

"Sure," she replied, handing me my cane.

We walked over to the main house. I was so grateful for having an elevator. Once upstairs, the aroma of Ona's cooking wafted from the kitchen, awakening my appetite.

"Ona, what have you cooked for us today?"

"Maggie, I have prepared papaya macadamia nut scones, and eggs any way you would like them, and Portagee sausage if you like?"

"Ona, whatever is easiest for you. Maybe if you prepare scrambled eggs for everyone, it will be easier, and the sausage will be wonderful."

"Sure, and coffee is ready for you on the lanai."

"That will be great. Come on, Brooke let's go out on the lanai."

We walked out to the lanai and settled into a couple of chairs overlooking the lush foliage beneath the big house.

Keoki came out with piping hot plates of scrambled eggs and the sausage along with a basket of the scones.

"Thanks for helping, Ona. Have you seen Colonel Elliott this morning?"

"Yes, he stopped by on his way down to the beach. Said he was taking an early morning swim."

"Okay," I replied but not sure what to make of that. *Since Mark's been here, he hasn't so much as even talked about a swim.*

"Mom, Mark mentioned to me he has been suffering from PTSD. Have you seen any evidence of that since he's been here?"

"No, I haven't, but then he hasn't been here a lot. He's been staying at the Waimea Plantation Cottages. The little he has been around here I haven't noticed anything."

With the mention of Mark's PTSD, I was a bit worried that something had gone awry with him. *Maybe I should look for him?*

"Mom, what are you thinking? You can't go walking the beach with your injured foot. Are you worried about him?"

"Yes and no. After all, he is an adult, though with his history of PTSD I'm not sure how safe he is. I want to be here when Patricia arrives."

Finished with breakfast, I said to Brooke, "I'm going to check the Anthurium Suite, which I have assigned for Mrs. Elliott."

"What about Mark?" she asked.

"I'll check the suite unless you want to go down now and start looking for him?"

"No, I'll wait for you."

"Okay, I'll be back in a few minutes."

I hobbled to Mark's suite and knocked on the door. No one answered, so I took the liberty of opening the door. Not knowing if he could be in the bathroom, I called out "Mark, it's Maggie. If you are in here, please give me a shout out." I walked into the room, but there was no sign of him. The bathroom door was open, and the bed didn't look like it had even been slept in. However, his personal belongings were in the room. *Next place to look will be down on the beach.* I closed the door behind me and went to join Brooke on the lanai.

"Brooke, there's no sign of him in his room, and from all appearances, it didn't look like he had even slept there."

"Where else could he be?" asked Brooke.

"Maybe he did go for a swim, but if he did, I would think he would be back by now."

"Mom, I'll go look for him, and you stay here."

"Brooke, I'm going to call Paul and ask him to join us before you start searching for him."

Dialing his number, I felt uneasy that something awful might have happened to Mark. Knowing he has PTSD made we think it had reared its ugly head and he was having an episode.

"Hello, Paul Sinclair."

"Hi, Paul, it's Maggie. Are you busy?"

"No, just going over paperwork. What's up?"

"Mark told Keoki he was going for a swim earlier this morning and we haven't seen him. Maybe I'm overreacting, but I'm concerned he could be having one of his PTSD episodes."

"Or," said Paul, "he could be having a bout of not wanting to face Patricia and suffer the repercussions!"

"Are you serious or being sarcastic?"

"A little of both. Mark is hardly one of my favorite people after all. With that being said, do you want me to come and help you look for him?"

"If you would, Brooke and I would appreciate it. With my foot the way it is I don't want to go trampling down onto the beach."

"Good point. Sit tight, and I'll come right out."

"Thanks, Paul."

"Anything for you, Maggie."

Good! He was on the way. At least with him here helping look for Mark, I will feel better.

I placed the phone on the table and turned to see Brooke standing with her eyes wide as saucers.

"Paul's coming?"

"Yes, he said he would come out right away."

"Mom, I know I just met Mark, but I wouldn't want anything to happen to him."

"I know, dear. Let's hope for the best that we find him." I looked at my phone and realized Patricia would be here in another couple of hours. Maybe just enough time to look for Mark and hopefully find him.

"Brooke, let's go downstairs and wait for Paul. Hopefully, he'll be here soon."

We took the elevator downstairs and walked cautiously towards the beach area. I was careful to protect my foot. The cane provided me with a fair amount of security but not as good as a healed foot would.

"Maggie, Brooke!"

I turned to see Paul making his way towards us.

"Hi, Paul. Fast trip from the hotel."

Greeting me with a sweet kiss, he replied, "Actually, I was at my place not far from here. I suggest you sit here on a chair while Brooke and I walk the beach."

"What a time to injure my foot! But who knew we would be hunting for a missing guest."

"Mom, you speak generally. His name is Mark, and he's my father, after all," declared Brooke.

"Sorry, Brooke. I didn't mean to sound so flippant about it." *She has undoubtedly gotten sensitive about him all of a sudden.*

"Come on, Brooke, walk with me, and let's see what we can find," said Paul.

I sat on one of the beach chairs where I wouldn't immerse myself in loose sand and watched as Brooke and Paul started walking the beach. Looking at my watch and hoping Patricia Elliott didn't arrive any sooner than we were expecting her, I realized that Paul and Brooke had walked out of my line of vision.

Keoki appeared and asked, "Miss Maggie, if Mrs. Elliott gets here before you're back upstairs, what should I tell her?"

"Good question. Right now, nothing. Please show her to the suite so she can get settled in. Let's give Paul and Brooke a few more minutes to look for him, and maybe they will find him."

I sat tapping my healthy foot as if that would hurry up Brooke and Paul. Best case scenario would be if they found him and, of course, the worst case if they found evidence that something had happened to him. I looked out at the Pacific Ocean in all its splendor, and a chill ran down my spine when a thought came to mind: what a horrible death it would be to drown.

"Maggie," I looked towards where the voice was coming from and saw Paul and Brooke approaching, carrying what seemed to be, clothing.

Not wanting to panic, they came up to me with faces that said more than any words could say.

"Mom, we found these farther down the beach," Brooke said, handing me a t-shirt with the Marine Corp insignia and a pair of cargo shorts. "Looks like Mark is missing," I said when a familiar voice spoke up, "Not so fast."

Mark appeared dripping wet in swim trunks and looking every bit as sexy as the last time I saw him. He said, "Anyone have a towel?"

"Odd you should ask for that now. Where in the hell have you been?"

"I told Keoki I was going for a swim. Got a bit disoriented and found myself quite a ways from here at Tunnels Beach. I didn't worry you, did I?"

"Don't be a smart jackass. With your PTSD, I didn't know what to expect."

"I'm here and you don't have to worry about my PTSD. I have it under control. I did a lot of thinking while I was in the water. Has Patricia arrived? I'm ready to see her."

"No. But she should be arriving at any time. Let's go back up to the big house and wait for her there," I said. Standing up, I tossed Mark his clothes and said, "You might need these," and off I hobbled, aided by my cane. Paul reached for my arm and said, "Here, let me help you."

"I would appreciate that."

As we walked, I could hear Brooke and her father talking but couldn't understand what they were saying. At this point, I was disgusted and didn't much care. Let Patricia arrive, gather her husband, and be off, back to the mainland.

Keoki had walked ahead of us to see if Mrs. Elliott had arrived, and hopefully, she hadn't. I needed to collect myself and calm down after this excitement. God only knows what could have happened to him. Once upstairs in the great room, I was surprised to see that Mrs. Elliott had arrived. Short red curly hair, medium height, and nicely proportioned for a woman of her age, she was dressed in a white pantsuit and matching accessories, including a wide-brimmed hat. I approached her and introduced myself.

"Mrs. Elliott, I'm Maggie Langham, and this is Paul Sinclair, a friend of mine. Hope you had a nice flight."

"Maggie Langham, huh! Mark has spoken of you often, and I wondered what was so special about you, that after all these years he would speak of you so fondly. I would like to see my husband."

"He's on the way up from the beach."

"The beach?" she asked incredulously.

"Yes, he had gone for a swim, but he has returned and…"

"Hello, Patricia," Mark said gruffly.

"Hello, Mark," she replied and pointing at Brooke asked, "Who is this woman?"

"This is my daughter, Brooke Langham."

"Your daughter?"

"You heard me!"

"I think you have some explaining to do, Colonel Elliott."

"More to the point, Patricia, we have a lot of talking to do," Mark responded brusquely.

"Let's get to it, then."

"Well, not here in front of everyone. We can go to my room," he said, grasping her arm, "This way!"

I stood there not sure about the exchange I had witnessed between husband and wife but then maybe their relationship was as he said. Unsure of my next step, I turned to Paul and said, "If you want to go back to the hotel now, it's okay. I think I can handle the situation and if it gets too out of control, I'll ask them to leave."

"Maggie, I'm out of the hotel for the rest of the day, so my time is yours if you want me here."

Smiling, I said, "Paul, I would like you to stay. Didn't want to take you away from your responsibilities though."

"I think you should rest your foot. Do you want to go back to your cottage?"

"No, I should stay here." Not paying attention, I hadn't thought about how the exchange between the Elliotts had affected Brooke for she wasn't in the room with us.

"Paul, did you see where Brooke went?"

"No, Maggie," he said as a voice said, "Looking for me?"

I turned to see my daughter and noticed she had been crying. I walked over to her and embraced her, whispering, "A little too much for you today?"

"Yes, Mom. Having met my father, he seems to be a bit erratic. I mean going off for a swim like that by himself and then the conversation between him and his wife. I'm confused and want to go to my room and rest for now. I have a lot of thinking to do. One thing I can tell you is that I have a better understanding of what you must have gone through all those years ago. I'm grateful you chose to have me and not abort me. I would have rather had the traditional mother and father family, but there are things I can't change. I must accept them, and I do with a grateful heart."

"I think I need to sit down," I said, walking tentatively out to the lanai and nearly collapsing onto one of the chairs.

Paul and Brooke followed me out and sat down next to me.

"Don't look so worried you two. I'll be fine after the Elliotts have departed. Brooke, you can stay as long as you would like to. I'm enjoying having you here."

"Thanks, Mom, but I need to leave and get back to New York to my job. But I will be back to see you and keep an eye on how you're doing."

Smiling with tears welling in my eyes, I said, "Brooke, you know you're welcome here anytime."

Brooke looked at me and then at Paul. "Whatever you two decide to do, I'll support you and wish you every happiness. Mom, I don't think you and my father have a future. He has too much baggage, including that wife of his. After all you have gone through with men, you don't need him at this stage of your life. You need someone who will love you and take care of you, and I think that man is Paul."

"Brooke, I don't know what to say. Paul and I are friends at this point, and I don't know what the future will hold for us."

"May I get a word in?" asked Paul, smiling. "Brooke, I thank you for your vote of confidence and want you to know I will do everything I can for your mother. Whatever will develop between us is hard to say, but I know I have come to care for her from the first day I met her at my hotel. I know how I feel, but she hasn't told me how she feels about me."

"Excuse me," I heard Mark's voice. He was alone and looking stressed.

"Maggie, may I speak with you?"

"Sure."

Paul spoke up and said "Brooke, how about you and I take a walk and give your mother and Mark some time to talk?"

"Sure, Paul," my daughter answered.

"Thank you, Paul," I said.

Leaning down to kiss me lightly on my cheek, he whispered, "I won't be far if you need me."

"Thanks."

Once they were out of earshot, Mark sat down next to me and took my hand.

"Whatever it is you have to say, I'll understand," I said, removing my hand.

"Maggie, I think it best if I return to the mainland with Patricia and get my life straightened out. I have doctors I can see there for my PTSD. Patricia and I must finalize our property settlement, and I want to get out of this marriage. If the time comes when I'm free, I'll be back, and if you have chosen to move on with someone else, I will understand. I can't expect you to wait. There are too many variables."

"I expected you to leave with her and I know that's for the best. But please, one thing for me, stay in touch with Brooke. See her if you can and become her friend if not her father. She needs you, and she wants to make up for lost time."

"Maggie, thank you for giving me our beautiful daughter. She's a fine young woman, and I don't intend on letting her go. Do you plan on staying here on the island?"

"Yes, I do. I have this investment and want to make it successful under my ownership. I know you are going to ask about Paul and right now all I can tell you is that we are very good friends. Where life takes us from here, I can't say. What is meant to be will be is a tired cliché, but I believe in it. When are you leaving?"

"Patricia is checking with the airlines to see if we can get out on a late flight tonight. Neither of us wants to hang out here. Too much tension, or so she says. Besides, the longer I am with you, the harder it will be to leave you."

"Mark, you can't be serious."

"Yes, I am. Patricia and I are over, and someday I will want someone to share my life with and, whether or not it is you, will only be a wait and see. So, until then…"

We were interrupted with Patricia calling out Mark's name, and I heard her say, "We are all set for the late flight out of Lihue."

"Maggie, don't forget me or what we could have," he said, leaning down and kissing me full on.

I pulled away, "Go, please, don't prolong your departure."

Mark walked away toward the guest suites, and as he walked, I looked wistfully after him. Maybe this was a mistake, and I should ask him to stay, and we could work out his health issues with the VA here. *Damn, here I go again second guessing myself. I'm a different person than I was all those years ago and mustn't live in the past. But he is oh so tempting.*

I heard a familiar voice, "Maggie, is everything okay?" Paul asked.

"Yes, fine. Mark and Patricia are heading out tonight. Best they return and not linger here although I feel bad for Brooke's sake."

"I think Brooke will be fine. She and I talked, and she has accepted it for what it is. At least she is satisfied knowing she has a father and who he is."

"Where is she?"

"She said she wanted to relax on the beach for a while."

"I would like to go back to my cottage. Will you come with me and stay awhile? Maybe Ona and Keoki will prepare some dinner for the three of us," I said, standing up and taking my cane I walked into the kitchen.

"Sure, Miss Maggie. Ona and I will fix dinner tonight. No worries about that. I'll let Miss Brooke know."

"Thanks, Keoki."

Paul joined me and said, "I heard Mark talking with Brooke in the great room. Maybe now is a good time to go to the cottage."

"I think you're right," I answered and, taking Paul's arm, we walked to the elevator.

Back at my cottage, I said, "Paul, I don't want to go inside just yet. Maybe sit out here."

"Sure, Maggie," he replied, "How about a glass of wine?"

"Perfect," I said as he went inside, and I sat down looking at the iridescent waves as they crashed onto the white sandy beach ebbing and flowing.

Acknowledgments

Writing is an isolating profession. Working tirelessly on our manuscripts before bringing them to culmination takes patience, time, and a devotion to writing. But in addition, it also takes encouragement from fellow writers. I am fortunate to have a wonderful critique group to work with. Meeting every other Saturday to discuss our ten pages was worthwhile but often frustrating. However, I couldn't have written *Starting Over* without the help of my group: Gay Totl Kinman, Gayla Turner, and Meredith Taylor. My appreciation to my editor, Johnny Hudspith for his patience and hard word on my manuscript. I couldn't have done it without him. Last, but certainly not least: I thank my husband, David. He has given me the support, space, and time I needed to pursue my writing and exercised great patience while on research trips to Kauai.

Recipes

Papaya's Macnut Coconut Scones

1 ½ lbs. pastry flour
½ lb. cold butter
1 tsp. salt
1 ½ T. baking powder
¼ tsp. nutmeg
1 c. toasted coconut
¾ c. toasted macadamia nut
    pieces

3 eggs
1 c. sugar
12 oz. milk
1 tsp. vanilla
1 tsp. coconut extract
1 tsp maple extract
½ tsp almond extract

Combine flour, salt, spices, and baking powder. Cut cold butter into flour mixture using a grater. Combine eggs, milk, extracts, and sugar. Lightly combine wet and dry ingredients. Drop about ½ c. each onto a cookie sheet and bake for approximately 15 minutes at 350 degrees or until lightly golden on top. Makes two dozen.

Hawaiian Benedict

4 slices sweet bread
8 eggs
16 slices Portuguese sausage
1 ½ c. Lilikoi Hollandaise (recipe follows)
2 c. hash browns
3 T. butter
Lilikoi Hollandaise
3 egg yolks

1/4 lb. clarified butter
¼ c. white wine
1 tsp. paprika
Pinch of Tabasco Sauce
1 tsp. lemon juice
2 tsp. Lilikoi concentrate
Pinch of cayenne pepper
Salt to taste

Whisk eggs, wine and Lilikoi sauce in a double boiler to the right consistency. Slowly fold in clarified butter and season with paprika, Tabasco sauce, lemon juice, salt, and pepper.

Poach eggs; toast sweet bread and top it with sautéed Portuguese sausage, poached eggs and Lilikoi Hollandaise. Serve with hash browns.

Serves 4.

Hawaiian Pineapple Pancakes

2 c. Bisquick
2 c. milk (at least)
2 eggs
2 ½ c. crushed pineapple with juice (canned or fresh)

½ c. butter (no margarine)
Maple Syrup
Oil as needed

Mix Bisquick according to directions and add 1 cup pineapple with juice. Before cooking, mix remaining pineapple with juice, butter, and syrup – warm over a medium burner. Add enough milk to pancake batter to ensure thin pancakes. Cook on a hot griddle that has been brushed with oil.

Serves 4

Hawaiian French Toast

1 large loaf Hawaiian sweet
   round bread
4 large eggs
1/2 c. milk
½ tsp. vanilla
¼ tsp. cinnamon

1 tbsp. butter or oil for frying
Powdered Sugar (Optional)
Maple or Coconut Syrup
   (Optional)
Papaya Pineapple Jam

Slice bread crosswise so that each slice is about 1-inch thick. Cut larger slices into halves or thirds, if desired. Set aside.

In a shallow mixing bowl, whisk together the eggs, milk, vanilla, and cinnamon. Mix occasionally to ensure it's well-blended.

Quickly dip slices (do not soak) in egg mixture and cook in frying pan until golden brown on both sides.

Sprinkle with powdered sugar and serve with warm coconut or maple syrup or papaya pineapple jam.

Pupus and Drinks

Rumaki Pupus
20 pitted dates
10 water chestnuts, cut into
   halves
10 slices bacon, cut into halves,
   partially cooked

4 tbsp. soy
2 tbsp. honey
1 tbsp. brown sugar
Pinch of ginger

Stuff dates with water chestnuts, wrap bacon around date, and hold with a toothpick. Combine sauce in a shallow pan, roll dates to coat. Broil 5 minutes each side in a 13x9 inch pan or bake – 400 degrees for 5 to 10 minutes.

Prince Kuhio

3 oz light Bacardi rum
3 oz pineapple juice
1 ½ oz guava juice

1 ½ oz. coconut pineapple
nectar

Mix all ingredients in a blender and serve over ice cubes.

Makes 2 drinks.

Special Acknowledgments

Talk Story Bookstore of Kauai and its owners – their suggestions for my research and reading were excellent.

The Kauai Public Library in Princeville for their assistance with my research early on when the idea for this book was a mere seedling.

The Kauai Historical Society for their Cook'em Up Kaua'i The Kauai Historical Society Cookbook 1993.

Printed in the United States
By Bookmasters